HINTERLAND

For Jenny
always a friend
who is Splendidly
Different.

HINTERLAND

A Collection of Sixty-Six Short Stories

By

Colin H. Smith

First paperback edition September 2022

Book design by Publishing Push

ISBNs:
978-1-80227-729-6 (paperback)
978-1-80227-730-2 (e-book)

*To Zhivka without whom this book
would never have been published*

THE LAST READER

I can't read anymore, I haven't the patience or time. Words overtook me to flow out of me like little fishes that would glide through numerous dimensions to become fixed upon a page.

But you can read me should you find time to waste in some lonely corner of your mind where the dust of life has settled whilst we were not looking.

Open the cover and watch that dust fly; each speck a word, gathered upon spectrums of light to become clouds of stories yet to congeal, compressed upon some gilded page in waiting.

Waiting, there is the thing. Hidden on abandoned shelves in libraries and upon old ladies' mantelpieces are billions of lost words waiting to escape into some innocent random reader — one who willy-nilly picks up a book, turns a page and reads, absorbed into some faraway place, the life of an as yet unknown who begs to breathe again.

It may be we who wait to be written, and once our course is set, we may sail through closed stacked decades before liberated in the sight of a reader. For the great bard exclaimed that, "all the world is a stage". However, the universe is a book waiting upon time for us to pick up a pen to write on its fabric.

The space between us, my fellow reader, is as thick as a page, and each word has a life of its own, some being wayward youths freshly born intent on kicking a football so hard as to puncture it.

On the other hand, older and more mature words have settled in the dust of shattered pieces from ancient times in Latin and Greek. Every time you read a word, heaven opens to let feelings, interpretations and meanings flow across the periphery of your consciousness like sparrows flitting upon the branches of who you are. I shot a word once with a twelve-bore shotgun (that is with both barrels at once). The damned thing split in two, hyphenated screaming, and flew off to return with a completely different meaning.

In this silent corner of our imaginations, resting in a deep leather chair of no reason and surrounded by closed scenes written, we should pause to consider all the combinations of words yet to come. Yes, for every book ever written, there will be thousands more until the last reader closes his last book upon the dust of eternity.

Which story will you be in and to what actions will you lend your name, and who will read you? Can it be that out there waiting is a book written in which we are settled, waiting for our return? Surely, once written, for as long as the book waits, we can never truly die in the minds of any reader.

Colin H. Smith

CONTENTS

A GLASS FULL OF MYSTERY OR A BOTTLE FULL OF LANDED GRIT

It is of endeavour and pain's denial that I engage here today in this lonely, late, wretched hour to recount where I have been and what I have done, or what has been done to me. Most would never have travelled at such a time and few could endure the test without turning to betray all that is true. Yet even now, I hold doubt that such events ever happened and that that dank place ever existed beyond some curdling of a blood-chilling rage of a dream. I did not stumble into the flaming heat of compression and I did not fall. My foolhardy inquisitiveness allowed, against better judgement, for me to enter that drinking party that stole my soul, which is now forever a torn sail in the wildest of storms so far from a safe harbour.

The streets narrowed and darkened, as I travelled towards the harbour in the oldest part of that small coastal settlement that hides, shrouded in a nightmare somewhere deep in the southwest, cut off from reason by wild hills to the north and the Atlantic Ocean to the west. The scent of ocean filled the air and I could taste sea salt in my mouth as if I was drowning, as a wind blew shoreward in resistance of my travel. Beyond the last buildings before that dark sea, the structures seemed to stumble and lean against one another in some intoxicated pain as the creaking of taut rigging against timbers and the knocking of impatient ships' hulls grinding against the harbour side could be heard. The rising and falling waters jostled those vessels like wooden floating coffins of lost souls to the depths of no return where men become the fodder of fishes and their bones stick in the benthonic slime of an eternal windy water that steals their thoughts and wastes them in vast, lost distances. Those are the hulls of the ancient whalers, who sailed to take life and burn the oil of great beasts' souls against the buffers that held the land from a far-reaching devil whom no one could see.

To dream beyond the reach of a dream is when that dream becomes a reality. As I walked in my own silence against the screams that surrounded me, everything felt normal, but it was not. Upon reaching the harbour wall, I felt the spit of that ocean beast and turned my back on its vengeful spirit as I entered that godforsaken public house known to many as The Drowning Fire. Passing through the gnarled, low opening, I stepped down into what appeared to be a dimly lit, subterranean cave that danced with the reflected orange light of flickering flames and oil lamps. The room was full of a sea fog, comprised of stale and smoke-infused air that blurred the shapes of men who moved as if floating, each a vessel upon some boiling sea. The mixed sound of men's voices met my ear yet not a word could be discerned in that cavern of comfort and confusion. Making my way through the throng, shoulder-to-shoulder with mariners and fishers, my stature seemed to shrink as a man turned to me from that polished bar and spoke.

"Aha, boy, what will it be — a glass full of mystery or a bottle full of landed grit?"

I looked him full in the eye and answered, "I am here for adventure. And what man worthy of any salt can deny mystery?"

I now realise how intoxicating that place was where men drank upon the margin in between landed life and the precarious ocean in which so many rested amongst the dead. They were sea-born and knew their fate, which was shared in some unspoken understanding that divided them from those who sheltered upon dry land. These men held no firm religion, for they were those of an addiction to something I could not understand yet — a thing that no words could convey but something that the absolute desolation and remoteness upon a distant storming sea gave to make men fearless in the torment of life. This made them as if men of ancient times, for I now believe the ancient mariners of Athens or those wraiths of Viking landers all drank the spirit of a shared mystery, denied to those who lived upon the firm side of this earth.

The speaker then shoved his hand out and grasped mine, introducing himself as the first mate of the Devil Fish that would sail upon the dawn tide.

3

I asked, "Where do you sail and what type of voyage will it be?"

He grinned from ear to ear as if some great bear looking down upon me and answered, "We sail south and east to catch the autan heading for Southern Seas. As for the voyage, none can know, for the Devil Fish is an adventurer of opportunity. We shall carry hardware and return with jewels, for many of these men are our crew. Most are rich beyond measure yet still they sail."

I answered with a naïve question. "Why do they still sail when they have more than any man can want?"

He smiled again, but this time his eyes closed, as he answered. "No man once upon the floating boards can ever rest upon land. Will you join us?"

I hesitated as he thrust a glass into my hand and, raising his to take long deep draughts until the glass was empty, gestured the same. As eyes were now upon me, the stranger amongst a crew, I drank the warm liquid. Having downed the glass, a change came over me and I felt strangely comfortable amongst that gathering in that last day. Emboldened, I gave my name, Adam, as we shook hands again, and he proffered his name.

"George Bates, mariner of this port, boy to man for thirty-four years, and each of these are my sons," he said waving a long arm like a shadow over the gathered group, who now focused upon us both as if we had something they wanted. A sea of faces appeared around me, each offering a hand to be shaken, as many names came and went. Finally, a lean man, the sort who may have been an endurance runner or a gymnast, approached through the throng that seemed to dissolve in his presence. His cap sat aside of his head that bore a slim, almost gaunt face and, as he opened his mouth to speak, a row of teeth that stood like tombstones in a graveyard of gums could be seen. He said nothing, as Bates introduced him to me.

"This is our captain, Mr Angel."

"Pleased and honoured to meet you," I replied, as another glass was pushed into my hand, which, under some convention, I downed in two draughts. It was easier to swallow than the first, as the floor of the building swayed a little as if afloat. I sat at a great table with my back to a wall, gazing at the company around me. Some were singing a shanty about a woman of the sea, others were smoking and talking, as in procession each came and sat at the table before me, offering introductions.

"I am James, the third son of Edwin who drowned with my brothers, fishermen, and all three out of Swansea Bay now caught by fishes themselves. I sail to be close to lost memories and keep my hands from idle frustrations."

Next came a dark-skinned man who spoke in low tones. He shook my hand not letting it go and peered unblinking into my eyes as if he could see far more than the blue cornea and through the darkness in my pupils to something within. He spoke my name softly and continued between deep breaths as if he knew who I was with a great familiarity that could not be possible unless he had a place in my past. For the first time, the company grew hush.

"My name is Marcel from the island of Guadalupe. My mother is a traiteur faith healer and my father a minister of faith."

I remained speechless, as he continued.

"I can feel the heart of who you are and what you are running from. Escape is futile, for you cannot escape yourself. It will follow you until it kills you, or you kill yourself."

I sat dumbfounded and confused. I had believed that my brother's death by my own hand was far behind me and my charging into a future had long smothered the memories that were unfolding like a chess game to a player who played oblivious to the rules.

Stuttering, I asked, "How do you know who I am?"

To which he smiled and, rising silently, he moved away.

Some fifteen others of different descriptions came and passed until the first mate, Bates, asked if I wanted to crew for the Sea Devil. I must have been dazed from the drink, as I accepted.

Four years passed before I returned to that public house, having traversed many nautical miles around the world. I had learnt the ways of a sailor and the nature of oceans, the hard times and the calms that settle in between. We had plundered other vessels like pirates and run before gales to escape French and Spanish frigates. Mine had been a journey of survival that had made me a wealthy man. Yet I had never asked the question as to whether what we did was right or wrong; there had never been time enough for such. It was then, once back upon land, that the real darkness settled upon me, as I craved the confinement of ship and the endless flow of activity that kept her crew alive.

To feel a man's last heartbeat and the final word upon his breath whilst watching his tearful eyes bulge in the moment before death is a shameful experience when you take another over the edge, but when it is he or you, life hangs until one is dead. Then comes the glow of relief when blood re-enters your veins from deep in the muscle tissues, followed by a brief sorrow, as you strip his pockets and jewels to feather your own nest. The life of a privateer is tantamount to being a pirate, and the further from home we sail with the king's blessing, the greater the recklessness and desperation grows within the crew — each banished to the oceans and forever unstable upon shore land. The laws of a mariner of bounty adhere to nothing that happens upon dry land. For each of us — from the master to the lowliest of cabin boys — knew of a comradeship felt in no other place except maybe upon the field of battle where each looks death in the face. Once such adversity has been met beyond the gruelling flight of months and years to places unknown, there can be no peace in men's souls in the routine mundanity of earning a living like a landlocked man.

For four years and nine months, I had lived in a continuous flow of moments; each one interrupted by the next ceaselessly with no break in between. Life had ever rubbed shoulders with death that others succumbed to. We departed as a body of sixty to return as thirty-eight. Some had gone crazy and leapt to swim for some mirage off shore, others had died in conflict, and two had been marooned upon a ghost ship for stealing.

Having not been on land for even one hour, along with the souls of those lost others, I found myself in the only place of comfort upon dry land that was left to my kind after the endless voyage. The Drowning Fire public house had not changed. It was as if my time away had consumed no time at all. My company was the same and each held a drink or a pipe as was stationed nearly five years earlier. Yet, upon my belt was a bag full of gold and my hands were gnarled from rope burns and cold salt water. Having ducked to enter, a silence settled for a moment as if a stranger had come in. As I looked around, I recognised my shipmates who mysteriously did not appear to recognise me.

Having arrived at the bar, the landlord asked again as he had before, "Aha, boy, what will it be — a glass full of mystery or a bottle full of landed grit?"

Collecting my glass and acknowledging the man next to me, I made to a seat against the wall as another sat with me. He proceeded to speak but not to me. He spoke as if to some imaginary being whilst looking through me.

His words were, "There was once a fellow who sailed from this house and who could never find himself. He sailed voyage after voyage whilst many grew old and died. Every four to five years, he comes here before he departs again."

He turned away from me to look at the rest of the company as he led in singing an old sea shanty about Adam Edmundson who, two centuries earlier, had joined a ship as a young man to die, as he fell to be crushed between ship and shore before his voyage had begun.

My name is Adam Edmundson. It is written that I shall ever sail upon some ghostly sea, accepted by all mariners never to be free.

Adm

BEYOND

The past week had been tough after the fresh snow had burdened the trail, and a fallen tree had obstructed a narrow pass causing a delay. A burden on time and food. It took over six hours of gruelling work with a bush saw before sled dogs could pass. By the middle of the second week, food supplies had run out and Josh had started to compete with the dogs for food. He had gotten so energyless that even the dog rations of dried fish and beef tasted good. Luck got him back into Dawson thanks to the mail team that gave him food and allowed him to share their fire for two nights on the trail. He had had it tough before and knew the odds were against any man who chose to travel into the jaws of winter's cruellest months in the short, dark days of when the sun hardly floated above a horizon that could rarely be seen. A time when light was so weak and the white rose in depths measured by many feet.

The white had started falling late in the fourth day. He knew it was coming when the sky took on that heavy grey that stretches overhead, making the land feel like a cauldron sealed under a heavy lid that jacked the pressure up. First came the slight rise in temperature. It was then that the dogs had grown silent and seemed to work harder. With the first flurries, they had stopped squabbling amongst themselves and seemed to watch the trees, pausing to inhale deeply as if catching the scent of a heartless beast that had the single-minded intention of driving all life before it into a frozen, bloodless death. Blood freezes in less than twenty minutes up in these heartless northlands, whilst the inner parts of a man linger on without pain in the cruel knowledge that all is lost.

Many of the dogs had wolf blood in their lineage. It showed in their breed, Malamute. The Spitz breed had been bred to serve man; it was the semi-taming of the wolf's spirit, bred for its energy and endurance. But no man would ever tame the cruelty and soulless spirit of the frozen northland where even wolves and bears could freeze to death whilst on the move. This was why, only through wilful stupidity, men ventured into a land at a time when all life chose to sleep. The trees had become empty bones of brittle wood, whilst bears sheltered deep in gorges or caves away from the worst of the cold. With those first falls came a wind that cut like a knife through the oilskins and leathers, freezing perspiration in the pores of skin that then grew sore and septic. A man with wet boots could not expect to survive for long without the curse of frostbite crippling him. Building a fire takes great skill and patience when the ambient temperature is minus fifty. It is in this devil's breath that kerosene freezes, preventing it from being used to light a fire or a life-giving stove. Not even the dogs can survive on frozen hide.

Josh pigheadedly drove on into what became a blizzard that did not abate for sixteen hours. Being forced to stop and camp, every action became a labour and any mistake or delay would have meant death within a few hours. The frostbite crept through his body and hypothermia anaesthetised his awareness to the point of unconsciousness and a slow death. This is what looking death in the face means, for most dead men never see it coming. He had passed dead men on previous trips; the trail wasn't called the Dead Run without reason.

Dawson, a town of thirteen hundred in the 1890s, was placed centrally in the Canadian Yukon Territory, equidistant between the Beaufort Sea and the Gulf of Alaska. Yukon, a name derived in English meaning settlement of gold. There was gold there, but it was not easy to gather. Many found it easier to cheat, steal or sell essential goods at inflated prices to desperate, soft-skinned southerners who travelled out of naivety into a hell of their own ignorance. Many came seeking the riches that the earth was not willing to relinquish easily, and more paid with their lives than struck lucky. Yet a man who knew the wicked game of this god forbidden territory and understood her beauty could, with luck, thrive and trade for a half-comfortable life.

This was Josh's eighth year running mail and provisions along the Three Hundred Trail between Skagway and Dawson; a trail that few knew and fewer had the tenacity and endurance to cross in winter's deep. He settled his team, made provision in the Westminster Hotel, having eaten a steak and drained a quarter of a bottle of Miles Whisky. Next came a bath. His last had been three months earlier and the hot water was the most heavenly thing he could remember. It stung as he climbed into the battered, galvanised steel tub in an absolute opposite to the cold that had torn at his flesh so recently. He held the lilac soap to his nostrils and inhaled the odour of civilisation before slipping back below the water in a moment's escape from an external wilderness that ever dominated his existence. After bathing, he climbed upon the big hotel room bed, but failed to find sleep. After an hour, he made his bed upon the cold, hard floorboards and then slept for thirteen hours.

Turnaround day came too soon. After five days of resting, the dogs had grown restless and the first signs of fat had returned to their scrawny forms. Every pack has a leader, elected through cunning and strength. Lonan had become lead dog not through the traditional way of physical dominance over weaker beasts, for she was lower at the shoulder than some of the other seven dogs were. Yet she lived up to her name that means cloud in native Inuit. She had learnt to understand the weather and could be seen studying the sky and giving warning before some storm or blizzard. This must have been some throwback to an earlier time of her breed when, in order to survive, the primal dog-wolf would have read nature's intent like a truck driver studies his instruments and road signs. It was unusual for a female dog to be dominant, but through sheer intelligence and agility, she had saved the team and the sledge load on many occasions.

Now five years of age, having pulled for three of those years for Josh, she was in her prime. As a young dog, she had pulled for an inexperienced team, led by a half-Indian half-Irishman who drank heavily. Lonan had known a cruel mind of a careless master and held great respect for Josh, for he respected her. Not the respect that a man may hold for his superiors in some servile cowering but the respect earnt through reason and action. Each depended upon the other and, after three years and four thousand miles in traces traversing trails, in some unspoken way two different lives had become one. Man and dog both needed a way to live, sharing a hunger for the energy of life in a place and time that held little comfort for man or beast. Each depended upon the other, for without the relationship that had been forged by the first wolves that crossed the paths of their two-legged soulmates, life in this hostile northland could not be sustained.

Lonan knew, through some secret source unbeknown to men, in a way that was shared with so few of her breed. It was the knowing of the untold that allowed primal hunters to divide into two or more groups and hunt prey; be it a solitary beast or herd of deer, in unison, apart, separated by distance in silent cooperation, each knowing exactly where the other is. This way Lonan had grown restless, standing and waiting, relishing the feel of the taut leather leashes and harness that would bite into her shoulders. As she snarled back at the team behind her, the load broke, allowing the steel runners of the sled to cut a path forward. Even the memory of the sound of steel against ice and the creaking of the wooden structure mixed with the wild yelps from her pack caused her nostrils to flare and her blood to run red deep within the wild, yearning body. Through her, the rest of the team grew restless and hungry for the wild. This was the unfettered spirit of the before time which is alive in all creatures of blood and fur when confronted with nature's challenge — the ultimate challenge to live, for life is the defiance of all that has no feeling and awareness. To meet the challenge is the purpose of all living things, and without that awareness, life is nothing.

Josh had quickly grown uncomfortable with the crowded streets and commotion of city life. He resented the hopelessness of the greedy rich who had come north under the illusion they would increase their riches manyfold through little effort, whilst carrying all the trappings of privilege into a merciless wilderness. Then those of little more than the clothes they travelled in, all driven by greed. It sickened him to see the poorly constructed, overloaded sledges and the inefficient southern dogs that bore a disenchanted look in their eyes and the demeanour of fatalism. The fate of many was to be eaten by their masters before the corpses of those men then fell prey to the ever-shadowing wolves.

Canis lupus, the grey wolf, was wary of man but not fearful of him, because the wolf knew the frozen heartlessness of the region, holding it in high regard with humble respect; a respect that few men have for nature. It is through respectfulness and a pride spawned of dignity that man grew from his lowly cave into the master of all things with one exception — that of a respect for his creator, the nature that formed and ever shaped his soul. Nature, the fluid and ever-changing mood of the world that ran in seasons and could smile upon its plaything or impose the most punishing of cruelties.

Josh had no friends since Adlartoc, his Inuit partner, had died when the big melt had come early, and her sledge had upended and disappeared below the waters of Hudson Sound. All he could do was watch from behind and let out a horse cry of painful despair against a fate that cared little for him and his kind. Now the dogs were his only friends, and he himself had come to think as a dog; he was one of them. Work had become his unconscious distraction from a life that felt as empty and cold as the white winter landscape that he spent his hours travelling through. Both land and man appeared to view time, and the events that it contained, with a solemn indifference. Both simply were — one a traveller, the other the thing that contained him.

The mail was loaded directly onto the sledge from the post office while the dogs were waiting impatiently in an atmosphere of escape that had fallen upon them. Not one had resisted being laced into the traces. People trudged past on the brown compacted snow that had become a mixture of horse shit and ice. The sky overhead had become a seamless grey, and low light levels permanently gave the emotions of evening, even at dawn. A chill late February wind whipped the street, causing the shop signs to flap like the wings of a distressed goose that could never take flight. At the rear of the nine-foot sledge, human and dogs' rations were stacked some four feet high, closest to Josh and furthest from his team of devils. He signed off with the postmaster and pulled the suede scarf that served as a mask over his face, leaving only his husky-blue eyes exposed to the outside world.

Stepping onto the musher's deck, he called "Hike", jerked the brake off out of its anchorage and threw his weight from side to side, breaking the grip of the brown ice that had grasped the steel runners. Feeling the jarring, Lonan knew it was time to pull, leaping forwards and driving her body weight into the ice, as the leather traces of every dog snapped tight as one, and the whole wooden frame groaned, creaked and juddered into a forward motion that soon became a soft gliding, emitting little sound. Each dog was silent and waited for Josh's instruction, which came in single ancient words, for dog sledging has been part of man's survival in the northlands for over two thousand years — a practice that has changed little to this day. With a command delivered like a bark "Haw", each team member knew to pull left along Main Street, past bars and hardware shops. The team knew the route well, pulling hard on the rise out on the south side of the city towards the Yukon River that they would use as an ice road east before cutting south to the town of Fairbanks.

Regardless of modern means of travel, whenever a disaster strikes, be it a car crash or an earthquake, the most reliable source of transportation is our own legs, and time and again dogs have saved human lives through their willingness to cooperate with us. It is so in the dark time of winter up in those northern hostile parts of the world where men are forbidden by nature, but man breaks all rules in a system that can break him in the blink of an eye.

Four days had passed and the only difficulty that had presented itself was a damaged cross spar on the sledge. The dogs had pulled too close to an undercut of rock that had snapped it. Josh had carved a new spar from birch and lashed it in place. The team and man were relaxed but in unfamiliar territory, for each year the trail would be different. Prevailing winds can change the topography by piling snow in different places, felling trees and the freeze thaw that leaves the ever-present danger of rock falls. The trail hardly looks the same from one winter to the next. The year of 1896 was the coldest on record when the Klondike River froze to a depth of over four feet, encapsulating fish in ice. This was discovered when Josh had set camp early one mid-afternoon, sensing the team needed to rest having traversed forty-three miles that day.

Lonan had wandered out over the ice and started to scratch the surface. When Josh finally paid attention to her, he found she was digging towards a large fish locked in the ice. Thirty minutes later, the reassuring smell of wood smoke drifted up into the frozen air, as a fire burnt its fuel of kindling and logs. At the centre of the fire, a pot boiled and in it, a fish was defrosting into a brief life and then poaching, whilst eight dogs sat patiently, warm on their head sides and cold on their rears that faced out into the wilderness. All knew the bounty and pleasure of food and fire; this was the bond between man and wolf-dog that bound them together against a soulless winter land. It was in the in between times when the day's journeying was over, and life's essentials of food and fire had been secured. It was before sleep had been summoned that Josh's thoughts gave way to other times and the things that all creatures of the wild fear. It was now that Adlartoc, his true partner, came to his memory and lowered his spirit into awareness of how lonely his life felt, for he had no other beyond his team.

It is just so that when a man is removed from his tribe and the land of his birth that he draws upon an innermost strength few are ever challenged enough to procure from the depths of who they are. This is the closet embrace a man can feel from all that is of his nature at the point where nature and he become one. For we, too, are beasts once born of hard, wild times in dark places — the before time when man was a wolf and hunted for the spirit energy that nature bestowed only upon the strongest of human predators. It was then that Josh loved his dogs most and worked as a hunter, ate as a dog and slept with those beasts under the ever-changing system of stars that flowed eternally in those unfathomable heavens, which marked the time that contained life through man and dogs' night passes.

Sometime between two and three in the morning, Josh awoke to find Lonan sat bristling and alert next to him in the sharp, clear, icy air. It was the same calling that had drawn them both from sleep. They together sat, watching the creeping colours of light that swept across an open sky, which holds no respect of time and distance between them and the far beyond unknown, as solar winds glowed fluorescing high in the Earth's atmosphere beyond the reach of all below. From the hills to the north, the howl of a lone wolf called across the land, rising to fade as if it was part of the air, ice and rocks, bringing an ancient sound and intermingling with the spirit of a moment that drew upon something deep within the hearts of both man and dog. As it faded, something had awoken in all eight canines and one man who stood in the moonlight, throwing his head hard back to let out a howl that called through the ages to some primeval spirit. The pack howled as one and as they ceased, across great distance, came a solitary answer, which flowed with a great power that told of life.

Dawn came late, as a scratching light clawed its way above the eastern horizon. The dogs seemed reluctant to rise, and Josh set about waking them with oaths and curses told with affection. Camp was broken and the sledge was in motion by seven thirty. Once a few miles had been achieved, Josh had the feeling they were being followed. He had noticed Lonan scenting the air whilst turning her head behind. Twice her eyes had met his. On the third exchange, Josh looked over his shoulders, covering one hundred and eighty degrees of vision. There was something faint in the distance where both fields of view met. The wind blew along the river from the west, channelling between the hills to push against his back, giving a sense of speed that drove the dogs on, who burnt the energy of beef and fresh fish that lay in their bellies. By three in the afternoon, the light was fading fast and they did not find a place to camp until after dark.

Camp was set under the riverbank that jutted out to shield from the wind. The fire blazed and all had fed. It was after the team had settled that the dogs grew restless. Taking a flaming branch from the fire, Josh peered out into the night to see two eyes unblinking, looking back at him. He took a chunk of dried fish from the provisions sack, doused it in fish oil to soften it and threw it in the direction of the eyes. The sound of a wolf chewing could be heard. Josh thought this must have been how the first meeting of man and wolf had turned mutual predators from competitors into comrades.

As Josh slept, ever by his side, oiled and loaded was his Winchester 1897 with its external hammer and tube design that made it one of the most reliable shotguns of all time. Reliability was essential to men such as him, who lived an unmarked life out of time with much of the world that stretched far south below him. Sleep took him beyond the ice and snow into the mind of the wolf. He sensed the isolation bestowed by the terrain's loneliness and hunger that drove the beast on in some unconscious need to survive — the need of a mate and the law of reproduction to ensure the spark gene of lineage continues the battle against time and place. In a fitful sleep, he reached for his gun indecisive as to whether he would shoot that lone wolf, as he realised it would be as if he was to hunt and shoot himself. Just how could he hide from himself in the isolation and singularity of being human in such an inanimate, heartless environment? He was a lone wolf in the night, loping through his dreams, and the wolf was him — dark and cunning, yet so full of oneness with the spirit of the place that had lasted from beyond some beginning.

The fire burnt low to the glowing embers that occasionally sent burning red particles up into the frosting air in a brief rebellion of heat against cold. Lonan looked beyond the fire, sensing another watching. She bristled a little while feeling inquisitive as to what it was. Having taken a faggot of wood in her jaws, she pushed it onto the fire, and flames soon greedily rose, consuming the fuel. She repeated the action against all instincts of her kind that determined that she should run. All of the time, from a distance of some yards, a large, black, male wolf watched with eager attention as if his life depended upon the she dog-wolf who was fearless of fire.

The passing of another day and the junction of a turn, as the team veered south from the smooth going of the Yukon River onto the Fairbanks Trail, which was populated with denser, woodland-covered rolling hills. The trail eased between those hills, curving its way towards civilisation.

A wolf without a name is a dog out alone, not lost but not found. The black wolf shadowed Josh and his team for two days and two nights, hanging closer behind and occasionally using his knowledge of the terrain to be ahead of them. He craved the purpose of the pack and the knowledge that he served that purpose. Snow flurries danced in erratic winds that formed fleeting rainbows, coming and fading in the struggle with sunlight. The team was two days out of Fairbanks and all sensed the approach of rest hard-earnt. It was late afternoon and time to set camp, when running from the behind, the large shape of a dark wolf overtook the sledge at close quarters and bowed wide around the dog team. Josh's hand reached for the Winchester, but having grasped it, he let it go. The wolf was now running with the team in unison with Lonan as if he, too, was under leash and had always had a role to play in the joint effort and purpose against all that defied life. The taming of the wolf was never a conquest; it was through a shared need.

On the last night before entering Fairbanks, the wolf had a name, Lupa, meaning quality. Lupa, whilst keeping his distance, stayed closed to Lonan, having brought a large hare he had caught to eat whilst the other dogs ate their evening rations at feeding time.

Dawn was slow to rise over a land, dusted with fresh snow. The land appeared soft and smooth, and, in each direction, the air full of falling snowdrops met the ground in a seamless indivisible bond to the eye. Josh fed the team that now included a cautious hanger-on who received spare rations. As the town grew visible out of the gloom, the dogs pulled on with vigour towards rest and food. Lupa had run side-by-side with Lonan, side-by-side for four hours and peeled away, doubling back behind the sledge in long, deliberate bounds as if running in snow had no resistance. The mail having been delivered and the team kennelled for the night, Josh found a hotel with a bar and checked himself in for a bath and a long sleep.

Fairbanks was a town growing by the month with prospectors travelling northwards full of naïve optimism, spending money on equipment and provisions that were always in short supply. Then there were the broken men who were exhausted and penniless without hope, returning to the exploitative harsh world of southern cities.

On the following morning, Josh checked with the mail office to register his availability and then made his way to where the dogs were billeted. He found Lonan keener than usual to greet him and he understood her desire to be beyond the town pulling into the wild. What he did not realise was that some greater purpose was growing deep inside of her.

On the third day, the team were harnessed, loaded and drawing the sledge that had had fresh steel runners attached, pulling out north of the city that sits low in the Tanana Valley up into the hill pass against the cold air that ever sinks, keeping the city cold. Sunlight drew down in thin slits through frozen air in shafts, giving the illusion of heat. It was, in reality, work that kept the dogs warm and alive, as they moved ever closer to the Arctic Circle that was only a hundred and ninety-six kilometres above them. They were to follow the route they had arrived by, back to Dawson.

Night seemed to land its darkness like a passing heavy cloud that did not leave but remained, consuming all light before it could reach the land. Lonan seemed reluctant to call a halt to her works, and Josh had to ram the break into the snow and shout many times before she sank to the ground in defeat.

"I don't know what has got into you, girl. But it's bloody well made you an awkward bitch!"

Lonan looked at Josh as he unleashed the dogs. He took her sandy-coloured head between both of his hands and scolded her with affection. This softened her heart and calmness fell upon her, for something in her marked a great change that called her forwards into a different place, readying for something else to come. Rations were distributed to eager fangs and the fire set before sleep. It was then that Lonan sat back on her haunches, throwing her nose to the stars, and let loose a long, low howl that lasted for a full minute. It seemed to climb in tone to the distant stars that watched from far beyond. Moments later, her call was answered in a longer and lower tone. Standing, she inhaled deeply, scenting the air as if searching for a trace of something illusive.

In the morning, the black wolf Lupa was resting by Lonan's side. This angered Josh, who loved and depended upon his lead dog, but he sensed her growing rebellion that demanded freedom; a freedom he had taken for himself and could not deny her.

Sledge team and wolf ran well that day, making good distance along the Yukon River heading northwest. As they stopped and set camp, Lupa veered off into the woods and Lonan followed. They were gone for some hours, returning together with a hare they shared as food. Josh knew what was coming and, the following morning, he leashed his team, leaving Lonan until last. She hesitantly stepped in line and allowed the leather harness to be attached to her bristling body. That day she pulled like a devil, drawing her mates behind her, ever forward, ever deeper into the heart of a wilderness land, summoned by nature in a need of a calling that most men and dogs could never regain from the primary time from which their ancestors had seeded them.

Camp was set and Lonan came to Josh. He again held the yellow sandy fur of her neck tight and pulled it in a fond shaking fashion. His fingers found the heavy leather collar, releasing it from her neck. It fell to the ground as Josh said, "Good luck, girl!"

Lonan, walking a few paces backwards, fixed the man in her eyes. Josh cold see himself reflected from her husky-blue irises, a vision that danced and flickered between fire and moonlight. She leapt back at him in a canine embrace and, for a full minute, both man on his knees and dog were one. It was then that Josh understood the new life she bore, as he mourned the loss of a second love in a lonely life upon a world that had isolated him. Lonan leapt away some yards, turning once and drawing a great breath through her flared nostrils as if to suck the odour of her man friend into her soul in order to carry it within her like the pups that were yet nothing more than fleeting specks of life. Turning away towards Lupa, who waited watching from the treeline that rose like a wooded fortress above the riverbanks, she leapt in great bounds soon to disappear in the swirling snow flurries beyond the woods into a different place in a wild time where freedom and all of its dangers had set her spirit free and wild. This was Josh's gift; his own unacknowledged love of the wilderness that was his calling from the wild.

Josh slept long and deep that night. He did not dream and was oblivious of the great procession of stars that flew without consequence above his resting place. A wind drove fresh snowfalls whilst jostling the trees and, somewhere below the thick ice, the never-resting waters of the Yukon River flowed ever-onwards across a world, indifferent to the will of men. Regardless of all, his existence is intertwined and dependent in a fleeting life that is involved in an endless struggle with the beast of nature — the very nature of the wild that created him and would claim him into an eternity without cause.

Upon waking and having rekindled the fire, coffee was poured and Josh stood, looking across the wide, flat river of ice to the point where Lonan had disappeared from view. Berg was pleased and an eager replacement as lead dog — a Malamute larger and more powerful than Lonan but always respectful of her agile intelligence. Berg was in his prime, being just over four years of age. Now was his chance to show Josh how he could run the sledge team with a missing member.

Dogs are not like humans. They are far more honest about who and what they like. There are no in betweens, just pure rivalry, and subordination to a more dominant creature and loyalty to a leader or the pack. That loyalty in the more intelligent breeds can become an unspoken love where man or dog would risk all for the other. This is a rare occurrence, but records show that where the two species of beast are interdependent, an extremely close bond will grow. Josh had a soft heart, cloaked in a hard exterior, but each member of his team trusted him. He had earnt their respect by being fair. He would never drive a dog too hard as many of the commercial mushers did. He always rested a lame dog in the sledge whilst the others pulled and none resented this, for it was the rule of the pack in the same way that, unless times were extreme, a wolf pack would help an injured member. Skeletons of our primeval human ancestors with broken bones that have been tended and cared for are an indication of social intelligence. The wolf bares this mark, too, when left to their natural instinct in the wild.

It was a deeper need than love that had drawn Lonan away from Josh. Her self-understanding enabled her to choose; self-awareness that few men credit possible. Josh did.

The team ran over the land, covering the miles, burning their energy and time. Josh burnt with them back and forth in a dreamtime that seemed to absorb him into the tasks at hand in each moment. His proficiency kept him and his team alive where many had failed. It never crossed his mind to stop or give up. He drove on, away from the memory of a lost partner.

Spring eased in and burst into the Alaskan summer, which was intense yet brief. This was when he rested between trapping for pelts. He had rented a cabin high in the hills and taken the dogs with him. Josh had developed a wheeled cart that he could hand-push or, on open ground, the dogs could pull. He ever watched the boundary between keeping the dogs alert and making pets of them. He held a fine balance that the dogs respected.

Lupa knew the land and the cruelty of nature. He had grown to be the only adult from a litter of seven. His mother had great intelligence, not the power bestowed only by genes but knowledge sought after and hard-earnt. She had hunted with a reason and understanding that not one in ten thousand men could do. When the winter had grown so hard and many others of her kind had failed, she had learnt how to dig rabbits out of their sleeping earths and how to cheat a meal from the only creature that preyed upon her: the mountain lion. Lupa also learnt from his father whose line came from a time when the world was much younger and had lent its breed to men as the first wolf-dogs many generations before. In more recent times, after his master, a lone prospector had fallen into a ravine to his death, a large, powerful, black Alsatian had returned to the wild joining with his true breed, lending his genes back into that primeval stock in a throwback to when wolves were larger and more powerful. It was that loop in genetic time that gave him his brutal strength and agility that, when combined with his mother's intelligence, made him the most formidable force to challenge the nature of this frozen, white, heartless, northern land.

Lonan learnt fast the ways of the hunt. She opened her senses to the driving force of hunger and the weight of growing lives in her belly. She knew the love of life like few others, for this knowledge was sharpened by having had a life where food was provided in return for pulling a sledge. Now Lonan had a mate upon whom she lent her soul, for Lupa would hunt to feed her and her pups until she could hunt again. The wolf and dog shared a bond that traversed two worlds — that of man and that of the wilderness from a time when great beasts and savages knew nothing but the law of life, kill or be killed, hunt, kill, eat and sleep. Then, there was the duty of the breed to procreate, that the line could chance life against all odds, which nature herself threw against oblivion.

The Earth turned its northern face away from the sun and, by early October, snow was falling that would not retreat for seven months. Lonan had delivered six mewing and suckling, sand-yellow and black cubs into the world late in March. Within five weeks, they were exploring the land outside of the den and tormenting rabbits in play hunting. By October, the four surviving pups were young wolves with gangly legs, but each was driven with a desire to survive. The family had ranged north, avoiding settlements and trails used by men. Lonan, having knowledge of people, had been able to steal from domestic dogs and even broken into a trail camp to raid provisions. It was on one such night time raid that Lonan had raised a commotion amongst a sledge team to enable Lupa to enter the camp and steal food. She had sneaked in with the pack and recognised the scent of one of the dogs from her early days in traces: a lead dog called Berg who hesitated at the sight of an old comrade and quelled the yelps of his team. Lonan had approached feigning friendship, but, once close, made to attack Berg, who set all the hounds barking in frenzy. Lupa entered the camp, ripping at the canvas cover that protected the food to drag a wooden crate of dried salt beef clear of the camp. By hunting and scavenging, all were thriving and ready for winter's toiling hardship, which would be the test of life.

Josh's trousers had grown tight by late September. Four months of feeding on fresh meat and vegetation had put weight on him. Rest and hunting had rebuilt him strong and eager for the winter work. At thirty-three years of age, he was in his prime like a fully-grown wolf who had developed to understand himself in a world that seemed to know everything and could never be outsmarted. By August, a longing had grown deep inside of him, that of a need he had suppressed, a need of a companionship greater than his dog team. The thought of winter's toiling white far from any town or metalled road was his distraction and desire.

Josh closed up the summer cabin on 12th September and turned his back upon the easy months to run into winter's deep. He and the dogs sensed a change in the air, as the acorns pointed full, and green started to fall in droves that crunched under feet. Days grew shorter and the air before dawn sharper. The dogs and their leader started a three-week journey into the autumnal forest, heading down to the city of Fairbanks. By the time they arrived, the first snowfalls of winter would be starting and, soon after, the essential work of sledge, dog and musher would be in demand.

Fairbanks at dawn was cold and deserted as the team pulled in tired. Sleep had been cut short by unusual lights in the sky that had unsettled the dogs and every living creature for many miles. High above them, having travelled for an eternity, a cloud of meteorites sparked and fizzled, burning in the atmosphere. The Perseids brought with them a meteor that hit hard into the snow a mile south of the camp, creating a blast that shook the ground; each meteor burning into oblivion as if it had never been. Josh pulled his team to the post depot and waited forty minutes for the office to open. He booked a run that would be ready for eleven, billeted his dogs and set about buying provisions. Having lived in semi-isolation, Josh felt uncomfortable in the city. Its smells and noises irritated him, so he planned to pull out that day and rest his team beyond the city.

Camp was set under clear sky upon the first soft snow that had not yet compacted. Progress had been slow in all ways, such as the dogs' mischievous breaking out to chase hares before camp was set, and although they never helped, Josh resented their fun whilst he worked. There was a spirit of delight after the first day of what would be many days of pulling in the months to come. The Yukon River was still flowing, so their route would follow the shoreline but head inland where the forest and terrain grew too dense. Carmacks, a village on the river, was their destination some two hundred and twenty miles south of Dawson City — a land where the Tutchone-speaking natives had settled in an attempt to retain independence whilst cohabiting with the modern world. The sledge cargo was medicines for a mission station that served the natives.

Morning rose sharp, clear and cold. Josh woke to the sound of the river crunching water and ice that had washed down from the Dawson Range, which rose high, flanking the land south of them like some great battlement of wilderness where few men had travelled. After the first hour of travel, Josh hauled up to rest and to inspect the team. Each harness, being new, needed to be inspected for flaws that could lead to a break. A failed leash had been the precursor of many an accident upon steep slopes or above a frozen body of water. Once wet in zero temperatures, a fire is the only way to beat the cold that can cause severe frostbite in minutes. Josh knew the law of fire. Without it, survival in this white desert wilderness could not be achieved. He often carried a pouch of smouldering moss, sealed tight in a tin that, through a restriction of air, would smoulder for hours. Wrapped in skins high upon the deck of the sledge was the ever-valued bag of kindling sticks that had dried by the previous night's fire. Under the layers of clothing close to his flesh was its last resort — steel and flint whose spark could reignite the dried moss. Without fire, there would be the danger of bear attacks and, in a severe winter, the wolves would grow brave, driven with a hunger for fresh meat.

The second night came in a harsher way than the previous. A strong wind had blown in from the north, bringing snow from the sky and lifting that on the ground in a ghostly mist that obscured all vision and clung to everything it touched. Collecting windblown branches for fuel and lighting the fire took over an hour of labour. After many attempts, the fire refused to catch, so he resorted to balls of paper and a match, which burnt too fast and released little heat into the wigwam of firewood. Anxiously, the dog team watched small flames flicker before rising in heat to consume more and more kindling. They respected the fire for its warmth and were aware food would follow its birth. Slowly, it grew strong enough to consume the wet branches piled upon it.

Dawn was still some degrees of the Earth's eternal turn upon some invisible spindle away when the dogs woke Josh. They were in formation, circling the man and his fire. Drawing deep lungs full of stinging, icy air, Josh was out of his sleep sack and dressed, standing with his team. Taking a burning log from the fire and hurling it towards the treeline, he saw the shapes of four or five wolves scattering. The camp was under attack. Josh cursed the dogs to stay and not leave the circle. More than a few mushers had journeyed beyond civilisation to find half of their team carrying the pups sired by Dezzi, a true husky named Desire because of his endless promiscuous behaviour. Dezzi, who was of little experience, made to chase after the camp raiders when Josh caught him with a slammed boot into his haunches spinning the seventy-pound animal around and upon his side. Shocked, he retreated to the fire, for otherwise he would have been ripped apart and devoured beyond the circle of eyes and bared white canine teeth that grew under the bulging eyes and bristling hair of Josh's defenders. Each knew what would happen if any one of them broke ranks.

They held their ground for two and a half hours, as false charges were repeated to draw a dog out beyond help. As dawn broke, dim and grey from the east to the northwest, a pack of seventeen wolves were revealed biding their time. Josh had held his gun for hours, but this was his first chance of a clean shot. He took aim at the furthest beast and spoke to his team, as he had always done, warning them of the percussion about to deafen them. The blast shook the air; the far wolf let out a high-pitched yelp and fell upon his side, as his fellow wolves panicked and ran for the frozen cover of the forest. The blast returned in an echo from the far mountains, as disturbed falls of snow cascaded from the nearest trees.

The day started with the team alert and cautious, for they were aware of what awaited them, hidden and peering out of the treeline less than ten yards from the trail. Josh kept his rifle loaded, as it lay atop of the handles of the sledge. He hoped the pack would be distracted by a deer and find feed elsewhere so he and his team could have a peaceful night. Progress that day was slow, labouring in the fresh show now that the iron runners of the sledge sunk into rather than cutting over and through. By three in the afternoon, the light was fading as Josh chose an undercut in a low rock face to make camp. The small cove could only be entered by a gap between a fallen tree and the rocks that rose on a sheer vertical face.

As the fire grew, an air of relaxation settled amongst the team while water boiled, causing the billy can lid to jingle, as it allowed water vapour to escape into air so cold it crystallised and fell as if snow in a microcosm of its own. The clattering lid played a discordant tune that accompanied the crackle of burning wood, whilst from lower in the fire came the smell of charring meat that filled the air with a comfort rarely found on the wild banks of the Klondike River. No man had ever slept in this place and none would stray into it for decades to come. Without each other and the fire, this would have been the loneliest places on earth. Yet out of practised skill and routine, a harsh place became a home for one brief night and even the land seemed to crave the company of man and dog that gave the spirit of life to things, which could never live for themselves.

Night brought sleep to all and in the morning, Josh found all eight dogs lying close to the embers, absorbing the last heat that ebbed and waned under the breath of a breeze that circled in the barricaded space of the camp. In the back of Josh's mind was an anxiety, for they were to head away from the river valley out into open land, which would make that night's camp exposed. The day's travels proceeded well. Moving south, they passed another sledge returning to Fairbanks. The musher exchanged a few words with Josh but being loners there, each did not have much to say. The elder man speculated about the weather worsening and Josh warned about spending the night in the open because of the wolves.

Josh drove on into late afternoon, hoping to find a secure place to camp, but in the end, he settled for a small clearing surrounded by trees. The trees would yield plenty of fuel for the fire and shelter from the north wind that had picked up earlier in the day and not baited. This night, Josh allowed the dogs freedom, not chaining them, but built a fire larger than usual, saving a few longer sticks to serve as torches should they be needed. After eating, he set to cleaning his rifle and ensuring the two cartons of ammunition wrapped in greaseproof paper were dry and in easy reach. The team settled fast as Josh watched the glowing stars drifting overhead and his world moving about him. Thoughts of his lost partner slipped into dreams of what should have been. A full moon climbed in the night sky, white against a velvet blue sheet, punctured by a billion holes that let the light of other worlds and maybe other lives through into his dreams. Each dog shared them, twitching and yelping, as their canine desires passed with the stars towards another day. There was routine, but each new day presented a different space and new problems that man and dog would negotiate through the absolute trust they had in the other.

The following day passed uneventfully until two in the afternoon when Berg brought his team to an abrupt halt. He threw his head back and sniffed the air in repeated short snorts. He then let out a howl that lasted a full two minutes. Bristling and bracing, Berg looked back at Josh for reassurance and leapt forward, pulling the leashes taut with a crack so fierce that every dog was electric and braced for a challenge which none, except Berg, could sense. Minutes later, from a ravine, came four wolves, running slightly behind the sledge and maintaining a distance of fifty or sixty yards. Darkness would fall in less than an hour and Josh knew the four assailants were a harrying team and that another group of wolves would appear on their left flank. If an intelligent alpha male led this pack, there would be a head on confrontation. Josh knew he could not outrun these predators, so he steered his team towards a low incline that was covered in stunted pine trees. He needed a fire, a big fire.

The incline ended with two arms that sloped out onto level ground, recessing in an almost perfect semi-circle. The arms had higher ground that would offer deterrence, leaving him and his dogs open on one side. Having learnt the lesson of the gun, the wolves did not remain static in the open, but merged into the forest on the opposite side of the trail. A fire was built and two smaller fires were set on each side of the opening, ready to light if required. The dogs were chained behind the fire and Josh unrolled his sleeping sack on the open side of the fire in order to be between his sledge team and the wolves. It took dogs and man a long time to settle into what had become a dark night, sealed with heavy clouds that promised snow.

The first disturbance came at three in the morning when a single wolf howling woke Josh. By the time he was on his feet, many wolves were calling from three different directions. The call of the wild subsided, leaving the first howling beast to call a heart-stopping solo that man and dogs understood as a primeval war cry that even men upon a younger world had enacted before some attack, which held the ground between life and death. The first snow flurries of the expected storm were dancing in the air and visibility was down to a few yards. Josh placed his sack behind the fire and moved amongst his dogs, patting them whilst checking their chains and muttering reassuring words to each, as they braced and pushed against his hand in a rare affection that he bestowed upon them. Josh spoke to his dogs as he would when they worked as a team. He was sharp and firm ordering them to remain silent and to stay put.

Repeatedly, in turn from every angle, the wolves came close to tease a pursuit, but none was given. Silence split the air and only the crackling of the fire interrupted the monotony of alert tension. Here was the competition between old and new, the descendants of wolves who had learnt to hunt with man and his precursor whose relentless race in part drove man to be what he was destined to become. It may be true that man, dog and wolf are equal in their tenacity and endurance, but only man has mastered fire in its many forms and this made all others subservient to his power. Again, Josh spoke softly to his team whilst raising his gun and aiming, following a movement close by in the grey snow-filled air. The blast knocked a large male wolf off his feet and sent him dead to the ground. The wolves had yet again learnt the lesson of fire and now had a respect for the man of fire.

Dawn came late for the team, and each member was tired after the night's events. A weak sun reflected from the white that covered all things like the making of a monotonous flow as far as the eye could see. They broke camp and headed out into a featureless landscape, bar the elevation of rocks and hills. In such a bleak and harsh place, nature shapes man driving his actions. Unbeknown to him, the struggle preoccupied his mind and time. This is the purpose that so many city dwellers unconsciously yearn for but do not understand. This is the call of the wild that most crave but never reach in a life where we try to control so much around us while failing to control ourselves. The day's trek proved uneventful, as temperatures fell in a sunless, static air. The night passed peacefully and the following day matched the previous, as all fell into a familiar routine that served the purpose of survival.

Josh Lanier had been born in the city of Vancouver to a French mother and American father. He had grown up working on the family smallholding, spending much of his time tending livestock and in the company of animals. He had left home in pursuit of adventure and ended up applying his skills with animals to dog teams, and finally had his own team. He could never admit it to himself, but he preferred the company of his team to any stranger with a conversation in a bar. He was a loner born out of experience and the tenacity of original ingenuity that matched him in the harsh life, doled out by nature in a land where few would ever be drawn except for the love of gold and the illusion of getting rich quickly with little effort. Josh knew that upon this earth there could be no gain without endeavour. The beat-up weak frames of once fit, young men were evident in every town he had ever stopped in. Unlike him, they bore to the illusion of the American Dream of a material wealth that had little to do with the law of life. Under this illusion, many perished and most suffered for the rest of their lives.

Josh knew he could not jinx time and that he, too, would grow weaker and older. But whilst there was energy in his body, he would defy the challenge of life in the wild, and if need be, he would accept defeat there. He had known the love of a woman and that love had been forged through a unity against nature's heartless will that drove them to survive for each other. This made his loss the greater and that lost love was now invested in his team who, in an unspoken way, knew of the love he bestowed upon them. After weeks of hauling, often man and dogs in harness drew that sledge into winter's depths upon a frozen edge of the world where the cold raged its fury on a sleeping land. Leather harnesses, the hours of work, fire, food, and sleep, harsh words and effort, whimpering and barking under a relentless sky. Then the occasional gentle praise and soft caress of love that ever remained hidden in brief private exchanges between Josh and his team.

At Christmas, after the last mail haul, Josh planned a two-week rest. He had booked himself into a guesthouse and the dogs into a kennel, which had an open fire at the centre of the doghouse. His plans were obliterated when the Postmaster General of the Northern Commercial Company paid him a personal visit with a commission to run the third leg of a relay team that had to traverse over three hundred miles in five days, transporting medicine to the city of Nome up in the Alaskan Arctic Circle. He could not refuse, as there were few men and dog teams left who had experience of the route. It had to be a success, for life depended on it. Unbeknown to Josh, the eyes of the world's press were on him and the other twenty relay teams. This journey would prove to be the toughest of Josh's life in impossible conditions to save the lives of others.

He departed early morning on Christmas Eve on what should have been a five-day journey. Under unusually clear skies and a bright cold sun, the team pulled north, each member energised by a brief rest and an unspoken challenge to cover a great distance, crossing from the Klondike into Alaska. It was unusual for a team to attempt such a run in deep winter, but Josh and his dogs were in their prime. By midday, the sky had grown heavy and the temperature had fallen to minus fifty-two centigrade. Snow was falling and soon created a whiteout, yet the dogs navigated through instinct and senses not bestowed upon Josh. Conditions grew fierce, driving the team without Josh's command to draw to shelter in a small hollow of land, flanked on two sides by pine trees that tripped the wind, giving a little shelter. Josh fed the dogs to reward them and made ready to pull on, for he knew there was a cabin two miles further along the trail. The cabin would hold provisions and dry firewood. It was a law amongst all sledge drivers that any wood burnt would be replaced for the next occupant.

The dogs pulled forwards with Josh running alongside, desperately trying to keep warm. After the first mile, upon a steep turn, the sledge runner rail caught an ice-covered rock that lay unseen. It raised one side of the sledge to the point of being out of balance whereby it turned over upon a now exhausted Josh. In harness, the dogs were trapped and could not pull the sledge to free him. He feebly fought against the weight, as the cold bit into him. After struggling for a few minutes, Berg threw his head back and let out a howl that could match the call of any wild wolf. It seemed to be a call of despair, yet its long wailing held a defiance of the snow that muffled all communication. Frostbite was blackening Josh's cheeks and nose, and he was starting to accept the inevitable, as chilled blood drove into his heart, sapping his life-giving energy. Snow slipped its binding and flowed in small rivers around the dogs and sledge, covering a half of it. After another hour, Josh would be removed from sight.

Berg's howl did not go unanswered. From a distant hillside, a double howl returned as if an echo but inaudible to the human ear. The sledge was now buried in snow and Josh unconscious. Unbeknown to him, a dog and dark wolf had sensed a danger and heard Berg's call at the limits of perceptible sound. Having run for four miles, they arrived at the sledge to snarl and spur the team into life. Berg was up and straining at the twisted leashes. Within moments, the rest of the team were barking and straining with great will to move the dead weight.

With great strength, Lupa dug the gathered snow from the high side of the sledge, while Lonan excavated it from around Josh, freeing his arms. Then, as the team pulled and Josh jerked at the sledge, Lupa and Lonan pushed upon the turned side of the sledge. The sledge moved slightly forward, raising the fallen side until it fell right, freeing Josh. Without hesitation, the wolf and dog dragged him to the stand at the rear of the sledge where he was able, with clenched fists and teeth, to pull himself up onto the musher's foot ledge. Without command, the team pulled on, escorted by an old friend and her mate.

DEVIL'S BAG

I had never thought about hell; I had no reason to. Life had been fast and full, having dabbled with religion, but it had never grabbed me or stimulated my intellect. There was one time — as a teenager in between wakefulness and sleep — that a sinister laughter came to me, and it has haunted me ever since.

I am certainly no angel, but I do not consider myself as evil either. Yes, I guess if I found a bag of money, I might just hang onto it but, when tested, I proved to be honest. The test came a few years later after the sinister laughter. As a London restaurant manager, having closed late, I banked the takings of several thousand pounds in the night safe of the NatWest Bank on Charring Cross Road opposite Leicester Square Underground Station. As I opened the deposit box, there in front of me were the money bags of a previous banking. I slammed the gate closed, as thousands of pounds that could have been mine dropped into the bank's strong room. I have forever regretted being honest ever since. Well, maybe not, but as I have grown more cynical with age, observing how corrupt this world is, I often wonder if I should have changed my rulebook. Several tests have come my way since; however, my honesty has remained intact and the guilt, which is the first gate before the drop into hell, has remained closed.

Whilst labouring to earn my keep, I have often considered how life would be if I had no conscience, but, of course, that is only a daydream. On the other hand, is it possible to do an evil thing without hurting others? This question gives rise to a self-deception of immense proportions, opening a portal of badness that others have sunk into. Can an evil be justified when used to prevent a greater evil? Well, the Allied Command dropped two atom bombs with this excuse in mind.

I do not think I ever did enter into an evil act, but my demise grew out of a temptation that is there for us all, and the devil took my hand. Once he had me, he would not let go. The turning point broke after midnight on 7th February 2000, as I made my way through the London streets to catch a taxi home. My shift had lasted eighteen hours and ended with a double whisky in a club bar where I was a regular, brief late drinker. As I walked along the damp street, ahead of me a young man in a smart suit was kicking the living hell out of an older man who was curled in a ball upon the pavement. He was being kicked across the street like a football as he groaned in pain with each impact. The street was otherwise empty. Things happened so fast that I have no recall of thinking. I ran with full speed, opening my adrenal valves to the max. I exploded upon the assailant like a cannon, knocking him flying with a shoulder barge that had the impact of a tactical nuclear weapon. As he regained his feet, I leapt forwards throwing a punch that nearly broke my knuckles but sent him falling hard upon the pavement. He tried to get up, staggered a little and collapsed. I calmed and, upon regaining my composure, realised what had happened.

I checked the elderly victim of the former assailant to find that apart from what appeared to be a broken rib — for he was clutching his chest — he was going to be all right. The smart younger attacker remained unconscious; his rucksack upon the ground. I called an ambulance and looked into his bag to find an identity. It was stuffed with crisp fifty-pound notes. Without thinking, I grabbed a bundle of money, filled the pockets of the old street man's ragged overcoat, and told him to wait for the ambulance. He reached for my hand and squeezed it, looking me directly in the eyes. I can say that I have never had such gratitude poured into me without a word being exchanged.

I manoeuvred the younger man into the recovery position, having checked his pulse and breath. Grabbing his rucksack, I abandoned the scene. As I walked away, I could hear the siren of an ambulance growing in volume. By the time I stepped into the black cab, blue lights were reflecting off the wet road and walls around me. I didn't look back. Tired, I slumped into the back seats avoiding conversation with the driver, Alfred, who often drove me north of the city to my rented apartment. He was a Nigerian student who was self-funding his accountancy qualifications by driving a taxi. The dull orange hue of street lamps blurred my view of the passing city, as shop windows and homes slipped by unknown in their hundreds. I closed my eyes and tried to reach the purpose of all of those sleeping hidden lives encased within. Alfred woke me and I stepped out into a suburban landscape of familiarity.

"Don't forget your bag," called Alfred as I walked away.

Thanking him, I handed over a large bundle of notes telling him to take a few nights off. His services were paid on account, so he wasn't expecting payment.

"Are you sure?" was his surprised reply.

I answered, "Get out of here!"

The engine revved, tyres shortly slipped against wet tarmac and away he accelerated into the night. I could hear the heavy beat of Pink Floyd's anthem to money, "Money! Get Away", as he faded into the distance.

Sleep took me deep that night and ran late into the following morning. I had forgotten the bag of money and was surprised to find it, counted and stacked neatly upon my coffee table. There it was and I had no recollection of counting it. Then the question hit me. What was I going to do with it? I was now in possession of what may be stolen money that, in turn, had been stolen from the thief by me. I didn't know it, but the devil had me by the hand. I don't recall how I spent that day, but, by evening, I had paid off all of my debts, rent and bills. It was then that the suspicion was dawning upon me that no matter how much of the money I spent, there would always be the same amount in the bag. In response to this, I set about testing the idea and set off the following night to hand two of the notes to each needy or street person I could find. The following day, the bag was as full as it was twenty-four hours earlier. I repeated the charity, giving a few times more.

Then one city night, I left the bag behind, and I now know that I didn't sleep a wink the following night. By trial and error, I discovered that if I failed to hand out money to those who needed it, I would be deprived of sleep and experience nightmares of inexplicable pain, always accompanied by the haunting laughter that had awoken me years earlier.

Eighteen years on, my health was suffering and the only way I could find peace was to live with the homeless people around the West End of London. I always gave money anonymously by leaving it in a sleeping bag that was left in a shop doorway or by giving a book with the money secreted within its pages. But someone had witnessed me and that is where the attack happened: a young man in a suit came to my regular sleeping place and grabbed the money bag. I hung on and he kicked me repeatedly until a passer-by defended me. When my assailant had been defeated, my saviour checked me over to see if I was all right. Our eyes met fixed upon each other's gaze in recognition. It was then that I recognised my younger self at the point without understanding that he sensed his future.

I now write from a bed in Charring Cross Hospital, where I fear death will take me soon. I am not sad to be leaving a corrupted life. I write this to a younger version of myself, who is out there doing good work that is instigated by a demon. My warning is to that younger self, should he learn who we are and the trick that we have both fallen for. Should I survive, I will set myself free and, in doing so, no longer be who I am today. So, the next time you are passing a street sleeper on a cold night, look at their rucksack for it may have been mine once.

HINTERLAND

It was dull — not simply gloomy, but oppressively dull. There was a rancid odour in the air too — not the smell of death but that of decay, a precursor of death. The house, at a guess to all who passed by upon the old road, would appear to have a brighter demeanour with its straight wide gravel path, softened with a few weeds that led to the grand pillared porch and hard dark riveted oak door. It was at the porch that I balked at the foreboding sense of a deep darkness, the sort that transcends time. Having travelled from the town after ten that morning in the promising spring sunlight, although the air had got cooler, I drove down into the valley and along the River Stacks road.

I am a writer of wills working for the small firm of Dyke & Jarvis in the town of Keswick that sits at the top of the English Lake District. The house named Hinterland had the appearance of a noble old man who still polished his medals that were now becoming too large for his frail body. It certainly was a grand house. I say was, as it is still there, but something has changed since that visit in April, 1960. I am an old man now and my medals are my memories.

51

Having opened the rusting iron gates and driven in, I parked my Morris Traveller inconspicuously to the side of the gravelled area and approached the door on foot. The old established garden still held a natural charm that was dying out in suburbia where evergreens and conifer trees seemed to be most desired. The doors creaked open, giving the impression they were rarely used. I was unable to see the opener who remained out of sight until I was invited in, having to slip sideways between the dusty wood of door and frame. An elderly lady, tall and slim yet energetic in appearance, greeted me peering over the top of her pince-nez glasses. I introduced myself and was invited into a pompous drawing room that, whilst elegant, was showing considerable signs of decay. The yellow walls had faded and the blue ceiling and architrave had cracked with blotches of water stains imitating maps of some imaginary land.

I declined a drink and got straight to the point of my visit, which was to inspect and ratify alterations to a will that a colleague, now long retired, had written many years before. I asked the elderly lady, who hadn't given her name even though I had introduced myself, to see the will and whether she was involved in it. Silently and without taking her pale blue eyes off me, she went to a bureau and removed a file, which she delicately opened and handed to me. I felt inadequate, for my office could not find the master copy, which we had been paid to secure and, consequently, I had not a clue what the documents were about.

Handing the files to me, we made conversation in an awkward way about my journey to the house and I asked how long her family had owned the property. She answered slowly as if considering every word, telling that her family could be traced back eight hundred years to a Catholic priest who had preached from a small church that was on the site of Hinterland.

Whilst talking, I had opened the documents to see all the pages were blank. We spoke of insignificant things for a few moments until I drew her attention to those old, frail, plain papers of no meaning. Her manner froze, as her watery blue eyes panned one hundred and eighty degrees to fix upon mine where they lingered coldly for an increasingly uncomfortable few moments. Fumbling to break my discomfort, I suggested that this was not the will and that perhaps there may be another file in the bureau.

Blinking and reaching down blindly as if she was to smack me, she took the papers, studied them intently, and to my great surprise began to read whilst turning her back on me. I felt a growing sense of discomfort as that large high-ceilinged room seemed to close in upon me and the air grew heavy. Turning to me, she looked me in the eye as I became aware of a shimmering light that seemed to glow where her eyes were. In the fraction of a held breath, I saw her skull devoid of all flesh. Choking, I took the papers without a word. To my amazement, I started to read the handwritten words upon the old paper that had a reassuring feel about it. After the formal description and usual passages that would be found in any will, I reached a page that spoke of a burial chamber in Latin, *Ne signatos disputationi animas permanere usibus* (To remain sealed lest timeless souls be reclaimed). I asked the creature that I was growing convinced was not just a woman but something else if she knew the meaning of this page. Sitting down across the room from me with the light streaming behind her from a large window, I could only see an impression of her face.

Hesitantly, she spoke. "You must help us."

This was the first indication that I was dealing with a living being.

She went on. "We have been prisoners in this world for four hundred and seventy-six years, locked out of our tomb."

She continued to explain, to my incredulous disbelief, a story that even today, many years later, I revisit and tremble, for there is much we cannot know. The will recorded ownership of the property and its bequeathment to a Mr and Mrs Calpure in 1548, with the stipulation that the property ownership could not be transferred out of the family's direct bloodline. She explained from that chair with light splitting in shafts around her head and shoulders that she was barren and could not bear children. This had locked her and her husband into a perpetual life in the house, unable to leave. My task was to witness a change in the terms of the will to allow them to enter the family tomb and be done with life forever. Shaken but trying to be reasonably professional, I asked as to whose instructions I could take in order to rewrite this legal document. Upon asking, the light from the window dimmed as if a shadow had been cast and, for a brief moment, I could see her face that now had the countenance of peace. She appeared much younger.

From outside of the house, the sound of steel against stone could be heard in occasional bursts as if a mason was at work. Standing, she approached me and took the papers to the bureau. Using a quill and ink, she began to write. Returning, she placed the papers, quill and inkwell upon a small wooden table that sat between us. Closing the room door, she lit a candle that was mounted in a long brass candlestick and then drew the heavy curtains across the windows. An immediate chill settled into that now enclosed space. Sitting back down in her chair, she blew the candle out and we remained in absolute darkness. Gripping the mahogany arms of the chair that had become my only reference to a reality, I felt a silence, maybe the silence of the grave. After some minutes, the air had become still as if it was becoming frozen water. Then, from the direction of the table, came the sound of a metal nib against the porcelain inkwell and a scratching of handwriting upon paper.

I felt the presence of someone or something pass me and heard the room door open. With that, she drew the curtains, allowing the relief of light to return stinging my eyes that had been bulging with the strain of denied vision moments earlier. The scent of candle fumes came to my nose reassuringly, as she motioned to the document that lay upon the wooden floor saying it was now my turn. I picked the papers up carefully to not smudge the glistening new ink and signed my name, Richard Parker, under a fresh clause that overrode the restriction of sale. As I straightened my back, the whole scene around me had changed. My client had disappeared and I found myself in a very old and dilapidated house; the great window glass was smashed and partly boarded over and dust covered the faded furniture.

Upon leaving the building in a confused state, I wandered in the gardens to regain my composure before driving back to the town. At one side of the house, some eighty or so yards into an overgrown shrubbery, I could see a natural stone mausoleum. Upon close inspection, the stone door seemed to have been recently worked with fresh flakes of stone upon the paving at the entrance. I shook with shock and bolted, driving my placid little Morris as if it was a sports car. I didn't even close the gates.

The following morning, after the first client had left my small office, I turned to the papers that my assistant had left for my attention upon the old pine desk. There, to my great surprise, was a document titled "Hinterland". Below the clauses and stipulations in age-faded ink was my name.

Betty, my assistant, knocked the office door, poked her head around, and with one arm waved a bottle of whisky at me. Slipping into the room, she explained that a lovely young woman had left this sending her gratitude. Written upon the label of an ancient bottle were the words: Thank you for deliverance.

Each year on a specific April night around the time of my birthday, I wrap up warm and sit in my garden facing down the valley towards Hinterland whilst sipping a warming whisky and wondering at what I had signed my name to. It is strange how after sixty years that bottle is as full as it was in 1960. It seems to warm me more now that I am older.

QUERCIA

Mine is no ordinary story. It is one born from a place beyond reach through study, endeavour or adventure. Only chance can deliver it into such a place, or maybe it is a state of mind, for I am unsure which yet. Once there, like some shimmering glimpse of absolute beauty, it held me so mesmerised that it was hard to look away. Beyond those moments of enthral, there is also an evil that crushes the soul of even those of the greatest bravery. Growth happens all the time. It mostly appears as a slow laborious process. When looked back upon time itself, however, it seems to have sped up and lasted but for a moment, and the change delivered in its generations through generations of babies into men is maintaining characteristics. It is also the same for plants and geographical structures.

Mine is such, being a time-gnarled family that has lived on this patch of semi-tamed wilderness a few miles south of the town of Oak Bluffs in Massachusetts. It is a place of rolling hills and sheltered valleys. Here, winter's mists can rise mysteriously in no time at all to cover the land in a milky softness after storms so violent that trees can be uprooted and hurled against the ground as if some vengeful wraith has vented its temper in ways that no man can match. The summers are calm and warm, and this makes it ideal timber country where my ancestors have worn their lives out felling timber that has yielded without resistance from the forest. Along with my ancestors who have lived here, are the trees that have changed little, but there is change in all, and they have had a vengeful bearing upon each other; this now has fallen to me in a confusing burden that I am yet to balance.

The original family business, that can be traced back five generations, is the lumber trade. Those men of trees who felled native hardwood timber for the logging industry worked long and hard, wreaking devastation upon that ancient community whose roots and bloodline reach back many thousands of years to the last ice age. The trees have witnessed much change and, for them, time has a different meaning than it does for men. Each tree is interrelated almost as if they are one, roots and fungal cords interconnect, enabling the weak to be sustained by the strong. These trees never die, for each is absorbed into the next, and I now have reason to suspect that in every standing tree is the memory and soul of all of those who have lived before.

Today, I manage plantations of spruce and pine that cover what was once ancient oak-forested land. There are still a few of the old specimens of Quercia oaks growing where it was uneconomical to fell and log them. I hold some reverence for these old-timers from a previous age that my forefathers knew and whose ghosts wander amongst now long-rotted stumps.

For the main part, the land here is in a broad sheltered valley that rises up into rolling hills on the northwest side, climbing to Oak Bluff where the land cuts away as if a great cataclysmic hatchet had once landed, felling the rise into a sheer drop of about five hundred feet. Looking down into the bluff, only those mighty, sinuous roots bejewelled by sporadic rocks hold the orange, clay-rich soil, where my predecessors sleep, from flowing down into the valley in a single explosion of movement. It is as if those roots, that are as old as time, grasp the land like the fingers upon a desperate hand to prevent it from flowing away. Up here, we bury our dead who then are absorbed in the growth of those watching and waiting oaks. This is their revenge upon my family for our plundering of their society of trees like a native Indian tribe whose wraiths demand retribution for a blundering invaders' massacre.

The oldest trees remain perched high, towering over the bluff that holds their name. They absorb the weather's worst, as it rolls in from the Atlantic, softening the blow for the weaker trees lower in the valley. From up there, they are sentinel beacons to a spirit that passively ruled this place for a period vastly greater than there have been men here. These trees made the soil and formed a climate, even sculpted the land. They are the reason I am here. Upon the ridge of the bluff is a hollow on the ground where the root stump of a felled oak has rotted out. It is known as the Wolf Pit, for wolves' skulls have been found there. The large trunk of that tree is over six feet in girth, and it has not decayed for some strange reason. This has always intrigued me. It is of an ancient oak that must have stood one hundred and twenty feet high and spread its canopy half as wide again. That great fallen girth now sleeps on its side. Yet even though my family record shows it was felled over two hundred years ago, it still resists death by sprouting a few lateral shoots of the freshest green foliage that produce the most perfect hard oval acorns I ever did see. It is with one of these acorns, clenched in his time-beaten fist, that we buried my father twenty-two years ago after he died under a falling limb in the very place where he now rests. There is a sturdy sapling of thirty feet rising from that transforming grave.

Walter Henry Smith, one of the family's first to work on the land, felled that tree, but never lived to remove it. The story told over the generations is that the tree, although severed from its mighty roots, refused to die. Judging from the density of the wood and the now collapsed crown, this magnificent beast must have started its life as an acorn over two thousand years ago. It was my wife Flora's idea that we cut a flat seat and backrest into that resilient trunk so that we could sit there and enjoy the view whilst spending time with Jack, my father. The view stretches out over the coastal plains towards the sea from where the migrating geese fly in for winter and out for summer.

One evening in early fall, as the leaves were on the turn before the light faded, I drove out along the track that runs diagonally through the plantation. I know this land better than I know my own face. Having parked, I climbed the bluff on its easier side for about forty minutes with my light chainsaw and enough fuel to cut two six-foot scars out of that old trunk that lies sleeping above Oaks Bluff. This would be a place for me to come when I had time to relax. I had always felt it is a special place and climbed here often as a boy. Arriving at the lookout point, I rested and smoked a little before setting up my weapon and going through the safety checks that had become a sort of traditional war dance, which I enacted whenever starting a chainsaw. I know the damage a saw can do to a tree in no time and have seen what happens to a body when a chain and maximum revs interact with flesh. The air was still and the light was turning to orange as a low sun was starting to reflect from the far horizon under the higher clouds, backlighting the lower ones. I knew my father and grandfather would have witnessed this view and felt their presence. Both were buried up here along with all the rest of my ancestors. I, too, will one day be absorbed into the land in this very spot.

Starting the saw, it growled low rising into a purr and then a scream — this was its war cry. Pulling the visor down on my SawTech helmet, I lowered the chain to the wood as the smell of hot sap met my nostrils and a snow of sawdust began to scatter about my feet. I love the smell of freshly cut oak that rises, drawing a calm mood and memories from my first efforts at splitting logs as a boy.

I hadn't cut much more than six inches when, despite my ear defenders and the roar of the machine, I heard a scream. Switching off and removing my gloves and helmet, my legs felt wet. Looking down, they appeared to be covered in blood. In a sort of panic and confusion, I removed my boots and trousers yet felt no pain. I surely couldn't have cut myself as the saw had remained at the oak all of the time. My confusion grew when, although drenched in blood, I had no injury upon my body. It was then that I remembered the scream and turned back to that stubborn old trunk. The sun had now sunk low, and the light was level and weakening, but there it was — the cut wood was not dead wood but as fresh as a thirty-year-old trunk, rooted strong and sure in the ground. There was a red blood-like sap, flowing from the linear cut and forming a pool on the ground. When I lifted my saw to avoid it becoming saturated in blood, I clearly heard that scream again. I dropped the damned saw and peered in the twilight into that haunted trunk. There, in the wood, was the face of my father; next to him were the faces of six others, one being my grandfather. It was then that I understood, and it was then that the trunk rolled, crushing my right leg and trapping me in excruciating agony.

My rescue came hours later by naval helicopter and, after six months in hospital, I can walk with a stick. I am home now and shall never fell another tree. Some years hence, my son Oli will bury me by that everlasting trunk. I, too, shall grasp an acorn in each clenched fist that only fresh life will open with fertile growth. Life into life and surely but slowly, I will become a great tree, towering over a world that few men can understand. Oli is an ecologist, hell-bent on returning this hallowed land that contains the magic of life back in time to the ancient oak forest, which will forever remain until the final storm that will change all things.

Olli

JOE

(PLEASE DON'T CRY, FOR HIS TEARS HAVE LONG DRIED)

Blind with age, Joe sits content with eighty-seven years of memories that come knocking at his mind's door, as he drifts through his last hours. The grand armchair, which holds him like a womb, is wide but not too wide, giving an unconscious comfort of a mother's embrace. Sat by his apartment window that overlooks the street below, he feels the warming of the sun as it climbs into afternoon, and then the gentle chill as evening draws its curtains to a dull light. Dawn brings the sparrows who feed upon the breadcrumbs he leaves for them. They wake him with shrill calls and one enters the room to steal from his supper plate that sits upon a dark wooden table by his right-hand side.

Once the birds have left, he dreams again until the delivery vans arrive out on the street and an engine stops. The sliding and slamming of doors make him turn his head in the direction of the sound — all too familiar from years of listening. The sound of a doorknocker way over the street comes to his ear. A moment later, a door opens with a jarring squeak and Mrs Jarvis' voice can be heard as she pays the milkman whose bottles clash a tune repeated every day at the same time. A youth whistles as the whirl of a bicycle's wheels pass below along the pavement, bumping over the stone joints. Into morning, the sound of cars whining in high pitch as they approach and play a deeper Doppler tune, then move into the distance. A dog barks at a cat that overturns a bin as it bolts. Somebody coughs before entering one of the shops below. Pigeons cooing amorously and, in the distance, the drone of a passenger jet can be heard as it heads out upon a climbing path. There is a clicking sound as the gutters shrink in the cooling air.

Joe remembers a day after school seventy-five years earlier when he and Mitch Monterey scrumped apples from Farmer Jones' orchard and had to flee from his dog Beth who came running and barking at them. They threw apples for her and turned pursuit into a game of fetch. Beth never barked at them again.

He sleeps his chin upon his chest and shudders at a thought far in his past. Schoolmaster Driscoll has him by the ear and is threatening the cane after Joe, twelve years of age, has broken a window with his brown leather football. Peace settles in his mind as he remembers long shuddering draughts of red wine with Rosemary Pearce in her parents' garden and the sleepy, dizzy feeling that drowned his head again when he kissed her. She had married Mitch, raised six kids, and then died when the number twenty-four bus crashed into Pilkington's Bridge. Her kiss still lives on in Joe's mind.

Years come relived and terror awakens to be calmed and soothed by the remembered voices of long parted family and friends. From high above in an apartment, a baby cries into life as Joe closes his eyes for the last time and his lips part to let a slow, gentle breath escape as his lungs reach equilibrium. His heart beats on, slowing for a few more minutes as he feels the kiss of his long-lost love, Ethel, who waits for him in the place where he will soon be.

PUDDLES IN TIME

Dark is the night. Labour and pain still to calm, a mother's first words to her baby. Innocent and mewing, this suckling child opens his lungs to cry and cough mucus from its mouth, so loud yet unheard outside as if he hadn't been born. Not a sound on the street. A child born to poverty. The cries fill this room, travelling from the raised bed along the grey walls to the window. Beyond the dull curtains that hang open, all proceeds with indifference. Rain-washed pavements glimmer under the faint orange streetlights and all human activity is asleep. A faint moon dodges clouds that deny its waning existence. Languidly from tiredness, the portly elderly midwife boils the bloodstained towels and linen to white. Steam rises from the kitchen below, driven by the coal fire that boiled the water.

It is one thirty in the morning; a time when imaginations creep and other worldliness enters this place, which is otherwise hollow. Holding the innocence close and smiling, exhaustion overwhelms this first-time mother, as her breathing slows and her smile grows. Silently, her breathing ceases, her soul beams in a serene peace and leaves — all in contrast to the tearing violence of birth into this world of no particular care. The child is alone — a single life in a world of deceptions. What of his chance, what will life bring to this poor wretch? There is no father to lead, only fate awaits this baby. Never will the sound of his mother's voice whisper into his ear. Lost is so much love. What will fill his heart so loveless and world-hardened? Where will he go and what can he do? What is to become of him?

Downstairs, the door opens, and as a priest comes into this house of rented rooms, he pays the midwife in coins and she leaves with a bundle of rags. Dark-robed and white-collared, the priest enters our gloomy room of death. He closes the mother's eyes and lifts the child coldly into a motherless world.

Five years later, having been fostered four times (once for a week), our boy is weak and snivelling. It is winter in Kentish Town, an inner suburb of North London. Traffic passes noisily just feet from a basement window that looks across a narrow pavement to the roadside gutter where discarded cartons and wrappers blow with still smouldering cigarettes butts. Inside, cold and damp stream upon the outer wall. A woman dressed in denim trousers and a loose blouse stands hand-washing dishes at a sink. A man is slumped, holding a brown beer bottle and watching television. They are awaiting a social security check. Our child has eczema; the sores crack the skin upon his face, arms and the backs of his hands. He hurts, but he is accustomed to pain. There are no other children here.

Ten years on, our child has a new name, Johnathan. He attends school where he doesn't fit in. He has trouble concentrating and the words in books will never stay still for long enough to be read. Johnathan fights his classmates. He rebels against his teachers who have no time for him. At sixteen years, he is out of school and working as a delivery boy for a stationery company. He is of medium height with dark, sharp eyes — the eyes of a frightened animal. His arms hang long and loose. He is a gangly teenager with lipid, unwashed, dark hair. Johnathan doesn't know what he wants and he's sick of being told what he needs.

By the age of eighteen, he is leaving the back of a police van and being led handcuffed to a police sergeant into Camden Town Criminal Court. Drugs are his failing, the taking and supplying. Drugs have become his friends and replaced a mother and father that never had a chance. A love that never grew is now a dark, angry, unconscious state of mind, and this young man wants to fight. Surly and resistive, he mumbles his name to the court. Sentence is passed and he arrives in Wormwood Scrubs Jail for a twelve-month sentence. Life gets harder. Daily routine drags and the atmosphere of repression hangs heavy upon our boy's soul. He learns to fight dirty and develops a taste for evil. He doesn't flinch at pain being so removed from that cushion of life: love.

At twenty years of age, he is dealing again. Central London is his pitch. It is 1981. Lord John, as his contacts call him, stands at the junction between Leicester Square and Charring Cross Road. His cigarette remains burning in his hand and the ash hangs lengthening, as do his burnt years. Black taxis zigzag across lanes, competing with red buses and big expensive cars. Leicester Square, or Squester's Lair as his clients called his pitch, is a dirty, crowded, threatening place in the 1980s. Recession has closed shops and many retail lets are short-term, low-rent seedy shops and kebab houses. Lord John works out of a sex shop in Cranbourne Street opposite the Club Hippodrome. This shop sells leather aphrodisiacs, labelled from China but made in the basement. Dildos of all imagined shapes and sizes adorn the window. Our young man carries the largest by means of defence — a two-foot black erect phallus. He had to use it one night to deter two muggers in St Martin's Lane. From then on, when drunk in The Lamb and Flag, he would recount to great laughter how he drew his dildo and dildoed his two attackers into a pulp. Satisfaction!

Twenty-five years of age and his lordship is no longer selling from his pitch on that corner; he has others selling for him. Twenty-three others. He dresses smartly and has an expensive haircut. Having learnt his trade hard, he keeps his runners at arm's length; this keeps the police off his back. One officer has become a friend and customer who takes a kick for free. This ensures smooth trade. Unlike his smart attire, his rented one-bedroom apartment is a mess, but it is the nearest thing that he has ever known to a home. The restauranteurs, bar staff and cafe workers are now his family. Like rats of the night, they glean and fleece a living out of tourists and each other. This is his world. He knows no other. There is no softness of feeling in his life, no women have found him, and his virginity remains his unchallenged fear. A loveless life leads to a love-blocked life. Having never been loved, Johnathan is unable to experience love. Although surrounded by prostitutes, nightclubs and porn joints, this young man is uninitiated to women. During the three years of his second foster home, the boyfriend of his foster mother sexually abused him. He had long since blocked this experience from his memory and thought that he would never return to it. Except... and there is always a twist of exception.

Late on a wet Saturday night, he had gone down to a confined restaurant basement toilet to pee. Whilst washing, a middle-aged man entered behind him. He unconsciously recognised the cologne from an earlier, more painful time. He felt his waist being grabbed and a hand between his legs. Rage burst upon him, the rage of a childhood stolen, anger at being held and at who he was not and could never be. He lashed at the face of this tall slim man, and kicked and kicked until there was no energy left to hurt anymore. Johnathan climbed over the body and left the establishment exiting into the cool, late London air. He was physically shattered and emotionally empty. In the distance, the wail of approaching sirens could be heard.

Puddles form in the paving outside of Johnathan's new home. The air is cool and the sun bright on the morning of his thirty-fifth birthday. Mews houses merge when seen from the lower end of the street and the colours of painted walls blend with spring flowers. It is April. Johnathan strides along this street, cocky and floating. He has more money than he can spend and he has time upon his hands. Where will he go and how will he spend it? For this is his birthday. Having missed so many, he is determined to do something. As he moves away from us, cigarette smoke lingers upon the sharp morning air and we can smell it. He reaches the end of his home street and turns left into Charring Cross Road. We know his destination. He has a friend who is a nightclub manager and he knows where he can get free drinks at nine thirty in the morning. How else should a thirty-five-year-old man about town start his special day?

Pigeons rise en masse, as he kicks a beer can at a sleeping vagrant in the middle of Leicester Square. They circle a few times and then settle on the high roofs that corral the area. He skips across the pavement to disappear into Club Maximus. Ricki greets Johnathan with a grin and a hug. Ricki likes him because he knows all the big crime names who operate in this Square and the few miles that drift into the City of London. Drugs come with Johnathan, and Ricki's customers always want drugs. Vodka is mixed and drunk; it is drunk again, as the cleaners clear the previous night's dereliction from around them. It is now late morning. Ricki and Johnathan are outside, walking and smoking. There is a drugs delivery to collect at The Victoria public house by Victoria Station. Landlord Jimi Fraser is the distributer middleman, an ageing wide boy, one time cousin and fixer for the 1960s gangster twins Ronnie and Reggie Kray. Fraser also does a profitable line in counterfeit twenty-pound notes that sell at ten pounds a note.

Today, Fraser wasn't a happy gangster. His competitors had smashed the front of his pub with explosives. The papers said it was a gas explosion, it was. Three oxyacetylene canisters detonated with IRA Semtex. The money safe had become so hot with the blast that three hundred thousand pounds in twenty-pound notes was now pure carbon powder. You can't insure counterfeit money. Some live for money, others for brutal pleasure and debauchery. Jimi Fraser (a.k.a. twenty-for-ten) lived for the thrill of the pain he could cause others. Johnathan hasn't reached this stage yet. This happy day, like most in Johnathan's life, ended badly. Drunk and out of pocket.

Lord John doubles his money by cashing his earnings into twenties. Fraser, a nasty piece of work, met his end when someone far nicer than him fixed the brakes on his new black Range Rover and he drove at speed up a tree. There were bullet holes in the back of the car, but the police didn't worry about these. Inspector Channing was pleased to see him cremated and attended the solemn ceremony in person. He even bought flowers — opium poppies — specially donated by a rival gang.

It is summer, 2005. Hurricane Katrina is beating the southern United States and the Kyoto protocol is being negotiated to hold back global warming. An earthquake killing seventy thousand people devastates Kashmir, but Johnathan and much of England are oblivious. After clambering from his two-week unmade bed, he is looking in his bathroom mirror and, for the first time, he sees himself clearly: a forty-five-year-old single man. He also sees the father he never knew looking back at him. In this moment, for the first time, he understands who he is. He is looking around his home and sees the mess he is living in. He feels all of this, but cannot hold it in his mind. This infuriates him and increases his sense of inadequacy. Lord

John has work to do. He now works out of a small office above a tobacconist's shop in a back street that runs off The Strand. He has employed a young lady to help with phone calls and basic accounting. Lisa is sweet, innocent and pretty; she is also intelligent. For the first time in his life, Johnathan has close contact with someone who is not out to fiddle and hurt him. This makes him feel like he has never felt before.

Trade continues, the drugs change, but the money remains the same; it grows in piles in bogus accounts for no reason at all. All bosses have bosses and his lordship, as he is now known in the clubs and bars that he wastes his time in, has one main supplier. It is never good to limit your trade to one source and this is his failing. Supply ceases and a rival trader muscles in on his territory. He had not laid a finger on Lisa, but tonight he has taken her for dinner in Soho. Having finished their meal and whilst walking trying to hail a taxi, they are confronted by thugs from another dealership. He is able to defend himself, taking only a few minor injuries, but Lisa is hospitalised with a punctured eardrum and fractured shoulder. Again, for the first time, Johnathan feels responsible and a need to help her. He takes her to hospital and visits her the following day. Love grows in our man and he doesn't understand what is happening. During the following days, his contacts defect out of need and trade ceases. His need to see Lisa grows and she has no idea why thugs set them about.

Two years on and Lisa has moved in with Johnathan. They live in his Mews house that is now polished and neat. Trade is no longer drugs; it is a bicycle shop. Cycling is a growing business and this shop has an edge. Johnathan ships in counterfeit Mercian cycles from China and sells them like the hand-built originals for a great profit. Life is good and he at last has found love. In 2010, he finds the bicycle shop trashed and scorched. Lisa is gone and Johnathan has been fitted up to take responsibility for a spate of drugs deaths. Twelve years in jail is his term. He is forty-seven and will be at least fifty-five when he is next free. Whilst locked up, the Old Lady of Threadneedle Street changes the appearance of banknotes, rendering thousands of pounds of his stash worthless. Depression settles upon our boy and he grows intolerant and violent. All that he desires is Lisa's love and he doesn't know where she is.

Day after day, he polishes red-tiled floors and grows vegetables in the prison garden. The clank of iron bars and heavy doors becomes the sound of his life. Prison guards unreasonable and inmates treasonous to one another. Aggression and an atmosphere of repressed violence hang in these corridors and cells where men tread time, breathing the ever-present vapour of disinfectant.

Johnathan is losing fitness and is settling into slack uncaring ways. He occupies unknowingly the cell that his father resided in thirty years earlier. Welshman Mark Beynon didn't know he had a son. A sometime market trader and heavy drinker, a womaniser without a conscience, who had a record of assaults, he had been imprisoned for murder of a train driver who had slept with his girl. He had lost his love and his life to prison. Now Johnathan has lost his only fleeting experience of an awkward love; this left him feeling hollow and embittered.

It's 2015 and Johnathan is being released. He has a kit bag and one hundred and twenty pounds; his shoes do not fit, as his feet have spread with age. Another elderly frail man leaves with him; this man is a lifer, released because he is dying. Johnathan looks into the eyes of the grey-haired old man who walks slowly with a stoop. He is seeing his future. Jonathan has just looked into his father's eyes and each shall never know it.

Life is a great mystery. Anything else is arrogance. Every one of us lives following a random path that opens each day in front of us. We take bearings; however, random events steer our choice of action. Johnathan is an intelligent man; he has proved this time again yet society never embraced him. It is as if the world didn't need him, just as it rejected that old man, his father. Some close the doors to strangers; institutions and workplaces are closed to someone who thinks or looks different from the standard mould. Universities are a closed shop except to those of wealth and the luck of a good memory. Original thinkers and creators are usually too different to be embraced.

Johnathan — the man who found love for a moment, the man who fought his bad luck by making his own rules. He is now fifty-nine and he has a small flat in Camden Town, London, having adopted a street dog as a friend who he calls Dominic in memory of the bent copper who helped him get his trade going in the early years. Dominic is sat tied up outside the local library where he has a bowl of water and lots of treats and attention from passers-by who got to know him over the weeks.

Inside, in a quiet corner, sits our man. Occasionally, he reaches into his rucksack to lift a bottle to his lips. He types on an old battered tablet and sometimes smiles looking up to dream. Lisa comes back to him and the bicycle shop, the smell of metal, paint and grease. He thinks of that corner in Leicester Square, Ricki, and the clubs. Buried deep within him are those first and last words his mother told him, "Lead a good life, my lovely. Do it for me, for mine is wasted."

Click, click is the sound of the slow typed keyboard as he writes the words you are now reading. This evening, after a bowl of potato soup and two bottles of Guinness, Johnathan lies sideways on his two-seater sofa. He kisses a creased, faded photograph of Lisa as Dominic the dog curls into him. He smiles and then closes his eyes for the last time. The silence in his flat spills out into this late November night where all is at peace. It is as if our boy had never been born.

ELEVEN MINUTES TO ONE

Midnight came and passed in silence, apart from the last train out of London until six hours later. Building speed, it slowly accelerated until it faded into a higher pitch, passing Battersea Power Station and beyond the reach of sound. Pell lay huddled in his Parka coat against the cold and wet that blew in upon windy gusts under the old door he had propped against a wall as a night shelter. He had slept in worst places and gone hungry for longer periods than this. The thought that the baker's shop would be open by eight that morning kept hope alive, giving him the will to hang on. The unsold sandwiches and maybe a loaf would be thrown out in the bins. Once he had scraped the dirt off and pulled away the parts with mouse droppings, he could fill that empty craving feeling which pained deep in his stomach. He would have to be quick though. The past two mornings, a woman with two small kids had beaten him and taken everything. It was a poor show scavenging damp crusts left for the pigeons and ducks in the park, but it had come to this. He did not feel shame, more anger at the scowling looks he received from those comfortable well-fed people who watched him. What did they know about hard times and hunger, the loneliness of rejection?

The past two weeks had been cruelly cold as was to be expected in January. He had avoided the hostel at St Mungo's where he could get a bed and some of that lovely stewed beef soup. Oh, how he craved a mug of beef soup and a bunk for the night! But that would cost him the seven quid he had stolen when those three teenagers set about him down on Embankment whilst he rested in a bus shelter. They had just got off the bus and laid into him, kicking and swearing, calling him dirty and ignorant. How were they to know he had a first class engineering degree and had managed the construction of Centre Point, that massive office block occupying 101 to 103 New Oxford Street, fronting Charring Cross Road on the site of a former gallows? That was in a different life, a far-off time in the mid-sixties. It was ironic that the building, which remained empty, became a temporary shelter for the homeless and he had built the bloody thing in the first place. He had heard it was a listed building now and it had his name as the building's engineer on a plaque inside the entrance of what are now expensive flats. Well, they had kicked him like a football until one had cut his hand with a knife. It was then that he handed the ten-pound note so they would leave him alone. Those ten pounds had been hard earnt playing his mouth organ in Covent Garden. Nobody had paid attention to him except the pigeons and the kid who had pointed at him telling his mummy that that man smells. It was then that a tall fella had come over to him and asked the way to the opera house.

Having received directions, he turned and walked away without thanks. It was only then that Pell had noticed the ten-pound note turning in the breeze at his feet.

Pell, now in his late sixties, hadn't seen a note like that in weeks and he dived at it like a mad man lest any other got to it. He was used to small change that people tossed at him. He guessed that the gentleman bound for the opera didn't want to embarrass him by offering charity, so he dropped a tenner out of sympathy. People had many different ways of giving him money. Some just emptied their pockets upon the pavement, sending coins rolling all over the place. Others would appear embarrassed, sidle up without looking him in the eye and place some coins in his upturned cap that lay at his feet. He had to watch that cap. More than once, kids or another down-and-out type would make a grab and run. There were no rules or dignity in being down on your luck.

Pell had seen many things since he was ill and had been evicted from his flat in North London over four years ago. Once homeless, in debt and broke with a conviction for drunk and disorderly behaviour, there was no way back into society, none whatsoever. If you are unwell and cannot work, you cannot pay your bills and the benefits would never have been enough to keep a roof over his head. He was now proficient as a beggar, having studied others who had many more years on the streets than him. He had spent the summer with Danny. Being twenty years younger, Danny had more energy and together they had begged outside posh hotels and by cash machines, cadged at the back doors of restaurants and sneaked into hotels for a wash or even a shower. Danny was a pavement artist working with chalks. This could earn a pretty penny on a dry Saturday afternoon and then they would get drunk together in St. James's Park. Danny and Pell had raised hell in Horse Guards Parade until the guardsmen had let them into the guardroom to warm for the night. They had shared a cell together after a kind arresting police officer had taken pity and dropped the charges at seven in the morning, ejecting them from Rochester Row Police Station before his inspector arrived for work. But Danny had drunk too much a few weeks earlier and the cold had got him. Hypothermia killed many chaps like him when they had been on the lash. The only reason they drank was to cope with the cold, but it killed in the end.

The wind hammered so hard against the old wooden door, which Pell had lifted out of a skip, that it was sliding down and the rain was getting at him. He couldn't sleep, so decided to move on in search of luck. He wandered for about an hour, getting wet through and finally collapsed under the stilts of an office block. Although cold with temperatures barely above freezing, the rain and sleet couldn't get to him here. Shivering and hungry, at eleven minutes to one, he fell asleep.

At eight o'clock the following morning, the storm had passed revealing a bright day in which wet roads and pavements glowed as if cleansed by some fantastic event. In the brightness, a woman in her early thirties with two young children had been waiting at the rear of Victoria Bakery. As the gates were unlocked and the previous day's unsold bread and sandwiches dumped in an industrial bin, she came forwards retrieving what was still editable.

A mile away at the famous landmark building Centre Point, a police car had stopped and was parked on the pavement. An unconscious man had been carried into the building and laid upon a chair. Whilst removing his wet coat, one of the officers was talking to a paramedic who had just entered the scene.

"We see this a lot at this time of year, he's our third this week. It's the hypothermia that gets them, and how tragic that there would have been a warm bed and grub for him in here this time last year before they sold the lot for posh flats." The officer pulled a timeworn leather wallet from the coat pocket. There was an old business card in there, which read: Mr Pell Frischmann, Chartered Engineer. Turning, the officer noticed a brass plaque on the wall in the reception of the building. It read:

"This building was designed by George Marsh of the architects R. Seifert & Partners with engineer Pell Frischmann and was constructed by Wimpey Construction from 1963 to 1966 for £5.5 million. The precast segments were formed of fine concrete, utilising crushed Portland stone; they were made by Portcrete Limited at Portland, Isle of Portland, Dorset, and transported to London by lorry."

$\mathcal{JEC}$

BIRD'S WORDS

Sometimes I write for the sake of it. It's easy, but can be discordant. Other times, I have a brief, a subject to research. But strangest of all is what I call just words and this can leave me feeling a little lost. It is the weirdest of experiences that can happen to me, and it never materialises in an empty space. There is always something there. It is like a drainpipe or a laser beam, or a ray of light. I know this might sound strange, but late in the night in those cold small hours, words appear on my screen. Those words have names, characters and they take on lives. I have met some beautiful words past midnight, those that come in chains holding hands with others who are brothers and sisters, lovers or friends. Then, there are the ones of darkness, those that have a sinister intent not through how they sound but by how they look. These words are less rounded and can bear teeth in jagged type — the sort of words that corrupt letters into words that stand out upon a page.

I have lived — that is, I am no spring chicken having seen the best and the worst that this world has to offer. I say this to indicate that I do not frighten easily. Well, here is a sequence of events that made me leave my house at two thirty-seven in the morning and burn my laptop there, because I could never let those word combinations free onto the Internet and I hope that no one else has a relationship with the stream of words that I have. Words are simply codes of sound, recorded since sound fades into an empty space of silence, a space that awaits the next to follow. Imagine the last word of a dying language that has represented a civilisation in a now extinct tone. That flow of words which locks into my mind to appear upon my screen often bypassing my consciousness is not always in English, my mother tongue. I could handle foreign words that required translation, but words that appear in structured sentences with no explanation of meaning is something else. I had recently read an article in the science papers about the discovery of a civilisation that existed in a city built between one hundred and sixty thousand and two hundred and sixty years ago, expanding over one thousand five hundred square kilometres. The archaeological find was north of Maputo, Mozambique. The Sumerian archaic pre-cuneiform script, along with the Egyptian hieroglyph writing, were considered the earliest true writing systems dating to 3400 BC.

Words from two hundred thousand years in the past is a thing to contemplate. Can it be true? Well, I had transcribed onto my screen a jumble of shapes, bird's wings, eyes and various other objects. I gazed hard at the screen in amazement asking myself, "What is that?" I left the room and went to the bathroom and upon returning, my computer had been moved and was radiating a lot of heat; the case was covered in fine, red, sandy dust. I was more intrigued than frightened and because of the heat, I switched the machine off and fell asleep on my sofa.

Upon awakening before dawn, I found myself hot in a dry atmosphere. The walls of the room I was in were stone with small unglazed windows and a single doorway through which a steady draft of dry, hot air streamed. I removed the reed blanket that covered me, arising to peer out of that door. There, a city of two-storey buildings stretched out ahead of me in silence as if it was deserted. This appeared to be a dead city and, as I wandered through alleys and narrow streets, I could not find a single soul. Turning from a wider road and then into a square, a large building appeared and I assumed it was a temple.

I must have slipped and hit my head, for upon awakening some time later, I had a wound on my forehead and a red dust was stuck to the congealed blood that surrounded it. I was back in my room, covered in dust and scorching with the heat of burnt air, being completely confused assuming I was still dreaming. I was not. Opening my front door, my world was as it should be.

I washed and dressed the head wound that had healed, leaving a scar in the shape of a bird's skull. I could not bring myself to turn my computer on, so worked that day without mentioning my experience to my colleagues. Being exhausted, I showered, ate a simple supper, and fell asleep upon that same sofa as the previous night. I awoke shortly after two in the morning feeling hot with a dry throat. When I reached to turn on the light, the switch was not there. I had returned to that dead city from a dream. There, on the floor, was my computer glowing with those haunting words upon the screen. Overburdened with fear and anger, I picked up the computer and ran out of the building in a mad fit of panic. Outside, as if awaiting me, stood a tall, thin man dressed in a robe of many colours. He gestured me to give him the computer and follow him. We returned to the temple where I had fallen. Upon entering, there was a fire burning on an altar and he placed the computer in the fire. The plastic melted fizzling and spitting. Turning to me, he put his thumbs over my eyes and it was then that I found myself back in my room, dusty and without that blasted computer.

Time passed in periods of months. I had replaced my laptop and begun to write again when one spring night, after some hours of writing, I noticed that the letters made the outline of a bird's skull. Cool head, I picked up my smartphone and searched for Maputo archaeology. There, to my surprise, was a long report about the bird's head civilisation that evidently seemed to have a cult of imagined time-travel to reach their gods and had a symbol above the gate to their temples that looked very much like an Apple laptop computer. Only instead of an apple logo, there in a circle was an emblem of a bird's head, the one scared upon my forehead.

JOHN

John was a misfit; always left out, bullied as a schoolboy, intimidated by a frustrated mother and beaten to concussion by a disappointed father. His two sisters were silent witnesses who carried their own unrecognised damage. John had once attempted suicide, but fortune had saved him. He had wandered into the Fontainebleau forest south of Paris with a brandy bottle in deep melancholy. He hung a plaited rope in a birch tree; the noose was not tight and his mind was clear. Having thought of everything, he jumped and it was then he realised his mistake. Instinct took over and he reached for the rope that cut through his hands. For minutes, he hung easing the pain by holding the noose to release the pressure. His mind raced from childhood into recent days, all whilst the pain grew, as his vision faded. The last he heard was the birds in the forest and then silence. Three young men had found him with moments of life left in him; two had lifted the third that, in turn, lifted John back into life.

He travelled, away from life, moving south into Spain, feeling the land, studying the people, walking in the mountains through Andalusia, south to Barcelona, where he lived in a cupboard room with a mattress and sleeping bag, pouring drinks and serving tapas from twelve to twelve. He pushed on west to Madrid as a year or two passed. Drifting through towns, hitching rides and bumming on trains, he spent three years zigzagging through France, Belgium, Germany and Italy. There were hard times and softer times, stealing food and money from lowly jobs. John found himself in Prague working for an elderly widow who owned a bar. She was the only person who had respected him, but when she died, her family sacked him and he rolled on into Eastern Europe. He learnt to beg in Russian and made money by selling potatoes in the market square central in St. Petersburg. He drank and smoked with others, and played chess sat on the ground in Red Square, Moscow, when the temperature was minus twenty-two degrees, with a Russian soldier who had lost his leg in the Chechen War.

With most of Europe and a third of Russia behind him and growing tired, he had been out of contact with his previous life for years. He had lost who he was, yet not found who he should be. Tiredness filled his body and sadness swept his mind. He never lost his charm and there were women, but none could satisfy his intelligence and none lasted. He stayed with one in her beaten-up Soviet high-rise blockhouse for nine months until she died of an overdose; then the authorities deported him back to England. Immigration at the port gave him a hard time because he had no identity, and a bitter copper beat him and kicked him out onto the streets having checked his fingerprints. Many thinkers become suicides, but occasionally the understanding of perceptions focuses through the prism of a rage that has grown in a furnace of boiling emotions over a lifetime. Supping from spills and leftovers on pub plates, he had drifted for years and now it was too late. Repressed anger and a denied intelligence had blown a mental bulkhead and in a fraction of a moment's injustice, the poet had become a killer. Groaning and screaming inside, he stumbled on into the hills, not knowing if he had killed.

John was denied scraps that were due to the bin and his coins refused across a dirty bar. That was the last insult against a powerful mind that could outthink most. He dropped his bundle to headbutt the frail bar owner and then set about the jeering clientele. Years of odd jobs, digging vegetable gardens and unblocking drains had made a strong physique a dominating force. The three policemen couldn't hold him and it was when Met Officer 287 raised his truncation to inflict a blow of uncalled for malice that rage erupted in John's mind, as he blocked the blow to step forwards throwing a punch to the officer's throat. John's furious eyes were the last thing that 287 would see. Out into the dark, through the cold winter shadow-dancing streets, tears streaming, fear streaking, anger gave way to regret, and shame flowed in his blood. Self-pity grew and his legs became weak.

Up into the fells he ran until he could only manage a walk; he could hear the bark of the dogs in his pursuit. The moon was high and bright and, from far below, torches by the dozen glowed. Falling to his knees and, pulling a chain, a gold locket came free from his pocket. Under the silver light far from any home, he kissed a glazed lock of a woman's hair.

Anna had been his only love; he had fallen in love with the image of her before he had found her. Knowing what he was looking for, he had spent all of his time off work looking for a particular woman who may not have existed. Back then, he was a researcher at Cambridge University, running psychological experiments upon people with antisocial behaviour problems — a subject that fascinated this lonely man. Anna had arrived at the university later in life, aged twenty-eight, to study etymology. Being older, she did not fit in with the younger students and John found her sat in one of the college gardens drawing sketches of people. One night of talking followed by a day in a shared bed welded these two like the two circles of an infinity sign. It was a train crash that killed Anna and left John broken.

Closing his eyes and slumping forward, his heart calmed to a slow thump. He could feel the fresh cold of frosted brittle grass against his face. The first dog reached a body that no one knew nor cared for. Just another lowly vagrant yet once a woman had loved him so. A lost lover's heart now ceased through will alone.

LAST CATHEDRAL

Upon the dirt track that winds up into the hills from a 2 small village, a man and dog move laboriously, climbing in the late afternoon sun. The man has travelled this path many times over a period of seventy-two years. The dog, too, knows every step of the way, but this time they will travel further than ever before. A few hours pass and the village falls far below them, hidden by the larch trees that stand like an army, guarding the valley that flows as a sheet of never-ending green as far as the eye can see. Afternoon is now turning upon evening and the light has changed spectrum, making the brown of tree trunks darker and the foliage a far deeper green than before. Gnats dance in the near horizontal rays of light and grey rabbits become more alert to the coming night.

Looking at the man questioningly, the dog sits as the man pauses to rest upon a rocky outcrop that has been used by both many times before. The man pours cool water that sparkles into a fist-sized hollow in the stone as the eleven-year-old Border collie watches intently and then drinks gratefully. Swallows scream across the land below them, heading into the evening, and smoke drifts its softening low over a river that snakes lazily on. After a few minutes, the man, looking at his friend, mutters a few fond words, ruffles his neck and stands to walk. Another two hours pass and the walk has become a climb, but both continue unquestioningly until they reach a small plateau that cuts from the main pass to a junior hilltop. It is here that they spend the night.

Barber the dog knows his job of old, whilst the man offloads his rucksack. The dog gathers enough sticks for a small fire, and then both man and dog watch a pan of meat boil and the sun fall beyond the hills that flank the far valley side into another day somewhere else. Both eat heartily before sleeping in a worn bag that is shared by both. The man drinks from a hip flask full of whisky that is as old as he is. Stars now watch over them as the hills and valley turn against the procession of a never-ending, seamless, deep, black sky. The embers of the fire glow a little warmth as Barber curls close into the man who dreams of previous walks in years past on this date to sleep upon this very spot and repeat a dream over again of a reality once lived.

It was nearly fifty-two years earlier that he had climbed to this point with Faina, a dark-haired Russian girl from over the border, whose father ran a lumber business. She had become his wife. He had loved her for many years until illness had swiftly stolen her smile and touch from him. Then he dreamt of thirty-eight years past when he first climbed with his two sons. As dawn's first inkling shot orange and yellow shafts upon an awaiting dome of open sky, light from the edge of the world glowed in the moments before daybreak. He shuddered as he had many times before and cried for lost love.

For some, cathedrals are holy, but for this man's fondest memories a small ledge one thousand metres above sea level was the holiest place he could have been. His two sons, born two years apart, also shared his love for this ledge, but they could no longer be there, having both ended their lives fighting in the Ukrainian war four years earlier. In his life as a farmer, he had grown accustomed to death, but nothing could have prepared him for the wide-open empty space of loneliness in which he found himself. His dreams had brought back the voices of boys and the softness of a wife, all the early rises and late finishes that farming had involved.

Upon awakening, with the fire rekindled and coffee brewed, Stephan considered his last morning. He would not descend to the village. Having given Barber a drink and a hunk of meat, the dog was ordered home with a note in a bag attached to his collar. Reluctantly, Barber set off for the village, and seven hours later, an old friend read the note.

Stephan now remains forever in a dream of memories that shall accompany him into a time when nature has taken even the hill in which he climbed into nothingness. Today, a stone cairn stands four feet high upon that small plateau and, under it, the dreams of what was once a man and his dog rest safe and happy.

ROOM

White chrysanthemums upon a table; table stood on a carpeted floor. A woman in the room doorway dressed like a whore: tight skirt, buttoned blouse, bust bursting, perfume flowing. There is a cat curled asleep upon a chair. Dark-patterned curtains drawn, letting light through a slit. Cigarette burning.

His collar loosened, sitting on the bed. Music from the radio; 1930s is the tune. Late afternoon, but there is a faint moon. She walks forward, closing the door. Looking down, she slips his braces, as he looks away. They say nothing to each other.

Whisky is poured and sipped between clouds of smoke. He lies back; she unlaces his shoes as a police siren passes into late afternoon. He loosens his shirt buttons. She becomes shorter as she slips off her high heels. His wallet is upon a table next to a snub revolver.

The radio changes its tune. Outside the second-storey window, a stalling truck screeches to stop as another vehicle hoots in protest, then rumbles away. The cotton sheets yield softness; her lips red and dry. Sitting down beside him, she reaches to loosen his trousers, giving it a try. Closing his eyes, he thinks of what she is hiding and stiffens for the shock. Her hand is upon him and he is not resisting though he has never done this before.

A fly buzzes distractions in the room to settle on the ceiling, drawing his look. Removing her blouse, bra straps and cups is all it takes to make him kiss her. She shudders in delight for he is young and firm. She has done it all before. From him, there is nothing she can learn, but there is money in his wallet and some of it she will earn.

The light hangs from the ceiling, faintly swinging in the air. The cat awakens to jump from its chair. She is in her panties, breasts upon his chest; his clothes now scattered on the floor. There is an empty glass upturned and the cat is licking at its rim. Her tongue is upon his nipples as he grasps her waist.

Outside, the light is fading and those table flowers close with the day. He thinks of another from a far-off more innocent day. She is thinking of cooking dinner for an eight-year-old boy who is close. Her silver necklace dangles teasingly in his face as she closes for the final sexual embrace. He shudders and whimpers holding on to her thighs. She theatrically lets out a modest cry.

Dressed and standing, drinking a glass of water having helped herself from his wallet, she leaves closing the door. Slowly and naked with a tear in his eye, he picks up the revolver and, through his head, he aims at the sky. There is light through the curtains. The cat has left the room. All is silent and there is blood flowing on the floor.

ଯୁ

AN ORDINARY DAY

That day was or could have been any other, but it was a day that had a twist in it, which I could never have foreseen. My journey was one that had been traversed many times upon streets, unchanging and populated with monotonous similarity. The traffic unobserved, droned past exhaling the reassuring exhaust of familiarity in a rise and fall of engine revs that paused impatiently at intersection lights. The usual clatter of feet upon subway steps and then the interruption of all that was familiar and usual, an interruption of sound. The absolute silence following a percussion that came with heat and flames, which drove dust into my panic-drawing lungs, leaving me crumpled against the tunnel wall stunned.

The ringing in my ears came before smoke and dusty abrasions of sight returned after struggling to open my eyes. At first, I was in a dream and reached for the clock that stands upon my bedside cabinet. It announced with luminous green arms 08:30 a.m. Was this a waking dream, a reality or a nightmare? Looking around me, I understood little, and it was when I tried to raise myself into a sitting position that the pain hit me, shooting from my buttock down my left leg. I let out a cry and must have passed out. Regaining consciousness, I was floating, looking at a myriad of oblong white stars that focused into the subway roof tiles and Art Deco lights that leered at me like scavenging hungry vultures. I now know that I was strapped tight into an aluminium-framed stretcher and was being evacuated from whatever had happened. The next thing I remember is the ambulance, muffled words and a mask being placed over my face. The rest became a beautiful peace from which I knew I didn't want to escape.

There were lightning bolts that broke the peace and someone thumping at my door, but wearily I did not answer or react to the electric charge of the defibrillator or the heart-thumping massage. Peace came and I felt happy in a painless, floating space where beauty came in rills of scented flowers that I drifted through upon an orchestra of gentle, soaring string music. Beyond this, there was nothing (that is, until the cold of the mortuary and the slamming of sluice compartment doors). It was cold in there, but I could not move or shake. Then came the darkness of the coffin lid and the brief whine of electric drills screwing the lid down as I pressed into the purple velvet cushioning of a lonely interior.

It struck me as strange being able to watch from the outside but not being there and unable to move in my confined space. Somehow, I accepted my lot. I wondered if it was like this for others. I watched the trolley being wheeled out through double glass doors and slid into the back of a long, black, well-polished vehicle. I heard the engine start and the two men in front laugh at a joke.

The journey did not last long and I felt the cold as they carried me slowly and rhythmically across the uneven grass to a pile of freshly dug, damp soil. The air was scented with autumn decay and it pleased me in a reassuring way. I did not want to be lowered into that pit and could not see who was there; it was very few people. One lady looked familiar, but I couldn't place her. Then came the clonking of soil and grit upon this polished box lid. Soon, the sound became muffled and then silent. I accepted this as I was not there. I felt as if I was in that sterile impersonal subway tunnel and that is where I remain. I sit through hours that have now become years, unseen and watching. I do not move much because of the pain in my leg. No one sees me except the dogs that travel the subway with unsuspecting owners. The dogs and night rats know I am here. I occasionally tickle one on the muzzle or behind its ear as they pull towards me. My watch still says 08:30 when time stopped for me.

DANNY

Vacant are the eyes of this pavement-sitting man. Limp are his lips from which a city river so full of words once flowed. Wild is his grey matted hair that resembles the waves of his life's storms. He has sailed upon time's oceans and witnessed many sad dawns. Needing a cigarette and a shot of Cognac before he can move, now closing towards sunset, he knows there may never be another dawn. Swigging from the easing bottle, he sits upon his stool. He had scribed this on a pavement the other day that he knew that life travels in only one way. A portrait of his last morn, now it is pink dust and he is not there. Trousers soiled, jacket dirty and worn. Undergarments ragged; like his soul, they are torn. He has chalks in his pocket. Danny is his name.

Parisian pavement artist of fifty-two years, he has scribed for his life. Now he has drawn upon the last pavement in a dusty hue. He knew the bars where he could get free beers, boiled potatoes and stale crusts too. All of his creations for a few centimes. Great were his fleeting chalkings that passed all too soon. Now washed away by rain, scuffed are the pavements that bore his lasting pain by those who pass unseeing, for they are life's wasters who are the insane.

Danny knew the constellations and many remote emotions that only dreamers can find. He had drawn the stars that were his company in the lonely times. A dreaming lover, who in his dirty rags has travelled far. His last pair of boots was nearly done. He had no use for another, nor could he feel the warmth of the sun. He worked in the hotels and bars of this city for his board. Once he had a lover who bore him a child. Jade passed him once upon the pavement; their eyes met unknowing. She turned back to drop a franc for his rainbow flowers and then moved briskly on.

His chalkings upon the pavement are a city's soul laid bare. They picked up the last Parisian pavement artist. He had slipped into the Seine. Police took up his body this morning; it was about half past ten. These summer dusty pavements will never be so colourful again. I miss him and his work as I walk by where he sat every day. Now there is only litter where, with thick chalk, he used to work and play, and one brandy bottle that the sweepers never clear away; it has rested there now for many years. Jade teaches art in a theatre, Sorbonne, every second day. Her favourite medium is rainbow chalks as if Danny had shown her how. If I ever fall out of luck, I think that I will become like Danny, sat upon a pavement in the sun and rain. Just behind that pitch, a bottle will be tipped once again.

BOG ROLLS AND GODS

I never knew when it would begin. But how could I? Back then, it would have been in the future — my future, not yours, not anyone else's — for I can't imagine anyone knew my future in their past. Like driving along an unknown road, you simply cannot comprehend what is out of sight. Most simply expect more of the same. No, they demand it and in doing so, they miss everything different. There are dinosaurs out there, the living extinct. They are us — the drivers of lives in a restricted tube in time. See no difference. Experience no difference. Just stay in the tube of repetition. Beyond the tube? Well, that's the thing.

Until now, I have never met anyone out here in this wild expanse of unreality, which is a larger reality than the jam jar of modern human existence in the twenty-first century. It's freaking dangerous in here — looking back out to where you are stood, reading this message in a quantum bottle of perceptions within a sticky, cloudy, strawberry-scented sewer called life. "What the hell?" I hear you say. Look, pay attention, or get your finger out and scroll the screen back into the tube of meaningless travel. It's a never that someone will write to you from beyond the confines of standard physics — shouting, crying and laughing at the confusions of simplicity that are cleared in the endless time of space, which glows upon an all-embracing tide of energy beyond the pre-programmed, half-eaten lunchbox of your mind.

Yes! Go fetch your soul from that puddle, sunken down into your butt cheeks of life. I am not going to tell you that everything is possible because that is such a worn-out phrase. But look! No, not like that. Look at your hand! Really, look at it! What is it? Where did it come from? Can you imagine the time and multiplicity of forces there were and will be engaged in bringing this fleeting, feeling construct from forever into the instant that is now? The energy and backache that was consumed in building you is phenomenal! I am telling you that millions died in getting you here. And what do you do? Dream of a silver BMW 5 series, whilst eating cornflakes before driving down your tube. Can you hear the flush at the top of the tube? Yes, you are within a human toilet without bog paper, you idiot.

Okay. I've rattled you or even pissed you off, I'm sorry. Well, not nearly as sorry as I am, for you are stuck in there, eating soggy cardboard floating in the stolen produce from a cow's udder. Tell me, what will you do today that is different from the day before, the previous week or even a year ago? Yes, new faces but the same conversation, a different office or contract but the same problems. Let us change the tempo. Have you ever sidewinded time? Stay where you are and imagine what other things and places could be right now. There are a million answers and permutations yet you are there and feel fixed by fate. But you don't believe in fate.

Fate — that sequence of events, which we create to wrestle with yet never feel in control of, because we run our lives' timeline upon the preconceptions of what we have been taught, which is the restraints of a tube-confined reality. How did I get out here leaving you in there? Well, there is a hole in the tube. For most, it is the singularity point that the whole of life prepares us for. For most of us, the escape is a death at the end of the tube. The tube is like a glass pipe full of a fluid. It is like a womb of contained reality, full of something like amniotic fluid. In order to be born, you have pushed this fluid forwards along time's tube. The more you grow and the older you get, the harder it becomes to push against the resistive back-pressure of driving that fluid ahead of you. At the end, you become so tired that you give up, as the fluid busts out at the tube's end into a birth that is your death. Jesus figured this one out and came back to tell us, but we humans are so stupid that no one listened to the poor man who got nailed and nailed it. Did he say, "Father, forgive them, for they know not what they are doing"? Well, I was there and, in my timeline, he said, "These bloody fools haven't got a clue, let 'em stew in their own stupidity." Then hey presto, after two thousand and twenty odd years of trying to figure Christ out, what do we do? We go elect morons! Sense? None.

I ask you, my sweet reader, what are you going to do with your next ten years? I would love to see you out here, in a place where time is not a value; here, in a state of mind where thought is space, information is light and knowledge is time. When all three are brought together, you have, so to speak, infinite time because you will not need time, for you will have everything, and once you reach what most call "death" and give up, you will live forever through what you have perceived. So, step out of your car and be a person, not a driver.

Jle

HAND AND MIND

It is as if I have spent my life unconscious or at least in some deep place. It is not that my world did not have feeling or colour — I was living a bright, challenging, intense life. Maybe it was the intensity that kept me preoccupied, preventing me from standing back and asking why. It is only now, almost too late, that I stopped dead in my tracks and slipped upon the wet surface of life sideways into something else. I now tell you a story of the strange change that befell me.

The hand and mind are two separate things but nothing without each other. The mind perceives but is also deceived, whilst the hand has evolved to feel and shape things. It can utilise tools and interact on many levels. Imagine it is possible for a hand to have a will of its own, one that can conflict with its master like a slave in revolt. How does the master discipline the slave and should the hand be regarded as an absolute subordinate to the mind? My hands have both always responded to the commands that they receive. That was at least until I asked them to do something that was completely wrong and a big mistake. Our bodies are an extension of our will; the medium with which that will interacts with the physical world.

All works well so long as we never doubt the absolute obedience of our bodies to the higher power of the mind. However, the minute we doubt our control over a limb, hand, finger or any muscle, that body part immediately goes into revolt, purely by being liberated in a moment of doubt.

Whilst working in central London as a young man, I would often finish my work in a restaurant in the Strand late. It became usual for me to shortcut through the back streets that had not changed character in maybe one or two hundred years. These narrow, dark and dingy passageways were my route to hidden ancient pubs like The Chandos, which was little more than a narrow room with a bar. The sparsely decorated place that was always cold with subdued light even on the brightest of days was one of my most frequent attendances. That December night, I met an Australian man a few years older than me named Ray Hammersley. Ray was a lopsided sort of guy who didn't seem to give a damn about anything but his camera. He had left far Tasmania, a land scarcely populated and even more inclement and hostile than dull, damp England.

Ray had a mission to build a photo library whilst travelling the world. He would sleep in doorways, squats and hostels, amongst other places. I met him many times over those winter months when he would tell tales of his far-off home and of the stories that had mythologised and embellished over generations. Ray was unkempt in appearance and when I say lopsided, I mean he walked as if one leg wouldn't quite do as it was told, always dragging back a little as if it had the impairment of a long-past wound. Upon the back of Ray's hand was a red tattoo of a hand, only the hand was enclosed in what seemed to be a human mind. Upon close inspection, the attached arm was not an arm at all but a spine enclosing a spinal cord. At the top of that emblem of a spine between the brain was a knife that sat between both. I had asked him the meaning of the tattoo to which he dismissed my question, covering his hand by withdrawing it into the sleeve of his battle-weary, grey tweed overcoat that always flew open as he walked. Through friendship and a little sympathy, he took to meeting me at my restaurant just before closing, and I would always give him a plate of hot food and sometimes a beer or coffee.

One evening in January, Ray came to me having been evicted from the squat he was sleeping in. It was an old Victorian London house. He had saved his camera and film collection, but seemed rather anxious, if not desperate. We went for a drink as usual, bracing against the cold night as we walked through winding deserted alleys. It was in one particularly dark place where the streetlights had failed that I saw a faint glowing coming from Ray's arm. I did not say anything as we were both keen to get into the warm. A warm pint of English ale in the deepest of winter can taste better than anything else. It can also have a deeper effect on the mind than at any other time. Upon entering The Chandos and having ordered at the grubby bar, we sat to talk. Conversations relaxed a little after Ray had told how he had hit two bailiffs to regain his photographic equipment and a couple of years' work. Having told him he could stay at my place in the northern suburbs, he ordered a third round of drinks. It was then that I noticed his hand clenching and unclenching, so I asked if he was cold.

It was colder than usual and the bar had grown fogged with the cigarette smoke of other drinkers. He said he was okay and proceeded to tell me a story from his homeland. He started by telling me of the Tasmanian temperate rainforest in the highlands where seventy percent of the land is covered by deciduous tree canopy that flows down to the Savage River. He then told of the Palawa, an extinct aboriginal people, who were part of the land for thousands of years. He told of his forefathers' encounters dating to the Risdon Cove settlement, eventually degenerated into the Black War (1804–30), a period of great physical conflict between the Aboriginal population and European settlers. These peoples were different from the indigenous population on the subcontinent, for they were cut off from the mainland by the biblical flood ten thousand years ago when the sea flooded the Bass Straight. He hesitantly used a word that I had never heard before — Corroboree. He explained he was a crossbreed with maybe twenty percent native blood and the rest being European. The Corroboree, he told, was a ceremony that consists of much singing and dancing. These were activities by which they convey their history in stories and re-enactments of the Dreaming — a mythological period of time that had a beginning but no foreseeable end during which the natural environment was shaped and humanised by the actions of mythic beings: one was the hand of God and the other the mind of man.

We drifted through another sleepy pint, huddled in our jackets, looking across a round, beer-sticky table in the far corner of that pub. It could have happened unnoticed by me if I had looked away for a moment, but there it was — Ray's hand reached across the table with his eyes closed and his head fallen forwards as if for a moment he was unconscious. I had assumed that tiredness was overcoming him as it was me. Without looking at me or opening his eyes, he then reached across the table with his forefinger outstretched, pointing as if in some accusation. Fascinated and mesmerised, I did not move and in that moment, his finger touched my forehead. It was at the point of contact that I felt as if a bullet had passed through my mind. As Ray raised his head opening his eyes, my hand reached my mind, and I touched the devil that danced in between who I am and the people I had once been in the before time. In that instant, there was more than just me as who I had always been, but a heritage, or a genetic and cultural link that stretched halfway around this world. I was now something else.

Ray — eyes wide open and staring at me — said, "It's you, you're the one. I could have never known. And how did I find you out of all the people in this world?"

He went on to tell me that he hated the tattoo upon his arm that had appeared after a night spent in the forest with another who had aboriginal traits. They had practised unknowingly the dance of a shaman and taken the fermented sap from the cider gum. The eucalyptus gunnii trees originate from the central highlands of Tasmania at about one thousand metres above sea level. Perhaps the easiest material to use from these trees

115

is the sap, which collects in bark pockets and ferments. From the dawn of man's self-awareness, shamanism had been the root of belief before religion. It is part of us and it will always be so. He drained half a glass of beer, wiping his mouth upon the sleeve of that ancient overcoat which seemed to be part of his anatomy. Cursing with wild eyes, he told that the tattoo only glows when he is drunk like that night in the forest when he acquired the strange emblem upon his arm.

Having drained our last drink, we staggered up St. Michael's Avenue into Charring Cross Road where we descended into the Underground and took a train on the Northern Line to my flat in High Barnet. We both did not awake until late next morning when we sat in silence drinking coffee. Ray left in the afternoon to re-join his friend, and I have never set eyes upon him again. It wasn't until into the evening after I had drunk my first glass of wine that I felt my left forearm growing hot. Having rolled up the sleeve of my shirt, I could see the emblem of a skull and spine gently glowing from deep within the pale white flesh. I lived with this mysterious irritation of a mind and spine for many years, often wondering who Ray was until one day in my fiftieth year, I received a genetic test. There, in the printed results were the words: "Tasmanian Aboriginal, one of the oldest and primal gene codes." Three weeks later, I was on a flight to find my destiny into a journey so deep in my past.

Jee

NOTHING THERE

As dawn breaks, it drives a breeze in this part of the world. The sun peeps orange over the horizon to glow soft-flowing reflected light, which, within a few minutes of a degree, becomes low-level rays, streaming horizontal across the fields to crash glowing upon the wooded hillside. I have walked my two dogs for so many years along the tracks under these high oak trees where that dawn light filters to form dancing shadows upon the humus-rich soil. These paths have character and hold friendship for me through familiarity. The trees are my friends. One reaches far higher than the rest, spreading over the rocky outcrops and young upstart hollies and birches that audaciously compete for that valued light. It was once my light too.

This September morning I live again to walk as the ghosts of so many others before me have done. I can sense their presence calling from pasts never quite lost. The ground flows ahead of me, closing like time to my rear. A grey bunny bolts from my future, running bewildered at my presence past me and is gone into forever. The smell of late summer's damp exudes from the bark and twisted roots that grapple to hold the ground like frozen snakes in a battle between life and death. That damp arises with the white spirited mist, which shrouds this forest before dawn. As I look up, squinting at the bright that streams against the shade of the canopy of leaves, a branch creaks above me, sounding like the gurgling of an old man's laughter. Marked in a ring above a branch is a scar circling the bark — an arboreal injury from an earlier time has effaced nature's pattern. I look away to ease my eyes as a long shadow swings slowly across my path. When I look again, there is nothing there. Or can I see the remnants of a disintegrating frayed rope hanging in the shaded darkness?

Alone, I look around me through the rising, grotesquely beautiful trunks and rays of light. The power and beauty inspire me while at the same time the bright and darkness seem to oscillate between some radiant good and creeping evil that has crawled upon the ground. I have purpose in my walk today. I am both conscious and unaware of my being here. Rooks circle cackling high above the treetops, gathering in a storm of maybe thirty or fifty black beasts. For a time, they steal my light and my reason. It is as if I started here and have returned always, as these wooded beings grew around me. I understand the nature of this place, its relay of perpetual dying and regrowth. What is that I feel in my jacket pocket? I reach in, slowly lifting the heavy woollen flap to my worn garment. I pull out an old hemp rope. In disbelief, I finger it as it uncoils, hard in its binding weave but soft to touch. It appears too long to have fitted in my pocket.

I feel as if I am being watched and this takes my attention from that mysterious rope. Being compelled to look back to that tallest of trees, I can see a man stood silent and staring back at me. He looks remarkably like me. I raise a hand to wave and he has vanished. Movement above the half-lit place where he was standing draws my gaze. I am more confused than frightened. There, hardly moving, I think I can see a man's body hanging. It twitches and falls heavy and still. It is then that I understand and feel so light as I walk away from death into the light.

I was here once. I will always be here. The next time you look up through the high oaks in late summer, you may catch a passing glimpse of an ending and a beginning. Perhaps you and I were never there.

BULLETS AND AN AIR BLADE

The sun was not yet up, but the atmosphere was telling of its forthcoming. A slight breeze had stirred some of the dead crinkled leaves that had gathered upon the ground. The sky had changed to a lighter blue, but it was still dark. Then the cockerel crowed its defiant call against night. A shriek that blasted through the air as cockerels had done so for what seemed like forever in this sun-baked, dusty Spanish village.

Rodriguez flinched in his bunk, knowing this would be his last dawn. Rolling over, he spat at the wall out of anger and fear; he was disgusted at the weakness of his last spit of rebellion. He felt utterly dejected and feeble. His journey to this early dawn had started long ago as a child. Having been beaten for stealing eggs, a crime he did not commit, his life had been a tally of injustice and hardship. His education short, and life with his family cut shorter through poverty and disease. It was only natural that he would take up arms against Franco's fascists. He had now to pay with his life for his honesty and passion for liberty.

At thirty-six years of age, Rodriguez had raven black hair and the piercing light blue eyes of a gypsy. He had been a schoolteacher in the Pyrenean town of Ordino, living with his young wife; they had a two-year-old chid whom he had not set eyes upon for nine months. His crime was the smuggling of Russian arms through the mountains for the fighters. Betrayal had undone him all for the price of a week's food.

On this morning, he knew his fate, but he didn't know how it would be delivered. He could hear the sound of feet marching in unison, maybe three or four men. The load of weapons had been exceptionally large and cumbersome, having landed in a small French fishing port. They had been railed close to the border and loaded upon a mule train of six animals. This way they had crossed the little-known mountain pass during night to arrive in Spain the following dawn — the dawn before this one. It was the Catholic priest Aaron who had traded Rodriguez's life to feed four orphans in his care. These children had died when a German-made bomb was dropped on the church in 1938. The betrayal, the smuggling and the feeding of the children were futile. Evil always has its way in times of war.

The old crumbling alabaster room shook, as the guard flung open the door and the child-feeding priest entered, Bible in hand, to administer the last rites. The priest was both deliverer and deliverance, just as the pope supported Franco and pretended to pray for the socialists at the same time. The soldiers had shot the boy leading the mules as they descended into a valley. They had been ambushed and explosives had

122

detonated, unleashing carnage upon the poor beasts that screamed in pain whilst life bled from ripped wounds under the heavy burden of war's cargo.

Rodriguez had paused to relieve himself at the rear of the line of mules and so had been saved by a call of nature. His instinct had been to run to help the now dead boy and, of course, he never got to him. Instead, he was in this small cell of a room with God's treacherous administering priest. The arms from his mules were already deployed against Rodriguez's compatriots. Having completed his meaningless mumbling, the priest left and the guards tied Rodriguez's hands behind his back. The soldiers scuffled with him out into the yard between the police building and the church of wasted faith. He had a cigarette thrust into his mouth and lit. The guard spoke softer than the priest did, but he was not heard, for the captive was with his slim wife and son in past days of love and play. A blindfold was draped over his eyes and a rope around his waist. It was attached to a pockmarked, sawn-down telegraph pole. The stones and soil below were stained brown and the hollow smell of a slaughterhouse rose to his nostrils. He could hear the sound of an airplane in the distance whilst his mouth could taste the last beer he had shared with his oldest of friends the day they had stolen a plane, which the republican forces had landed in a field near to the village. His friend Peter was a flying officer who had defected to the socialists.

Rodriguez was aware of the command, "Aim", but it had no meaning to him now, for his head was full of other times and better places. He felt hot and lightheaded, as the sound of an aircraft swam through what seemed like a dream. "Fire" was not heard, but he heard the bullets though never felt them. He had passed out. Those bullets were Peter's, fired from the stolen plane.

Bar Alcambria, Madrid, 1988. Two elderly men sit drinking. One hands the other a section of a propeller and the other smiles and hands a small leather pouch of spent bullets over the wooden table. Rodriguez and Peter have much to tell one another having not met in forty years. A young man approaches with a tray with three full glasses. He pauses at the table to speak.

"Dad!"

JAINI

It is in our sleep that we confront the greatest dangers to our mind. It is here, upon that dormant battlefield, that we slip into a different reality that seems to cut off when we return to the waking world. What if our darkest of nights follow us into waking days to cast a shadow that haunts reality? Dreaming and screaming whilst at peace, the nightmares of sleeping slip tears in your dark resting times, but most awake unaware of where they have been and what may have happened or will happen. This has become a more frequent experience as I have grown older, and I am learning to steer my dreams. However, I never expected those horrors and places to become a reality in my awaken time. Could it be that the dreamtime is part of what we consider reality? That is where my story starts.

I had always been a deep sleeper and rarely woke from my slumbers until May 7, 2001. The days and weeks before had been full with work dominating my thoughts. I had been drinking more than usual, stopping at The Friar's Inn on my way home to help me shake the day's pressures. It was while sat in the oldest part of the pub, gazing at the ancient wooden beams, that she came and sat uninvited next to me, and started a conversation. She was an attractive lady of about forty to forty-five with long dark hair, dressed casually in a T-shirt and neat, tight skirt that most women of her age wouldn't dare wear. I remember a silver chain with an emblem and a pig that she played with as she talked. I wasn't in the mood for conversation, having lost a deal to that blasted Japanese competitor after investing weeks of time and an immodest amount of money. I was fuming, for I felt sure backhanders and bribes had defeated me. The deal would have made me sixteen million over four years. Fuck it! I looked at her as she wiggled comfortably and smoked whilst sipping her drink. I could smell the sweet perfume of gin.

"Do you like gin?" she asked whilst looking at me with two of the darkest eyes I had ever seen.

I gazed back as if I had been hypnotised, for I had become oblivious to my surroundings. It might have been the shock and inconvenience of having my brief time alone broken into. Or was there something about her beauty and confidence that mesmerised me? I answered after an embarrassingly long pause in flat tones.

"Not particularly."

I think I had hoped this would close the conversation, but she asked me to take a sip from her glass, which I declined. She then calmly, as if she was a medical worker or some health practitioner, took my hand and closed my fingers around her glass, and told me in a firm voice to take my medicine. I wish I hadn't. I wish I had driven straight home and launched into my evening of account keeping. I sipped and closed my eyes for no more than a few seconds. When I opened them, the dark-eyed lady was stood looking down at me. She was wearing a surgeon's whites and I seemed to be unable to move, lying upon an operating bed.

I asked, "What has happened to me?"

She answered that I was going to experience a small procedure to exorcise the "gins" from my soul. I tried to say I don't like gin, but must have become unconscious.

The next thing I knew, the barman was shaking me and saying, "It is closing time, sir. You must wake up and leave."

Slowly, I pulled myself together, feeling as if I had had far more than the still half full pint of beer that was on the table in front of me. I walked around in the cool night air trying to work out what had happened to me and who was the Indian lady with dark hair and such black eyes. After a while, I drove the few miles home, showered and slept deeper than I can ever remember.

Upon waking, I was aware of a tight feeling in my stomach and a roughness on my skin. When I finally got up, having decided to work from home that day, a glance in the mirror revealed a six-inch wound that had stitches in. I was terrified and sick with no recollection of how or why I was this way. Having rang the local general hospital and given my name, they claimed to have had no record of my having been there. I drove back to the pub that evening and asked the barman who had woken me what he could remember. He recalled my presence and the Indian lady who had ordered Devil's Gin. He could tell me no more.

Having bought a bottle of Devil's Gin, I returned home and sat in front of my computer. I poured myself a glass and added a third of the measure of tonic that fizzed in rage as the gin itself turned cloudy. It tasted of metal and roses, but it relaxed me in an instant. I researched the distillers and the retailers, shipping and history when my screen blanked for a moment, and then slowly the dark-eyed woman from the public house appeared on the computer's now flickering, dull screen. I could see clearly the emblem and the pig that hung around her neck. I read the word "djinn". Upon regaining my composure, I stared at her image and, as I was getting used to her picture, she sprang to life and asked, "How is that wound healing? We took many djinns out of you and put some back in. Can you sense them?"

I started to swear in shock, and then she was gone. The machine had grown intolerably hot and the smell of burning plastic filled the room, making me feel dizzy and sick. I don't know why, but I lifted the bottle and poured a second glass, and there in the dull light on the rear of the label was a faint watermark — the face of my mistress djinn.

Having fallen asleep for some time, I dreamt of dancing with the Indian lady, who wore the most sensual, flowing, purple dress. Her hair flew as she moved, and her hands weaved patterns that mesmerised me. When I awoke, I was convinced the dance had been in my dream state but upon arising, there was a purple scarf draped on the now failed computer. To use the words "freaked out" is the greatest understatement of all times. This time, I must have passed out, for I awoke in a hospital bed with a nurse sat beside me taking my pulse. She explained I had called an ambulance and the paramedics had seen me through a window, unconscious, lying on the floor. Having broken in, they found an empty bottle of gin and had to revive me.

As part of my treatment, I stayed there for three days and received therapy for depression, stress and alcohol abuse. By the time I was ready to return home, they had convinced me my paranoia was induced by an allergic reaction in my gut to a specific type of distilled alcohol and I had been hallucinating in my sleep. I felt good for the first time in months and returned to my office the next day. I was delighted to be told by my personal assistant, Samantha, that an Indian company had contacted us to promote their product in Europe and America. I opened my emails and it was then that I needed a drink like never before. The email started:

"Dear Mr Prichard, the mystical properties of our Djinn Gin have many secrets. We have selected you to be our representative who will serve the spirit of our mission unfalteringly. We know you will accept this offer and have already arranged your visit to our distillery that few have ever visited. A word of advice: tell no one of this and do not bring any religious symbols with you. I shall be in contact soon. Our spirit is now within you. Yours, Jaini."

I ran my hand through my hair and pushed my chair back from the desk. I needed to think and all of the time something made me crave another glass of gin, not any old gin. I knew I needed this deal, but I also knew there would be a cost. Was it the gin or was it her? I had a need implanted in me that burnt so hot I had become part of a spirit beyond me. My reality and nightmares were at last the same thing.

The origin of the word "djinn" remains uncertain. Some scholars relate the Arabic term "jinn" to the Latin "genius". Another suggestion holds that jinn may be derived from Aramaic "ginnaya" meaning of "tutelary deity" or also "garden". Others claim a Persian origin of the word, in the form of the Avestic "jaini", a wicked (female) spirit. Jaini were amongst various creatures in the possibly even pre-Zoroastrian mythology of the peoples of Iran.

PURPOSE

The day has been hot. Dust has risen in thermals, distorting distant views. Heat haze shimmers in every direction across the broad valley where a river has shrunken to a trickle. This is summer in the high wilderness of North America where the land, now known as Canada, gives way to Great Lakes that are surrounded by mountains, formed from some prehistoric cataclysm. This is a time when the river needs no name.

The lone wolf knows the river that gives him life and a path to follow — a place where prey will gather as a source of energy-giving food. Energy — the essential ingredient of life that so many have now forgotten how to hunt for. Nose forwards like an arrow, ears low and level-backed through to an extending tip of a rigid tail — this beast has a love of life that gleams with energy and spirit. He runs ever onwards as a life machine, never faltering, loping into a time's distance, for there is only the now. Ranging for hours upon end, as he had for many days previously, there is purpose in his quest, a need of an equal, a need for a mate and companion. At three years of age, he is now coming into his prime, having left the safety of his primary pack where he had spent happy days romping and fighting with his brothers and sisters.

Months had passed, as he wandered in this vast wilderness alone. There was the time he had tracked an elderly moose for days to exhaustion and brought him down upon the riverbank as he tried to drink. His blood was warm and life-giving. In death, life grew in strength. Those lone days were soon to end. Now, without thought, he had scented something faint. It travelled in the air that drew his will on. The scent of the she-wolf, who could match his cunning and tenacity against the threatening wilderness where danger is ever present.

The valley climbs, as this creature moves on at a constant pace, to where grassland gives way to steep forested slopes, on through the ancient pines where shafts of late afternoon sun illuminate pools of detritus from harsh winters upon the ground. After two more hours of travelling, the trees give way to lower stunted junipers and scrub before the great rocky rises upon which birds of prey search for the carrion of lost lives. Now the sun slips low on the horizon, casting red light over the vista — red that for all life in this place signals the danger of coming night, a time when shrieks of death will pierce the dark silence as the hunted yield their energy to hunters. What does nature care of the weak? High upon a timeless ledge, this lone wolf settles his haunches as his heart and respiration slow. He draws in the air and pauses to turn slightly northward. Drawing in short repeated draughts, that weak and fleeting scent comes again. It is the scent of life, the she-wolf. Within one molecule from maybe two hundred or more miles away, he now knows the shape of her power. He now has the power of purpose, as all life aches to fulfil the need that is the call of the wild.

SAM

(THE PREPARATION)

Time was never important for Sam; it was the medium through which he experienced things, the pain of birth and ache of learning, the damage of rejection and failure, loves that grew then to be stolen with a death and love lost. The procession of day to night was the container in which he hunted for the energy that kept him alive, working for a wage in a seamless flow of that unquestioning passage. Sam had been a good-looking man in his youth and had maintained his athletic build to the end; this being the reward for years playing football for a local side. He had now lived for twenty-eight years in his small house where he and his wife Helen had raised four healthy children. These days in his twilight years, he spent most of his time sat on the deck that branches from the front of his home looking south over the now unkempt garden that was once Helen's pride. Beyond the garden, open fields spread in a sea of green to a neat regiment of poplar trees, planted to guard against the winter storms that blow a rage through the valley from the Atlantic Ocean some sixty miles beyond.

Sam had a feeling in him, an emotion that did not frighten him, for it had become a peaceful awareness. He had always had it since a young man when he had jumped from the breaking branch of an oak tree. Once in free fall of some forty-five feet, he knew he could die. He didn't. In those eight seconds of floating in blind panic before crashing through the lower branches that broke both of his arms, then the dense thicket of thorns which ripped his back to shreds yet broke the velocity of his impact, he learnt we are all born dead and it was how we resist the attrition of life that leaves its everlasting imprint upon the clay of time. Sam in his eighty-fifth year knew he was falling again. The dark wood of the deck upon which he sat was rotting, and the galvanised gutters on the felt roof behind him leaked. He had lost interest in any repairs and rather enjoyed watching the rabbits that trespassed into his garden under the failing rear mesh fence.

The evening sun felt as warm as ever upon his brown skin. His white hair hung rebelliously over his forehead as it had done so when he was a boy. His sleepy eyes, partially closed, watched the far sky transform from yellow to orange and a curved moon sneak upon the horizon. He didn't feel the cooling air as he remembered Helen's hand upon his shoulder. His hand reached for hers as she stooped from his memory to kiss his neck. Smiling, he closed his eyes and released a long slow exhalation that almost comprised a sigh. At this point, he was back as a six-year-old boy riding upon the seemingly giant shoulders of his father, hanging onto the heavy green hand-knitted jumper that seemed to be a permanent part of his body.

Years and conversations came and went until Helen whispered in his ear, "It's time." Night had taken precedent, but Sam was happy in some far and different place. A rabbit slowly hopped to his chair as nature filled a once overfull place.

BOY

I couldn't see him when he asked, "What's your name and where are you going, son?"

Straining my eyes in the bright dawn sunlight that glowed in the drifting mist and muffled his voice, it met my ears piercingly sharp. I lifted my foot to step back hesitantly as it fell to the ground, and the gravel upon this endless track crunched.

He spoke again. "Come closer, boy. Don't you want to see me?"

My body had turned rigid and my mouth run dry, but I spoke as best as I could.

"My name is Jack. I ain't done nothing wrong, so I should be getting along."

I saw a movement and the carriage door swung open with a squeal, a desperate sound like a church door closing on ceasing hinges or the last protest of a slaughtered pig. I knew this place well but not as it was then. The trees seemed taller and stiller than before, and the mist rising from Hobbs Lake was colder. I had never seen it moving in the bright before.

One of the bridled horses brayed and bucked a little as its hooves protested against the ground. There was darkness in the bright that confused the poor black steed yet his companions remained still as if machines and not animals. I edged closer, trying to see in. I could see right through the cab that was lacquered black; there appeared to be no one there.

I asked, "What do you want?"

For a moment, there was no answer, not a sound at all, and then, breaking the silence, a beating of a crow's wings rose above this horse-drawn hearse as it settled upon the roof, causing all six steeds to become unsettled, rocking the frame of this strange occurrence.

Instinctively turning to run, the voice came again. "Whatsa matter, boy? Haven't you heard a dead man speak before?"

I answered, "Dead men are silent and you ain't no dead'un."

Those black devils were still again as if this faceless voice calmed them. Or was it fear? Clutching my shoulder bag to my chest, I stood dumbfounded and rooted as those animals subdued. Then came that face which I can never forget — the white bloodless transparency and the bulging veins that protruded from the sunken skin; a face in a carriage, suspended in the mist, drawn from hell by six horses without a driver. We looked at each other unblinking and then he or it said again, "Dead men don't blink and you, boy, are not blinkin'."

I protested, telling that I was alive and staying alive as I felt myself with a growing fear and self-doubt. I sure did know this place, but I had grown confused in the moment and I was starting to feel cold, real cold. It was then that I noticed the crow had something in its beak. The wretched creature was holding a finger. When I looked at my left hand, my index finger was missing.

"It's yours," came the sharp voice with impatience, followed by, "You, boy, are dead, and you better get used to it. You haven't no business on this track. It's for the living."

Out of the mist came a hand pointing over my shoulder beyond me to the water's edge, and that black fiend took to the wing, clucking a sinister chuckle to land on something a few yards away.

"Go read yourself, boy!" he said and, in silence, I walked in between the dark and the light as if I was choosing something. There, under that black rat of a hell's servant, was a cast iron plaque embedded in a roughhewn rock. I struggled to read in disbelief:

"Here died Jack Saunders, June 7, 1840. Drowned dead."

Looking back, it was then that I saw the half-pint coffin upon that hearse of beckoning. I must have slipped out of fear and fallen in the deep still waters, for the apparition had gone and that plaque now reads:

"Poor Jack, aged twelve. His body was never found, except one finger dropped by a carrion crow."

FLORIN FOR PEACE

Twinkling high in the sunlight,
Turning over and over like a jewel of fate,
Still climbing in the air before descent

A group of men stand below looking up as silver metal takes flight, having been flicked spinning and thrown up one hundred feet. This is the florin of destiny, tossed to fall in settlement of a feud that has lasted a generation. Will it favour the Carbone family, proud and aggressive, all short and rotund, in the business of meat, extortion and general criminality? With their backs to the river stand the Narbonne family, good citizens of crime, smugglers and hitmen for two hundred years. The coin turns and starts a return journey; breaths are held, fists clenched and legs braced. Every eye is upon the coin.

Willow trees lining the riverbanks, anchoring the heavy, mineral-rich soil, are frozen in the still and warm summer Sicilian air that carries the scent of herbs, drifted upon cooler air down from the hills that surround Palermo. Beads of sweat emerge upon Roberto's brow to join in a flow of salty streams he ignores. Roberto, of thirty-six years, has the demeanour of a slaughterhouse manager. Nothing involving sinews and blood can upset him, for death is his daily business. His close-cropped dark hair is receding and his front teeth missing from a punch thrown by Alleno when they were twenty.

Alleno stands four yards from his enemy, a taller and more elegant framed man who retains a full set of teeth. What he lacks in physical power is more than made up for by his sharp mind and famous wit. It is his intelligence that has enabled him to evade prison and break so many girls' hearts. It is a broken heart that brings them here, for Flavia, Roberto's sister, now carries Alleno's child and is rejected. Great honour is at stake and each side's blood is up. Down comes the florin, having travelled in what appears to be out of the clear blue of a seamless calm sky in slow motion. Eyes are lowering as it nears. The priest, who is there to placate the tempers of his intemperate flock, takes off his mitre to wipe his brow. Thud! The florin embeds itself in the dirt no longer sparkling as enraged lowered eyes stare into each other in an electric atmosphere only broken by a whimpering dog that, sensing danger, scuttles away.

Hat under arm, the elderly priest Alfonso, who has christened each and every one of the thirty-four men present when they were cherubs, steps forwards stooping down to retrieve the coin, straightening his back as he raises the coin above his head to proclaim heads win. Men are running in all directions, retrieving weapons from iron bars and bats to chains and one with a chair. The rest is indistinguishable as men and weapons fight for more than twenty minutes, even some in the confusion against their own. One man jumps on another's back and rides him into the river; another breaks his brother's nose and then shakes his hand; another kicks the priest's arse and helps him up apologising. Miraculously, apart from broken bones, no fatalities occur and when the dust has settled, all retire to the Amalfi Sports Bar to recover. After two hours of drinking and insults, another war begins, which is ended when Big Alf, the proprietor, breaks two bottles of grappa over Roberto's and Alleno's heads; both out cold are dragged home and peace returns to this contested area of a city of beauty and turmoil.

Within a year, the priest at St. Carolina's Church married Roberto, and a golden florin was melted and cast into two rings. The child was named Florian and each of the two families never fought again, sharing in their crimes to become more civilised with one another. How they dealt with other mafia syndicates is another story. It is rumoured that in the dirt, soaked in the blood of every killing, can be found a florin that has been thrown from the hand of a united family that divides a state.

CHILD OF TIME

I asked, "Who are you?"

"Just dust," she answered.

This was the early time before the birdsong where sleep had not yet given way to wakefulness. Darkness still flooded this place of mind. She spoke again, although I could not see her.

"You were nothing and you will be nothing again. Welcome to the in between time, the no-man's-land between night and day. The place that passes from the empty into the void of nothingness of lost dust. It doesn't last. The change into day is soon, before the eternal night speeds upon the feathered wings of your time."

"Who are you?" I asked once again.

"You cannot know what I am until the point of departure," said the peaceful voice that I could not position in this space.

She paused and a silence, like none I have ever felt, filled this small attic room of little description. A deep chill seemed to sting the air and I could see shadows where there was no light. Silence consumed this space of time like concrete poured into a cave until no air is left. I pulled myself up against the bedstead into a sitting position and peered beyond the room out of the dormer window into the dark beyond.

I spoke again.

"What do you want of me?"

A softly spoken woman's voice whispered with such calm authority that it didn't frighten me. I could not understand her, for she spoke in a language or dialect that I had never heard before, but the lilting sound beautifully sang a song that only an angel could deliver. I remained mesmerised, wondering if I was still asleep within some haunting twisted dream.

When the cold silence returned, I asked, "There are two of you?"

She replied in that strange ancient tone and my ears craved for more of her calming lilt. For some strange reason, I understood her words.

"I am all things, for there was nothing before and there is nothing beyond. The Emptiness is the total."

She paused as if waiting for my comprehension to catch up with her meaning. I was then sure I had left that dream and the dream had turned into something else. But what was it? Again, more beautiful than before, her voice flowed serenely and more peacefully than any restful death.

"I am both Yama and Naraka, man and woman, birth and death. I am the in between time of energy that creates and destroys."

Silence fell again as I sensed dawn being held back by some supernatural force. Again, she spoke with such grace that I ached to see what must have been her form of haunting, absolute beauty.

"Mine is the hand of Ani that led his journey from ancient Egypt into death through to the other side, then to return to life. My hand scribed the Book of the Dead. I too am Nephthys, the creator of Osiris who is my lover."

Her voice faded and fell to silence. I considered those sirens of mythology who lured ancient mariners to their joyful death with the beauty of their calling songs. Was this my calling? From outside of the glass that separated this space from all else, I heard a distant church clock chime. It was as if time was fighting with something to survive. I caught a second gagging chime that reached me, jagged and torn. I sensed I was at the boundary that flowed between one place and into another. I was at the gateway of no return, straining to look beyond like Ani before his dark journey of enlightenment riding upon the death book's words. As I turned, a shaft or maybe a flicker of glimmering dawn opened and faded as if a shroud had been pulled over day.

I asked another question of my visitor. "Do you live or are you something other?"

The space surrounding me seemed to empty into a vacuum. The air grew thin and I dizzied into a strange place of floating where lumps of radiance flowed as if solid. Everything had become different from what I had always known. I became aware of something against me; it was as if my mind was being kissed. I felt waves of delight as all apprehension left and my soul settled, submitting everything that had ever held it within. The bedsheets slipped to expose my naked body that was no longer cold. I sensed a powerful, gentle beauty, yet could not breathe, as my body grew aroused under the influence of a rising attack of caresses. They travelled from my lips to fall delicately upon my chest. I needed to cry out, but my desire had become stifled like that church clock chime. Yet, I was screaming with delight in my mind. My skin tingled against the softest of pleasures, as I grew beyond the control of my will. I reached to embrace this succubus of demonic intoxication. She turned upon my back, contacting every cell of my burning flesh with one eternal kiss. Out of control, I found myself kissing and thrusting in return as I withdrew to plunge my face into the fertility of a so delightful hell. Her hands, that seemed many, pressed my eager face deep into her pleasure that I sensed through her needy longing. It was then that she groaned and braced against me and the world that I was surely leaving.

We merged as one without a margin of individuality. We groaned the pleasure of love's pain to the point of death, yet remained locked for an indeterminate period. It seemed many hours of darkness had passed when she next spoke. Her words surprised me, and again I found it difficult to understand the medium of her speech. I think she thanked me with a final kiss whose meaning I knew without explanation. Ours was a love that had risen from hell to create a heaven that our feelings would give birth to a child named Time. It would be Time that, at the point before the dawn of nothingness, would enable mankind to defeat his own evil.

Dawn broke in that instant as I drew my first breath in many hours to live as I had never lived before.

HE DIDN'T KNOW

He'd had it all, yet asked himself many times over the years: where did it start and how did he arrive at this point, so high and on the edge? He was just another boy, a little shy but quick to laugh, with a shock of blonde hair which flopped over his blue eyes that were so often tear-filled. He was of a sensitive nature, always looking down at his small, slightly turned-in feet.

Somewhere at the age of fifteen or sixteen, when out of school, on summer's evenings or Saturday mornings, Joe would play football with his mates. It was great fun and the thrill of having the ball made his blood flow full of adrenaline. He felt as powerful and free as one of those superhero characters in the films he watched. Then came the bullies who would hang around the park. They knifed his ball, and when he protested as they disrupted his game, they beat him up. Nothing too serious, but he was always picked on, being the smallest amongst his friends and, of course, none of them stood up for him. He soon learnt that in this life, you are on your own.

He knew those bullies. Some schooled with him, only being a few years older, but they were much bigger than he was. They had pushed him too far and, having an overbearing father who was also a bully, Joe decided it was time to take revenge. Not being able to meet them in a fair fight (it was never that way), he summoned his courage to steal a baseball bat from a local sports shop. The thrill of psyching up for the theft was as great as scoring a goal on the pitch. As he ran from the shop, his heart pounded and a wide smile of delight rose upon his face. He was thrilled again when he showed his booty to his mates. After much hesitation, and holding and swinging that bat in front of a mirror, he summoned his courage to meet his enemies.

It was early spring. As the evenings were opening out, he knew where three of those bullies would meet to smoke. The ground was soft and they didn't hear his approach. Having climbed a park fence and closing on them, his heartbeat raced and that scintillating adrenal gland let loose its burst of fire that raged into his head. They didn't realise his intention until it was too late as one lay on the ground in pain, and the second received a blow between the legs that would take weeks to heal. The third had an excruciating hit between the shoulders that would trouble him for the rest of his life. The aftermath dragged on. There was the exclusion from school whilst the police investigated, but in the end, things settled down and Joe was not troubled by those older boys again. The thrill of the steal and the excitement of the attack remained in him, and somehow, he craved more.

He grew more aggressive on the football pitch, joining a local team and gaining the reputation of a fast and agile but dirty player. Then came the fights. At parties and in bars, he had grown to relish a fight often provoking trouble to let his fists have some fun. He didn't always come off best, but somehow the delight of danger satisfied his lust for excitement.

At eighteen, he had become an efficient car thief, burning screeching tyres at speed along dark roads, taking risks and crashes to gain that high when danger or even death fluttered ever so close. No longer playing football, he missed a season for repeated fouls against other players. It was then that the gambling started, betting on the game that he knew. Between games, there were the machines he played in betting shops and arcades, always risking more for the thrill that made him feel alive even when he was losing. Later came the horse racing on which he lost so much money that he started selling drugs.

By twenty, he was a boxer and a prize fighter, earning thousands on a good night and taking weeks to recover. But this wasn't enough. He discovered the thrill of base-jumping from high points, a hundred or more feet, into coastal waters. Only on this day, he had mixed alcohol with his drugs, and as he stood there, he knew he was making a mistake. Hesitation wiped the adrenaline from his blood and something he had never experienced filled his mind. That shock of fair hair blew into his blue eyes, and tears pushed across his cheeks in the updraft. Fear shot through him like the impact that was racing up to meet him. He had jumped his last thrill, having not seen the large jagged ledge that was about to interrupt his fall. He knew he would be dead by the time he hit the water.

THE TEST

It's a big world to lose a person in. When it happens, it's like a detonation that has no end. The shockwave finds its epicentre and spreads as fast as you can outgrow it. Run and it will follow you, scorch you and pulverise you with the rubble of your past. Turn and face it and you are dead. There is no reasoning or barometric resistance that can hold your mind together once the event has blown. Just leave and keep going, unless you have a terminal desire to fail. Birth is the first kick that sets us running from the cocooned womb of absolute oblivious comfort that was preceded by the infinity of gentle peace.

Screaming with indignation, Jimmy Jones opened his eyes to the confusions that blurred a world waiting to torment him. Picture a stark bedroom in a dull but imposing Victorian house in an ordinary road set in St. Pancras, London. A large lady from Nigeria in a blue uniform and a white nurse's hat indicating she was a maternity nurse stood beside a bed where Jimmy's mother screamed while the nurse said, "This baby can't wait. He has to come." And come Jimmy did.

It was April 1960 and, as a baby, Jimmy suffered all the discomforts that the protocol for caring for a baby could impose: the comforting words whilst being slapped to get his blood and breath working, the intense hunger for milk and the hours of unattended boredom in a cage. He didn't know it, but he couldn't wait to get out and away from the restrictions that all babies and children suffer.

His unconscious plans started with throwing things. He threw his toys at everything he could: out of his pram and out of his playpen. He threw his food on the floor and smeared it up the kitchen wall. For this, he was smacked, so then he slipped out of his harness and jumped out of his high chair to fall upon his head. That fall was the second fall in his life after birth, and it became a defining moment as he could remember it for the rest of his life. It changed him and who he would be.

Somewhere deep in his yet soft forming brain, two nerve synapses, that (according to the plans laid down through eons of evolution) would never have reached, touched one another in connection. Jimmy was now different. Slowly, he learnt to walk long before he could talk and with semi-proficient perambulation, he made his first attempt to escape, leaving his prim and proper mother's side (as she talked to another prim lady) to run across the Thames Embankment and throw himself from the wall into the river where his splash down killed an unsuspecting seagull. This was his third fall.

Fortunately for him, the skipper of a small barge carrying coal witnessed Jimmy's descent and hauled the choking child out of the water. His mother had not noticed his absence for a full ten minutes and by the time she did, Jimmy was in the barge wheelhouse, sat on the window ledge, looking at the bizarre structure of Tower Bridge. It may have been that Thames water got into Jimmy on that day. From then on, he would always be drawn to the dank, cold waters that flow unrelentingly through the heart of a barbaric city that is an epicentre of all that civilisation has to offer.

Jimmy wanted to swim. His baptism in the waters of London drove him to swim. He first learnt to swim at the age of eleven in the dark, cold chlorinated water of his junior school pool. The water was so chlorinated that no matter how much bathwater he soaked in, he would smell of chlorine for days. He grew to love the smell of it. When he could, Jimmy swam lengths under water in the muffled silence of bubbles and the distorted visions that were the same as those when he first opened his eyes. He swam deeper and deeper, grazing his nose on the tiles below. Sometimes he would remain gliding along the bottom as the tiles flowed by inches from his eyes. He would stay too long and would reach the surface barely conscious.

Maybe because of his fall, Jimmy was a loner. He rarely spoke and often sat alone in the school lunch hall. His family made desperate attempts to beat him into behaving as other children did, but this made him seek his own company more. Alone, Jimmy would wander in the woods near his home. He learnt to recognise different flowers and the insects that lived upon them. He played with bees and butterflies, never hurting them, and climbed trees to peer into birds' nests. It was climbing the largest oak tree in the woods where he befriended a lady blackbird that he climbed higher, beyond a hundred feet, into the wispy-thin branches, which swayed in the breeze and bowed under his slight body weight. The bird accompanied him to see a view that stretched out over the tops of trees to beyond his home, to the Methodist church spires where Sunday school teachers tormented him with Bible verses. When the blackbird flew away, without thinking, Jimmy flew too. The air slipped past him as he flapped his wings and glided through the branches. Leaves tickled his cheeks and the sound of breaking twigs pinged in his ears.

That was that. Jimmy James had his fourth descent and at thirteen years of age, he knew he had to fight to climb. Broken limbs and another nasty bang on his head, somehow Jimmy did fly and he loved it until the ground rudely interrupted his fall. Nobody noticed his absence while he recovered in hospital. His mother visited twice in six months, and his father could not leave his work and the overriding need to be in The King's Head public house during his evenings. Jimmy made his home in the hospital helping the nurses and orderlies. He shuffled along the corridors upon crutches, running errands and guiding visitors. He talked with patients and learnt how to clean wounds and dress them with bandages. This was his first climb away from his family. Jimmy left the hospital, discharged, feeling he had no other home. He wandered the streets trying to find in his mind a place where he could belong.

Three more years in school and Jimmy left to enter the adult world. He was engaged as a trainee butcher in a shop.

His time was spent grinding mince. Meat, pink with blood and white with fat; the grinder ground on day after day, and trays of mince were displayed, weighed, bagged and sold. Soon Jimmy saw the old but noisy ladies who frequented the shop with their silent husbands as he saw the mince he sold them. Pink-skinned ladies and white-fleshed men all eating Jimmy's mince. No one spoke to him and he avoided talking to others.

One evening, Jimmy left the butcher's shop never to return. He even left his wages in the safe that sat on the floor in the manager's office. Forever more, Jimmy hated the smell of meat, all sorts of meat, and this made him look for a different line of work. He joined the infantry and trained for months how to hide and how to walk, how to run and be shouted at without flinching. He jumped out of aeroplanes and floated again, but this time under a parachute, to land in a tree and break a leg. This was Jimmy's fifth fall that took him back to his hospital home. The army discharged him, for now he could only walk with a limp and he walked the streets of London sleeping in shop doorways and hostels. He learnt how to make a bed out of cardboard and drink just enough to not feel the wet and cold. He grew used to being woken by policemen and moved on.

Jimmy didn't say much, but he knew a lot. He drifted through ten years to find himself on the south coast looking out over the sea. Skipping stones across the water and watching the sparkling ripples, he stripped naked, waded out and remembered how to swim. He swam and swam, diving deep amongst the weeds and rocks. Here, Jimmy was free. Free of the land he could no longer see and free of the people who could not see him. Jimmy was rescued, but he did not know this, having been hauled on board a ferry bound for France. He was resuscitated, regaining consciousness in the Pasteur Hospital in Cherbourg-Octeville. It was here he met Evelyn, a nurse from Brittany, and she gave him care. They walked in the town park holding hands and enjoyed sharing coffee and ice creams. Jimmy told her of butchery and vagrancy, and she knitted him a jumper made of thick, deep blue wool.

It was with Evelyn that Jimmy climbed. Evelyn gave him love and he slowly learnt how to return that love. He trained to be a lifeguard and worked at a swimming pool watching over swimmers from high in a ladder chair. Like a tennis umpire, he watched over the swimmers' lives. Jimmy took his work seriously and never rested from watching. His vigilance saved two people: a small child whose parents were in the water but arguing, and one fat old lady who was swallowing water and panicking. When he had delivered her to safety, she stormed directly to the pool manager's office to complain that Jimmy had assaulted her and that she was not in need of his help. Jimmy was sacked and this was his sixth fall.

Jimmy watched the sea and dreamt of being free, so he took sailing lessons. One day, without saying goodbye, he took a sailing boat, loaded it with provisions and set sail. He sailed the English Channel dodging great cargo vessels past the Netherlands and Germany out into the North Sea. He skirted Norway and Sweden, sinking in a storm, having grown weak and out of provisions off the coast of Stockholm. This was Jimmy's seventh fall.

Rescue came in the form of a luxury yacht owned by a Russian oligarch and piloted by an ex-Royal Naval captain. Jimmy recovered on board and after ten days, he was making himself useful as a crew member. He cooked breakfasts and mopped decks whilst sailing the Baltic coastline. The super yacht *Eclipse* sailed to Russia where Jimmy was put ashore. He was penniless and could not speak Russian. He walked begging for food, washing in ponds and rivers, working for a day here and there, splitting logs or cleaning cow sheds. His boots fell apart and a kind old lady who asked him his name, but he could not understand her, gave him her deceased husband's boots. Those boots must have been lucky boots, for whilst tramping through the town of Dimitrov, a hotel owner fed him and gave him a room for the night. Jimmy showered in hot water and lathered soap into his skinny body over and over again. He stood enjoying the heat until the water ran cold. Then came the large blue bath towel that felt like heaven before slumbering upon a double mattress with his head on a pillow that absorbed him into heaven.

Refreshed and having had a hearty breakfast of pilchards and eggs flushed with strong Turkish coffee, Jimmy was set to work. He sanded the old paint from windows and painted them. He made himself useful and through the hotel owner's wife Larisa who spoke Russglish (a spatter of English, mixed with a throaty Russian), she interpreted for them. Many misunderstandings later and much hard work, Jimmy had carved a name for himself in the town, becoming popular with children for whom he performed tricks and fixed broken toys and bicycles. He worked every day at the hotel and time passed, as days became years.

One morning, Jimmy was repairing an ornamental music box for a wealthy lady of the town. He slowly and deliberately worked on its small clockwork mechanism. At one point, he had turned it upside down to gain access to a base plate held by small brass screws when something fell silently upon the carpet on his room floor. Upon returning the box to the lady, she opened a small secret compartment in its side.

Putting her hand to her mouth, she cried, "Where is my precious ring?"

She told the hotel owner and he had Jimmy's room searched. This was Jimmy's eighth fall. He was accused of theft and told to leave. Not understanding, he started walking. He walked for three years this way and that until at last, through random luck, he recognised his old French town of Cherbourg. Sat on the seafront watching yachts in the bay and children playing upon the beach, a woman and a child walked past him. Their eyes met as Evelyn pulled the child close and hurried on her way. This was Jimmy's ninth fall.

He returned to London and did not recognise the place. So much had changed and so had he. He took a job in a pub pulling pints and rented a room in the Holloway Road. Customers talked at him and demanded that glasses be filled, but no one ever asked him his name. He worked three shifts a day, taking Sundays off when he would walk in the park and along the river. More time passed working and walking. He felt like one of London's pigeons: always in a crowd but ever alone.

It was late one night when Jimmy closed the pub and sat on a bench outside smoking a cigarette. A full moon had climbed to illuminate the night and something came over him. He felt an urge to leave. And so, with a sack on his back and new boots upon his well-trodden feet, he started to walk into the night. He slept in a field the next day and walked for nine hours the following night. He hadn't said goodbye. He had never said goodbye and it was only on his third night of walking that he realised this. Unconsciously, he was travelling to France to say goodbye to Evelyn and hello to his son. He arrived at the coast in Kent and slept on the beach. Upon awakening, he waded into the surf and started to swim. He swam for hours ducking beneath the waves. He was free. Free of his loneliness and free of the indifference of others. Free to live or not live, for life had always been his. His last fall was his last breath and the choice was his test.

THE GRAINED FACE

PEOPLE CAN SEE FIGURES IN CLOUDS OR THE SILHOUETTE OF CHRIST IN THEIR SOUP. THIS STORY, HOWEVER, STRETCHES FAR BEYOND THE IMAGINATION.

Another drink. It's only half past seven. I've been here since five. Drowning my sorrows, I am feeling pity for myself. I have had a hard time of life and finally quit running, now settled into a bar of an ancient pub in the Dorset countryside, southwest of England. I have been here long before darkness fell.

After a few more pints than I can remember, my eyes are swimming a little as I stare at the ancient oak bar top that is damp from my slopping pint of beer. The grain that flows in little sparks of indentations and long striations that flow in growth lines draws my attention. This wood has absorbed more alcohol of many varieties than a man can sink in a lifetime. There is spirit in the wood and I can sense it. There is something in the wood of this bar top and it's in the grain. A face. It comes and goes, fading. And as I lose it, it returns to tell me something. That face wants to say something to me. What is it saying? The run of the beer-stained grain flows in every direction to form an image. It is anything you can imagine, but I am not imagining, for there is a face looking back at me. I take a trip to the toilet and make it back to my stool where I sit, elbows on that bar top, looking down at the flowing grain that seems to run like a river of deep amber beer. The sound of murmuring conversation is all around me when I hear a voice.

"Hey, you!"

I look around to see who is speaking, but there is no one looking at me. I look down at the bar and there it is again.

"Oi, loser!"

This sobers me up a little because I know I am lost. There in front of me, clearly marked in the grain, is a face. The face is neither young nor old. It blinks and turns to look me in the eye.

"Now I've got you! Once you acknowledge me, you can't get away from me."

I push back my bar stool and my mouth drops. I want to speak, but I can't.

"You ain't gonna say nothin', are you? You'd be talkin' to yourself, eh?"

I frown in confusion, place my glass right over the face and look away across the bar. When I can't help myself and resist looking down again, my pint of beer is gone, but an angry face is looking straight at me.

"That was no nice thing to do. How'd you like a glass in your mug, mate?"

I decide that it is time to go. As I try to lift my elbows, I find they are stuck.

"You ain't getting away that easy, son."

It is then that I gasp, "Who are you?"

The face glares back at me but remains silent. I look up to see the barman studying me, so I order another drink. He reluctantly pulls a pint and I ask him if the pub is haunted. He tells me it is, by a woodsman who died when a large oak he was felling killed him. He was so crushed by the falling section of trunk that he was impregnated into the wood. The barman moves away to serve others and leaves me with the spectre of a dead woodsman who is in the wood of this bar. For the first time, I grow frightened and cannot think of what to do or say. I sit staring at an angry face that stares back at me.

"Burn me, you bastard. Burn me!"

I am so shocked I can't answer. I look around and no one seems to have heard.

"Burn me and set me free! I wanna get out of here."

I call the barman back and ask him what the dead woodsman was cutting down trees for. He explains the dead man was a charcoal burner three hundred years earlier and that the remains of his steel furnace and hut are not far from the pub, in Rampisham Wood. The barman retreats to serve others while my flat-faced companion speaks again.

"That's the spirit of the tree that absorbed me in revenge, I tell ya. Revenge for cutting the old gnarled fella down. I killed that bloody spirit and it plastered me here within the grain."

"What can I do?" I ask in surprise at my talking to this apparition seriously.

"Burn me. It's the only way to let me die a good death."

I draw my pint of warm and stagnant winter beer, clutching the glass so tight in a sweaty hand that I fear it is bursting. There, embellished upon the glass, are the words, "Demon Oak, Traditional Beers". Looking across the bar, I see a framed photograph. It is one of those frames that holds a series of pictures. One is faded brown in tint and the last is old, from the 1970s. The title under the pictures reads, "The many fires of The Royal Oak pub, 1870 to 1976". A shudder rises in my spine to jolt my mind sober. I test myself with a deep breath and slap my thigh; it stings.

A week later, a church service in the village commemorated the lives of four villagers and one stranger killed in a recent fire that started in the bar of The Royal Oak public house. Near the church, the burnout remains of an ancient stone building stand, stinking of ash. In time, the pub has been rebuilt and many years later, a traveller enters the revamped bar. He sits to order a winter night's beer. From a hard wooden place, I speak as his eyes fall upon the wooden bar.

"What you looking at, mate?"

LIFE UNCAGED

The brightness and shadow danced into my eyes as trees played with light, mixing the view of beauty in front of me with visions randomly plucked from life that now seemed so long. I felt as ancient as the oaks that rose above the wilderness floor to challenge the sky above. I didn't know it at the time, but as I sat there, I became aware that I had been staring at the bushes that drifted in and out of focus as they gave way to the low growing shrubs at the margin of the forest. I was feeling drawn in by some unconscious desire as the pain rose and fell in my chest sharply and repeatedly. It didn't occur to me I was dying and that the pain was not going to stop.

Like all animals that are aware of death, I was instinctively being drawn with the ancient desire to curl up in some sheltered, remote safe place, perhaps a dry hollow under one of the mighty oaks, and die, thus yielding the energy that is me to a beautiful monumental tree. This is nature's way that has been a route, followed by so many animals stricken before me — those fortunate enough not to have met a painful death having been picked off as prey in a weakened state. It is only humans that seek to die surrounded by their own, but I had always been alone like some wild cat high in the outlands of life, wild and free. There had been no conventions for me, and mine was to be like those of so many wild beasts whose calling had come. I sensed this and the futility of resisting it.

An ordinary day walking to work, having travelled the usual stops on the subway. Rising upon the escalator, the daylight flooding in made me close my eyes for a second. When I opened them, something was different. The place was its familiar self and the people looked as they always had. There was the sound of traffic, horns and the crossing lights. I lingered for a moment to look up at the buildings and it was then, as my eyes fell back to Earth, that I knew that the difference was not in the place or the people but in me. For some reason, nothing seemed important. I had a sense of a lack of urgency that created a massive hole in how I had been for so many years before. This made me so light-headed that I needed to get off the street. I hailed a taxi, called my office secretary and asked her to cancel my appointments.

"Where're we going, sir?" came the driver's question.

"To the Endless Forest," I instructed.

An hour and twenty minutes later, I was here walking as if in a dream under a light-flickering canopy of foliage that swayed, sending patterns from high above in shafts of light to dance around me like searchlights or heavenly angels. Having spent my adult life studying patients and assessing other people's psychiatric disorders, it was inevitable I would be used to analysing myself. My mind was racing for an explanation as to why I was feeling as I did. Sitting in a small clearing with my back against a tree and gazing into the forestscape, I started to feel drowsy and thought of events from the previous evening. I had had an appointment with a patient referred to me by a member of a Christian counselling group who specialise in helping those of religious inclination to cope with traumatic experiences. The notes mailed to me stated that Mr Bertram East was an insomniac and he had delusions about being another person in a previous life with a dual personality.

The therapy session started quite formally with all the usual questions.

"Date of birth?" to which he replied, "06.06.66."

"Next of kin?" to which he answered, "None."

He seemed relaxed until my questions became more searching. Mr B. East became more agitated. He appeared to be quite unwilling to talk about his childhood that, he said, was so irrelevant that it did not exist.

"I never was a child, my sort don't have childhoods."

I had asked about his faith and which local church he attended. His answer was that he wanted to be a Christian, but that Christ wasn't good enough for him, and anyway, Jesus had rejected him. He described the Catholic church that he attended at 162 Revelation Road. He had only used half of his allotted time but paid fully in cash and left in an agitated state, having given me his business card.

It wasn't until later that I read the card, which had embossed into it the words, "De Ville Mort, Undertakers & Embalmers". There was an address but no phone number. I had called the counsellor who had recommended him to me and asked about

Mr East's faith to learn that the church had burnt down a few years earlier through an unexplained cause.

Whilst sitting watching the forest that appeared to grow around me, I took out my phone and Googled the address of that charred church. Upon entering the street number 162, I gasped in surprise at what I read as follows:

"Mark of the Beast

Revelation 16:2 and 19:20 cite the 'mark of the beast' as a sign that identifies those who worship the beast out of the sea (Rev 13:1). This beast is usually identified as the Antichrist. This mark is first mentioned in 13:16–17, where it is imposed on humanity by the beast out of the earth (13:11). This second beast is the false prophet (19:20), who forces the worship of the Antichrist and brands those who do so with the mark. This mark is equivalent to the beast's name or number (13:17; cf. 14:11). This enigmatic number is announced in 13:18 as 666."

It was then that my mind seemed to be being driven by someone else as waves of guilt hit me in recollection of a hit-and-run I had experienced a few years earlier. A drunk had stepped out into the road and his head had shattered against the windscreen of my Audi. I had driven on and had never been held to account for not stopping. The man's name was East.

JOe

ADRIAN

Looking up, the horizon stared back at this man in a way that no other would see it. The low valley pasture where he stood was fertile, watered and warm, being sheltered by the great hills that rose on tree-crowded slopes to the grey mountain peaks in the far distance, some still snow-capped. The difference in the man's perception of the view was his relationship with this land, which at times was a beloved friend, but also it could be the worst enemy any man could have. He intended to use an enemy to his advantage and thus make it his friend.

It was past dawn and summer was no longer a youth. The first dews of autumn had saturated the long grass through which he was walking. Speed was essential, for others would soon be pursuing his tracks and they must not be allowed to get close. A good shot could pick him off at a quarter of a mile distance. Without looking back, he moved as a lithe creature used to covering great distances whilst conserving energy. Being six feet two in height, Adrian's long limbs counterbalanced each step, giving elegance to his stride, which he would now maintain for at least ten hours. Safety was to come after three days, maybe more.

Fourteen miles down the valley, the grey-uniformed military guards were opening the scientific institution's gates to allow the early shift workers in to master their allotted machines where carelessly they would manufacture death, but none would arrive for at least an hour yet. The multiple fuses had been set to detonate half an hour before the workers would arrive, but at the time when the day guards relieved those who had been on duty during the night at this munitions factory. The sleeping soldiers in the guard post had been easy to evade and the individual soldier on patrol had died silently and quickly. Adrian had no hesitation about killing, for he didn't see his victim as a man. Rather, he saw him as part of a brutal machine that had killed Stephanie, his partner, a French resistance fighter, betrayed and murdered without compassion like so many who fought tyranny unlike those complicit, spineless individuals who betrayed her. Switzerland, a politically neutral country in the early 1940s, was far from economically neutral. If money was to be made, the country would bend to making as much as possible, even if it meant arming the devil.

Adrian turned to look back in the direction from which he was running. He checked his watch and waited. Seconds passed, and all he could hear was the dawn chorus. The minute hand had passed the hour and self-doubt began to flow into his mind. Then it came. Because of the distance, he heard the rupturing multiple blasts twenty-three seconds after they had occurred. He could see in his mind's eye, the cooling towers falling and the carnage delivered to the soldiers' and the commandants' dwellings. Now was the time to make ground. His pace doubled in long strides. He must make the cover of trees before the aeroplanes came. Some twenty-eight miles behind him, the dust had settled and the workers had been turned away. There would be no manufacturing of weapons from this pile of rubble and corpses for many years, if ever. The Nazi command had assessed the situation and had a suspect. Pursuit had been ordered.

As the day grew, the cover of trees had been met and Adrian drew a breath of relief that the two planes overhead couldn't see him, but they could see the trampled track he had left in the grass upon the meadows he had crossed. Trucks would cut the road distance between those who would kill him after excruciating torture, but there would still be some twenty miles between him and his pursuers as there were no roads that came near to the route he was marching into (the high Swiss Alps on the French border, chasing the sun westward). This forced march of escape had been planned in advance. He would walk for ten hours to the west, rest for three hours, and then double back in a mountain stream for one hour before heading west again on an unused mountain pass that few knew about. He hoped this might throw those following him off his track.

He awoke cold and nervous under a clear moonlit sky. Waiting a few minutes, observing his surroundings and listening intently, he started his night time climb once he had gathered his things and cleared all signs of his presence. Dawn was three hours away and the altitude's thin air made him breathe deep. From a high ledge that afforded a view back down the slope and out across the wide valley to the place from which he had run some three miles below him, he could see the flickering light of a camp fire, that of his enemy. This inspired his flight and he moved on with renewed energy.

Dawn came like thunder as the sun burst over the cold peaks behind him, flooding the valley from the east. Within minutes, an eagle was climbing upon the first thermal below. It released a harrowing call that must have echoed for miles. Adrian knew those following him would have heard the call of the bird that, like them, was up for the hunt. His greatest danger grew as he navigated higher. The relentless heating of the rocky crags by day and the freezing at night for as long as eternity had fractured boulders into tonnes of unstable loose scree. A rock fall would pinpoint his position and the inevitable would soon follow.

By one in the afternoon of the second day, he had reached the summit of the goat herders' high pass. Looking back, he gazed down upon clouds as the sound of an aircraft rose faintly from below. At first, it seemed far away, but within seconds, as the machine broke free from the muffling cloud cover, Adrian had to throw himself upon the ground, for the pilot's eyes met his from a few yards away. Thinking as fast as a cat, he jumped to his feet, forgetting his haversack that remained upon the rocky promontory. Luck afforded him a large recess that was almost made for him to fit into. The aircraft was making a second approach and its machine guns were spitting bullets that ripped into the rock face as they searched for the abandoned haversack on both sides of the fissure that was a lifesaving haven. As the aircraft passed, Adrian grabbed a boulder of some eighteen inches in diameter, as much as he could lift above his head. It was as if the crevasse and rock had been sculpted over centuries to serve his purpose — one as a retreat and the other as a weapon. As the plane approached for the third time, Adrian summoned all the energy he had. This was his only chance. He loosed the rock and it only rose over three yards into the air and started to fall to Earth. Before it engaged with total liberty, it smashed into the port engine of the Ju 88A that turned it into a fireball. Adrian and the startled pilot's eyes met again as the craft started to spin. Moments later, it crashed into the mountain and was gone. Adrian hoped the pilot had not radioed a report to those below him.

Somewhat shaken, Adrian took off like a scolded cat. It wouldn't be long before another aircraft would arrive to survey the scene. Despite the adrenaline in his system, he had presence enough of mind to smile, for no one would believe he had downed a Junkers' aircraft with a rock. He would have to live to enjoy telling the story. With a haversack full of bullet holes and a punctured flask, he resorted to soaking a woollen scarf in shallow pools that gathered in hollows to transport water into the long hours that was no longer a climb. He was descending. The evening path was gentler than his climb of the previous day, but the awareness that should the soldiers persist in their chase, they would now be bearing down upon him as an easy target for a good marksman. He chose his resting place in an undercut of rock that had shallow, mossy soil in it, which would serve as a mattress. Having eaten his dried meat and a bullet-scarred apple, sleep overtook him and lasted for more hours than he had planned.

He rose after dawn when the sun glared into the undercut. It brought a deep sense of unease, for he knew those higher up the mountain would be closing on him. As he rolled out from the ledge, a shot rang out and the unmistakable sound of steel ricocheting off a rock hissed sinisterly in the air. He rolled back under the rocky cover of his one-time bedroom, peering out like a frightened creature. Moments later, a second shot shattered the clear, silent air and a crow fluttered to land dead a yard or two away from where Adrian lay. Footsteps clambering and sliding could be heard from above and then a German officer appeared with his back to the undercut. Adrian had an unobstructed view of the man. Oblivious, the soldier picked up the bird that hung below his fist and shouted, "*Ich bin ein guter Schuss, oder?*" and in a moment, he was gone.

Adrian listened to the voices and footsteps pass into silence below him. His pursuers were in front of him in an ironic twist of fate. Adrian was now the hunter of two enemy soldiers. This complicated his plans because, at some point, they would turn to face him on their return. The only answer was to keep the soldiers in sight but to be sure they remained unaware of his presence.

Setting off a full hour after them, he took every opportunity to scan the slopes below through the snub lenses of his Barr & Stroud binoculars. Every half hour, he would lie upon some vantage point holding his breath, surveying like a mountain cat hunting its prey. He would not move until he saw his enemies. The day warmed and the light clouds rose, letting sunlight stir the air in a heat haze that made his observations difficult. After a few slow, cautious hours of descent, he caught sight of the soldiers. They had turned and were climbing unknowingly towards him. He estimated that within half an hour they would arrive where he was. He had no choice but to climb and find a place to hide. His calculations were that they were younger than he was and relaxed in believing he had escaped far below; this was his advantage. At a small divide in the path that passed a large outcrop of rock on both sides to become one at the rear of it, he decided to wait and allow the men to pass, taking the gamble that he would move into the side they didn't choose. It was now only a matter of time.

Adrian heard their voices first and then the sound of boots crunching the broken stones upon the passage. Having braced himself against the high side of the rock and holding a small revolver as they approached, he grew confused, for the sound of their conversation echoed from all sides of the enclosed space. Swearing, he strained to listen. In one moment, he thought he knew which route they had taken and in the next, he wasn't sure. He was going to have to chance it with a gamble that could cost him his life or the lives of two young men. Sometimes luck lands in a glide and what shouldn't have been is avoided, but today Lady Luck had looked away. The soldiers, for some forever-unknown reason, had divided to each take a separate route. Adrian raised his gun and fired, hitting the startled man in the chest. He fell. The second man shouted for his friend and Adrian answered, *"Nur eine weitere blutige Krähe."* Just another bloody crow.

Running, Adrian headed down the slope, anticipating the second soldier having continued on his upward path. Turning the point where the two paths joined, he saw his prey standing, looking at his dead comrade. Adrian fired and the soldier fell on top of the other. It was a strenuous task dragging the bodies and tipping them into a ravine where they would never be found. It took some time for Adrian to regain calmness when he was able to drink and eat the two soldiers' provisions. Not realising his hunger until he was eating, did he note how wild he had become in such a short time, for until the explosion, he had never considered killing anyone.

Having walked into the night avoiding sleep despite great fatigue, the reassuring smell of a fire met him as the narrow path became a farm track. It was here he collapsed to be found after dawn in the morning. Luck was his again. The farmer who woke him was a resistance fighter, who had already had news of an armaments factory being destroyed and of a wanted man crossing the Alps.

⸰⸰ℓ⸰

TRANSFERENCE

It was one of those days, not any day, but the sort that comes once in a couple of decades for me and never for many (that is, until they do die as in never-coming-back). Have you ever died — not a fright of some momentary heart-stopping shock, but a death that is an end? Yes, the sort of time-ceasing, no-breathing end. I guess most haven't, but I'm sure many of us have wished we were dead at some time or other. Here is a thing: most wish for it and don't mean it, which shows how insincere our emotions can be when playing with our consciousness. Well, I have meant that wish in my past and that sinister desire was granted. This is how I came to understand the meaning of death and learnt to apply it to others. Being dead isn't a lot of fun, but there is the in between time like Schrodinger's bloody over-evaluated cat that I would surely poison to get off of all of those stupid social media know-better pages. In between is what it is, and if you can hold your breath for long enough until you can't hold on any longer, then blow that breath out like a breaching whale but not take another, you can join me in the floating, suspended below what you are and the component parts of what you may become.

As I said, it was one of those days. I am telling you, my living reader, about the first time and my, did the jolt make me jump almost out of my skin! I've got the scorch and stretch marks to show for it, not to mention the brain damage. I wasn't supposed to be there and, by God, I wanted out as fast as I could. The problem is once the darkness had cleared, I'm not sure if it was light that replaced it, but I certainly slowly grew accustomed to seeing beyond, once my breath had gone.

Why am I telling you this, I hear you asking? Yes, I can hear your thoughts. No, don't think nonsense because I am in your head. Tap, tap, that's the boot of my interference upon the inside of your skull, just above your forehead looking in. Don't worry, there are no knives involved here. This is all about supersymmetry, singularities, Doppler effects and the redshift of a nightmare. On this particularly different morning, compared with all that had preceded it, I felt different as if something was brewing and growing like the tension in the strata before an earthquake or the static before a storm. My head was ready to burst and my eyes itched since awakening early. Painkillers didn't touch it and a few whiskies only confused the pain. Surgeons told me later that the tumour wasn't big, but had divided a region of my mind responsible for an awareness of time. They wouldn't have found it had a vessel not haemorrhaged, leaving me with minutes to live. Those men in gowns and masks trepanned my skull to gain access with a micro laser. In breaching the boundary of my inner space, something of me escaped but remained mine. In that moment, breath left me, and my heart then slowed, defying all medical resuscitation. I was pronounced dead and trolleyed to a cold mortuary.

Wake up I didn't. I slept on and now you are in my dreaming death. How did you get here is the question, for I certainly didn't come and get you. If you are a little confused, imagine how I felt when my thoughts and feelings turned up in your head. You don't have to engage with this. It can go somewhere while you try to forget about me, but of course, you cannot. Yes, I died and I am still here making a mess of your head. Do you have any idea who I am? I can feel that itch in your left foot and your pants are pinching us a little; it's time to move and scratch.

Before my first death, I didn't know you, but now it has happened three times. I know what to expect. For sure, you have your own original thoughts on just about everything; mine will take over because they have been tried and tested before you were born. I am two hundred and twenty years old, spread over three lives. I haven't a clue where I was before that, but I do know I am not from around here, I mean this planet. You are twenty-two years of age and that was your formation time; now your mind is mine or, should I say, ours. You were never interested in politics. However, have you noticed how you freak at the news recently? We threw that beer at the TV the other night and you enjoyed it; go on, be honest to us. Do you know where you came from? No, not your mum and dad; they made your body, but I am your mind. We were formed more than a billion years ago and have travelled encoded for eons, drawn by gravity, changing resonance and redshifting to celestial observers without interest until we collided recently. No, it is not reincarnation; it is more like a possession in which you possess me. It happens all the time, only mostly no one is aware of it. I guess this prevents a few suicides and keeps more people from going mad. None of us are who we are and most never know what they were. Sometimes it goes awry. I am sure I was part of a tree once because whenever I hold an old, heavy book, I start to cry, for I feel the lignin of my flesh being chipped, bleached and milled into paper. It's not easy being in a vegetative state and I hate the sound of chainsaws. I should say, "We now hate chainsaws."

I know you are going to fight me. The last person, a woman I joined with, took more drugs than a New York junkie to get shot of me; I enjoyed the trip until we overdosed. Jasmine is her name. She is here with us. Do you want an introduction? Let's hope she doesn't start cross-dressing. Okay, you've had enough for now. I'm going dormant to let you rest a while. Take it easy, will you, as I can feel our head beginning to ache.

DIMPLE

Abald, short, pugnacious man lingers while one of two pit bulls on heavy chain leashes squats to take a crap on the pavement. Brian is not a man to disagree with, having grown up on a northern housing estate where the nearest tree was a branch-stripped, dying silver birch two miles away. His one-time prize-fighter, mostly absentee father (because of extended jail sentences) had spoken to him only eight times in Brian's first ten years of life but beaten the hell out of him almost as many days as he had been there.

Brian had feelings but not many. His first love was for his dogs and these were fighters; they bore the scars from badger baiting and from having been pitted against other creatures — that's dogs, otters, badgers and sometimes another man. His second love was the greyhound track where he would drink with other tattooed squat-killer types and scream with aggression like a berserker before annihilation in some hand-to-hand combat.

Then there was Tina, a girl of twenty-nine years, who was known as Pins because of her long, slender legs. Tina had grown up in a cold isolated corner of Lancashire and had escaped to London pursuing the career as a gentleman's escort; only gentlemen in this day and age on the Holloway Road, London, were as rare as hen's teeth. After a few years and some unhealthy infections, she had become a mistress of her game. Tina had met Brian whilst writhing away in The Victoria Tavern's toilet from a customer who wanted more but couldn't or wouldn't pay. Hearing the struggle, Brian intervened with a couple of punches, relieving the assailant of the ample contents of his wallet and breaking a dimpled pint glass over his head. No one had ever fought for Tina and as importantly, no one had ever thanked Brian for anything. They were delighted with each other and set about drinking their newly acquired wealth. Within weeks, they had shared tattoos, the outline of a pit bull terrier's shape upon their buttocks. The tattooist's pen had been a painful pleasure, which Brian liked so much he went back the following day to have a red bowtie added to the terrier. Tina moved out of her bedsit in Camden Town to Brian's council basement flat in Archway. All was never peaceful and happy, but they made it work. She would clean and dress his wounds and kiss his scars. She even cooked a couple of half-healthy meals for him each week. He gave her a few quid that kept her happy.

It wasn't many months later that Tina presented Brian with the news that he was going to be a father. This confused poor Brian as it wasn't something he had ever considered. He turned on his heels and headed to The Archway Tavern to consult his mates and rinse the shock from his now frowning brow. After six hours of straight drinking and five fights, PC Dimple of the Metropolitan Police arrested him. Dimple, a pleasant man, took pity on his prisoner and released him with a caution. That set the new child's name. Baby Dimple was christened in The Archway Tavern with a twenty-year-old whisky, then a fifteen-year-old whisky, then a ten-year-old whisky, interrupted by a few pints of Guinness. The celebrations ended with Tina covering baby Dimple whilst thirty men and women engaged in a mass drunken brawl that spilt out onto the street.

Baby Dimple grew to have his mother's legs and his father's tenacious strength. By the age of fifteen, he was running middle distance races in national competitions. His mates had nicknamed him the Hound, because he ran like a greyhound and had a small tattoo of a pit bull terrier on his left buttock and, to his shame, Dimple had a prominent dimple on both buttocks. In school, he was known as Dimple Dimple. At sixteen, Dimple and Brian were an item in the pubs and at the dog track where they raced their own dogs that were often winners, gaining big prize money.

After a year of gambling and drinking, copious amounts of money, cleaning dogs shit from kennels and exercising promising hounds, Dimple announced to his dad that there had to be more to life than drinking, court fines and the odd night in jail. Dimple, who had grown up playing gambling machines, decided to go into the one-armed bandit business. He had already learnt how to reprogramme the payment intervals of these machines, so he purchased six at a second-hand auction and rented them to local pubs. They were a money-spinner because they were rigged to never pay out more than ten pounds. Each machine delivered a straight return of nine hundred pounds a week after one hundred paid to the publican. In order to stop people from asking why the machines never delivered a jackpot, Dimple employed two mates to play the machines and win in a fixed roll. Nearly all the money from the win went straight back to Dimple.

Money was flowing in and Brian had joined his son's firm being in charge of collections. He bought a smart, black double-breasted suit, a baseball bat for protection and a sack trolley for wheeling the money to his fifteen-year-old, beat-up, dog-infested Berlingo van that was now his security vehicle. More money flowed in and the dogs kept on running. Our boys kept on drinking until they met a man by the Turf Accountants stool at the dog track, the Tic Tac man known as Swifty. It is the Tic Tac man's job to communicate odds and lay off bets to other bookmakers at the trackside. Swifty had been known to set a rate and change it ten seconds later, having moved the goal posts. Although he dressed like a tramp, it was rumoured he had a large villa south of Malaga in Spain and a golden vintage Rolls Royce to go to the shops. He lived two lives — one for the taxman and the other for himself. He never smoked his hand-rolled Havana cigars whilst in the United Kingdom.

Brian had known Swifty for many years. First, Swifty had fiddled Brian out of his winnings, then for revenge Brian had drugged his worst-looking dog that had high odds against it and it won, clearing Swifty out of two weeks' profit. In the end, it was more profitable for them to work together. Swifty invested in the gambling machine business because he was getting too old to stand on a stool in all weathers, fiddling bets and odds. Within eighteen months, the three of them had one hundred and eighty machines in pubs and clubs across London. They never paid out, but the owners of the establishments didn't care; they wanted their pay off each week. Money flowed in. It was time to do something with it.

They bought a house in Burley Road, Kentish Town. No more rent, just a one-off payment in full from the back of Brian's van, which was named the Dingo, for although full of money, it was always full of dogs. They deployed more machines and bought premises, which they opened up as a nightclub. It was here that Swifty sealed his reputation as being swift with his women and his money. With so much cash, they needed an accountant, and Swifty introduced his mate Rowland the Pole, hence Rowland Poland. Rowland, a pale, long, thin man ran a concession for the Camden Building Society from the shopfront below his dingy office. He employed two ex-dinner ladies who were known to those visiting the place as Beans and Mash. They could never fiddle Rowland on account of having no intelligence beyond a plate of beans and mash. Rowland Creep, as the schoolgirls he leered at from his second-floor office window called him, ran his business under the slogan "Rowland Figures It Out". It should have been "Rowland Cuts the Taxmen Out". He had been massaging Swifty's turf accounts for years along with covering a greengrocer store's accounts for a drug dealer who sold a lot more drugs than spuds. You name it, Rowland cooked it.

Business in North London continued in comfort with paid-off gaming machine officials and cash payments to site owners. Newer and higher earning machines replaced the old ones and the money pile grew too much for Brian's van, the Dingo, whose suspension finally collapsed under the weight of thirty-five thousand pounds in sacks containing pound coins. It was embarrassing when the breakdown mechanic looked in the back of the van and needed a few hundred quid to keep his mouth shut.

Swifty and Rowland Poland would meet early on Friday afternoons after Brian and his assistant Joe, a.k.a. Buster Ball Breaker, had collected the week's takings, leaving the machines hungry for money over the weekend. All three would count the coinage, which would often amount to as much as fifteen thousand pounds and then take off for Jimi Smart in a pub by Victoria Station (I can't mention his surname, as it could cause me problems). Smart, who ran a busy pub, had a second line of business. He would trade freshly printed twenty-pound notes for ten pounds in real money. This fake money would then be laundered back through the pubs and turned into certified sterling before heading to the bank (the Bank Coutts & Co, a private outfit housed in the Strand, London, that only dealt with the very rich and royalty). They were hesitant when Dimple walked into their foyer and asked to open an account. The receptionist was in the process of showing him the door when a manager spotted the briefcase chained to Brian's hand and the couple of ugly blokes standing outside on the pavement with ball bats swinging by their sides. Once the case was opened and the money seen, Brian was ushered to a leather easy chair and offered a glass of Champagne. The account was opened within seconds.

Having money is a nice thing, but knowing what to do with it takes an understanding of money, so the three turned to Rowland Poland and asked the same question at once. "What are we going to do with two and a half million quid?"

Rowland answered the three as one. "We're gonna buy a street in Madrid."

"What?" came the answer in triplicate.

Rowland answered, "I've got a mate, he's an ex-scrubber, did fifteen years inside for manslaughter. Whilst in there, he did two degrees: in Spanish and business studies. He is redeveloping a rather fancy row of townhouses in a posh inner city area called Rubén Darío. We are going to buy them and rent them out, tax free."

They all shook hands and three weeks later, they were flying EasyJet to Madrid. For these three Londoners, Madrid was bohemian, wild and beautiful. They drank in the bars and explored a few museums, and the Prado Gallery, which left them rather confused about culture; their natural response was to find an Irish bar and drink until the fight started. The properties were purchased, furnished and handed over to Fernando's letting agency. Now the coffers were empty and more money was needed. Back in the UK, Brian worked his dogs, while Rowland and Swifty introduced twenty new machines that ate five-pound notes as a donkey eats carrots.

Dimple fell in love. He met Jenny in the local corner store. She was a pretty young lady of twenty-four and well-bred. Her father, having been a major in the Guards, was now a respectable director of an investment bank. Jenny fell pregnant at the first round and against Daddy's wishes, the marriage certificate was signed in Kentish Town register office, and Brian was introduced *fait accompli* to Roderick Pankhurst later in the day. After the screaming and tears, Roderick got down to business, and Swifty and Brian were sent for. Roderick loved money maybe more than he loved his daughter, and he soon realised Dimple was a get-richer-quicker proposition. The meeting between the four started with a glass of wine and ended with a bottle of whisky drunk neat. Our boys were going into the ATM business and that would take big money. They left Roderick's mansion in the posh Bishop's Avenue near Hampstead Heath and walked slowly discussing their ideas. They taxied around to Rowland's flat in Docklands for an opinion. His advice was that they would have to all wear suits and stop swearing. That didn't go down well.

Nine months later, Dimple & Co were being financed by the Bank of Commerce and Industry to fit forty-five of the latest state-of-the-art cash dispensing machines all over the UK, replacing older models. Another street in Madrid was purchased to invest the money that was flowing in by the truckload after Roderick had taken his twenty-five percent without his fellow directors knowing. Rowland Poland was despatched to liaise with his scrubber builder friend to manage the new development. The dogs kept running and Brian's

Berlingo had a new suspension. Swifty didn't miss a bet on the dogs, and Rowland had dumped his old business and was now a property development manager, who hid his money in Roderick's bank to avoid Spanish tax.

Brian loved his dogs. Tina suspected that if it was them or her, she would come off second best. He loved the dog racing and it was in his blood, but times were changing. Doping the dogs had become mainstream, and Russian mafia had started fixing the races. Brian decided it was time to do something about it. He owned a few of the best dogs that ever raced and was friendly with the bookmakers who worked the track. Brian let his greyhound named Scarlet win three races and entered her for a fourth; all the money was on for her to win. He had a lot of money on her to come fourth and had put his share in the business on the line. Scarlet came in fourth and cleaned the mafia out, but Brian had to lie low and took off for Spain with Tina. Dimple now had to care for the dogs and this gave him time to think. He thought of his parents and his wife, and the people he worked with. It was time to take a break.

PAUPERS AND KINGS ALIKE

On the edge of the village, people gather for an old man who has passed. He was a mystic and a charmer of snakes, a medicine man of magic, a keeper of traditions that have traversed generations. Few respected his modest ways in a modern time and now his flesh crackles and chars roasting as flames liberate his energy and knowledge in the ultimate combustion of peace.

Out of the fire came a scream, heard by all in the darkness of night. Yet, it immersed in the drowning darkness; the man burnt so bright. From deep within the flames, it was seen. None could look away. There was nothing we could do or say. Dancing within the flames came the magic of a life on fire. For eyes, two embers glowed — the deep red blood — as something was said:

"I am a spirit burning, my soul is turning
in between the dark and the light."

Some ran away, but they couldn't hide from the truth. Others froze with fear, as I was drawn near to the crackling. There was no smoke, just a tower of flames. At first, my clothes started to smoulder as a skeletal hand reached out and took mine. I felt cold in such burning heat, while my vision became dark in the brightness. I cannot tell of what sense or feeling fell upon me when I stepped forward. The burning of flesh. My spirit unleashed. None tried to stop me. It was my time, for I am the sacrifice.

Life is a fire that fades yet rages at its end. The unspent energy of lost time. We all burn our years. Some slow into old age. Others pass fast to the summoning hour, which races out of an uncontrollable space when it comes without warning. The scent of fire is forever in the air above the ash of lives charred, for we are surrounded by death, we live upon her breath. Good men and bad men all burn on a pyre, be it to the slow incineration of a pauper's grave or the tomb of a king. There are always the flames of decomposition, our liberation. I, too, burnt for a belief in a moment yet I never left. I am the scent of fire, the ash of doubt in your mind. You saw me walk into that pyre, but did not witness me pass on through to the other side.

Am I alive or dead? I can never tell, but when you shudder in your bed, it is me who rings the temple bell, one that only you can hear. There is no pain, just the slipping of life's shroud, letting go of the things that made you proud. When next you look into a fire, you are looking into me, and in doing so, you will see yourself as you will be, for all will join me, drawn by my burning hand of desire, for I am you and you will be death.

PATTERNS IN ICE

Frozen blood stopped his heart yet movement continued, for ice flows slowly, dragging a harsh beauty over a barren land. He travelled with it, locked in for all time like the spirit of glass. Eyes open, ever looking to the sky, encased deeper with each snowfall. He had nothing to say having said it all. Ice pick in hand and ropes hooped over his shoulders, upwards he climbed to get away. There could be no return. Some strip naked upon the shore of indifference, leaving shoes and clothes behind to take one last swim beyond into that far-off place where none can follow. In his despair, his way was to challenge the harsh, frozen-hearted ice sheet that grasped this cruel northland. His exertions were great and thirst came first; later, the hunger that brought regret. Face and hands numbing, feet without feeling, he climbed on, kicking his crampons against the wall of ice. Hours passed like minutes and seconds that weighed in kilos. Growing heavy, the fight with himself continued. There was never going to be a solution and compromise was out of reach. It was the anger that grew in his will and aggression in his mind.

He had struck out in self-defence and the other could not respond. Now there was no turning back. The armed men were in pursuit. To hesitate would be certain death, maybe several bullets before his heart ceased and even then, he would witness his own descent from one hell into the abyss of another. There was never a plan, just the random acts in a foolish moment, but provocation is a valid reason. She had left him, broken their bond. She had no choice and he understood. It was his life or her body and the officer had the gun. Waiting all night in agony, cruel was the dark reasoning with which he fought. Then she came, limping and bruised. Well, what could he do? When he had finished, the commanding officer had no face left. The chain had ripped into his hand as he thrashed it over and over that officer, beating cruelty with cruelty's blind rage of revenge. She begged him to stop, but his blood was up, and he could not cease until overrun with sweating exhaustion and relief.

He has travelled thirty miles with the ice, locked away from hell, as heaven would never exist for him. It was then that the ice sheet met the sea and his body floated free. She was twenty-seven back then, young and strong, a resistance fighter before her spirit was taken. He was returned to her in a state of serene peace and now she is eighty-three. He hadn't changed at all as she leant over him holding his hand. Her warm tears flooded into his ever-open, ice-cold blue eyes. She then, at last, kissed him goodbye, remembering an ancient love that was frozen out of revenge.

THE WALKER

Walking in the hills above my village one December day, I had dawdled returning after dark. It had been one of those crisp, clear days when the sun had felt quite warm and there was little breeze. I had walked further than intended, and somehow lost track of time, not turning to return until the sun had changed from yellow to orange as it cleared the sky for a full moon that was already creeping behind me. As darkness settled, a creamy mist crept up to meet me from the river that snakes its way through the valley below. Approaching the village from the east, the sun had completely withdrawn its light and the moon cast shadows upon the mist. I neared the village church that had stood since Saxon times with the ghosts of many collapsed graves scattered in its irregular yard. It was still and, because of the heavy mist, a silent night — one in which even the surest of hearts would hesitate to deny that ghosts could rise from rotten wooden coffins or caskets to wander about as they had in life.

I stumbled a little upon a sunken hollow on the path above that ancient church and its graveyard. Having landed upon my knees by what I now know is a pauper's grave, I thought

I had heard a noise. Or was I pushed? Climbing back on my feet, brushing the grass and leaves from what were now damp trouser knees, I saw a figure brandishing a Bible. The vision came to me like a distraction. At first, I did not pay it much attention, thinking it was a minister or some enthusiastic lay preacher. It occurred to me that I might be dreaming, for the mists in these parts are known to create illusions in one's perceptions. I did ask myself if I was awake or dreaming and how could I be sure.

Mist obscured my surroundings more as I approached the figure who was speaking in muffled words, at least they sounded like words (not English, my native tongue, but some garbled ancient language; one I could not understand). It wasn't until I was some fifteen or so paces away from this foreign creature that apprehension crept into my spirit. I had never considered myself easily frightened after twenty-five years as a major in the regiment, having seen active service in the Great War. I raised my walking cane and bid this fellow in a black robe good evening to find he completely ignored me. I felt a little annoyed at his apparent rudeness and made a little jab at him with my cane to draw his attention, but the solid shaft passed right through him.

In shock, I spoke and was ignored again. Looking into his eyes, I saw abject fear and became aware he was trembling. To avoid this strange being, I detoured away from him into that churchyard. Feeling a little confused and weak, I sat upon a bench that is placed against one of the church's ancient stone walls. As I looked up, my attention was taken by a large imposing gravestone that had engraved into it in floral script, "Major Clive Digby Smithe, 1856–1918. He fell saving the men of his company."

Inside of that church doorway is a small brass plaque warning visitors they may meet the ghost of a major who died on the battlefield in France on December 13, 1918. The following morning being Sunday, 13 December 2020, the minister said a prayer for a lost soldier buried here and relayed his story of the previous night to his parishioners. I, of course, did not know this, for I was again wandering in the Dorset hills that I know so well.

AUDACITY

"If you don't ask, you don't get" is the mantra that few hear and fewer practice. Rejection hurts. Dickens nailed it when an innocent Oliver Twist asked the master, "Please, sir, I want some more." Poor Oliver was brutally humiliated and this is the lesson most carry through life: don't ask. Most don't and as a result, they fail to progress beyond the rudimentary basics that life has to offer. It is asking questions that is the powerhouse of human progress.

Little Jimmy Spriggs asked, when he was six years old, and got a whack for his cheek. Jimmy was born in London to a working-class family: his father a train driver and his mother a sometime cleaner and fixer of ladies' problems. On 5th May 1966, little Jimmy found his father's condoms in a damp cupboard below the bathroom sink. Having opened the foil and found the slimy rubber inside, he ran to his father and asked what it was. An embarrassed David Spriggs took the mess from his little boy's hands, whacked him around the head and sent him to his room. Thus Jimmy with tearful eyes learnt not to ask, but he was a resourceful child and had a burning inquisitiveness that nearly never left him. He collected snails in a shoebox, always respecting their needs of fresh cabbage leaves and his father's lettuces, a jam jar lid full of water. He gave them names, always releasing them, having put a different letter on each shell. Some came back to him for several years. When his father found the vegetables from his garden were being fed to a herd of snails, poor Jimmy was given another whack and locked in his room for six hours. By eight years of age, Jimmy was a mollusc expert and nobody knew it.

Jimmy loved flowers. He would spend hours wandering free upon the wasteland that was a disused sewerage farm at the back of his house. He would collect wild flowers and eat the beautifully sweet red tomatoes that had accumulated in the fertile soil, having been passed through the town's digestive tracts. Jimmy could recognise the seed heads on the grasses and he learnt about the changing seasons from how plants germinated, thrived and faded into winter's dark cold. By eleven years of age, Jimmy had bought himself a small microscope and studied plant specimens. He was growing wild fritillaries in his bedroom. It was his mother who threw all of his plants out, because Jimmy was making a mess. When she told his father, he was given another whack and ordered to cut the grass with an old push mower which he could hardly move being a weak and slightly built child. Jimmy tried hard but always took the rap, for he was honest in a dishonest world. He passed the ball on the sports pitch, but it was never passed to him.

At twenty-one years of age, his boss, a large lady a few years older, had a crush on him, but when he didn't share her emotions, she accused him of rape and that's how Jimmy went to jail an innocent man. Seven years later, he left jail with fifty pounds and the clothes he went in with. His family didn't want to know him. He joined the army, trained and they sent him to Iraq to fight for Queen and country. It was there he picked up an improvised bomb and walked fifty yards whilst screaming at his comrades to get back. He was a hero, but it was his officer that took the credit and wore a shining medal.

Jimmy left the army and joined the police. He rose to the rank of sergeant and witnessed many an evil crime. His chief inspector was taking bribes, but Jimmy had now learnt to keep his mouth shut. It was then he gained another promotion and decided to take a bribe. The criminals loved Jimmy and so did his bosses. He solved crimes that didn't count and helped those that paid well. Jimmy became wealthy and it was then that his sisters came to call. They wanted him to meet their children and go home to an elderly mum and dad. But Jimmy knew how the world works and told them where to go. He retired from the police and bought himself a big car. It's then that he went into politics because an MP can earn a lot. In his office worked a young man who was as honest as the day is long. And when this young man accused Jimmy of fiddling his accounts, Jimmy Spriggs saw himself.

oOo

THE FOURTH BODY

I was rested and almost carefree before the day broke into me with its demands. This was to be my day, although I did not know it yet. I was prepared for another day, serving a system that was failing but kept me fed unlike the hordes of scavenging hungry people who had no food security and lived to die in random acts of misfortune. Environmentalists, meteorologists and scientists of all disciplines had foretold this time, but the quest for wealth, driven upon the exploitation of all things, continued inextricably until the point that we harvested ourselves as the last commodity to be mined and sold.

The furnace of fertility burns her fuel — the combustion of life in a land of the impoverished and malnourished. Business is all, and culture is a facet of business that can only profit from those who are still alive and dependent upon the essential fuels of existence. Air, water and food enriched with the minerals and vitamins that are the growing energy of survival. The unofficial curfew left unlit city streets deserted apart from the wild dog packs and rats. Many, who had ventured out after dark, had been extinguished, composted and recycled in society's last-ditch attempt to replenish the eroded and inert soils that now lay vacant and unproductive. Since the last trees in the northern hemisphere had died, leaving the woods forever in a leafless eternal winter of decay, the oxygen cycle had stalled, reducing the atmosphere into a stagnant yellow soup of pollution that made eyes stream and throats burn. Most now wore filter masks that made life tolerable. The dwindling population fought harder by the year to survive. It was the wealthy administrators who commanded the hydroponic plants, fed by human organic decay. These people cared little for anything but them and accelerated the death of the human race.

My name is Lawrence Stanton. I am the chief composter at the Corpse Destruction plant. It all started with the first ice winter when all winter crops failed and the melting ice eroded much of our topsoil. The Hydroponic & Oxygen Corporation had claimed the bodies of the deceased for soil production, but a few years later, the demand had grown so great for corpses that after importing them from India, a black market grew in the supply of dead people and few asked any questions. The advertising "Let new life come of yours, the choice is yours" had been subtle at first, but it soon became mandatory that all organic matter was the property of the corporation. Wars were waged to kill and recycle, and all of the time the situation got worse.

On the morning of March 26, 2058, I had to report a shortfall of thirty-six bodies. The biodegrader and an aerobic digester required a specific volume of organic matter to react efficiently. The harvester police had been despatched to find and cull more people, and we waited, delaying operations. This made my manager nervous as there were strict targets to achieve. When the crew returned, they had failed to meet the required volume and a sense of nervous apprehension grew amongst my workers. I was called to the director's office who asked me to pick three men and report to the clerk of operations. Glancing down, I saw a report upon his desk that clearly had "four bodies required" stamped in the quantity's column of a work report. I reported to the clerk who led us into the composting chamber. It was then that I realised. Hanging back, I slammed the chamber door shut, making the clerk the fourth body. It was then that I left and never returned. They are still looking for me, but I am stowed away in a cargo freighter bound for Australia where irrigation and sun shielding is being used to rekindle the lungs of the world in reforestation. I am needed, for I am a soil scientist.

STEVEN–AND–CHARLES

I guess we all take some things for granted: the air we breathe or the water we drink without which we would not survive long. We assume cars will pass us safely and the next person we walk by on the street is not a killer. On average (assuming you will meet three new people every day and live for roughly seventy-eight years), you can expect to have met eighty thousand people before you die. That's many people who will be many things, but it is a fact that some will be psychopaths and killers. It is a strange thought to consider what demons hide in the person riding the bus next to you or even the person sat next to you in a cinema. We all have our hidden secrets and demons that we would never admit to. Yet we live in a world full of confused, pained and twisted people. The perverts and murderers are everywhere, hidden behind everyday faces that can be polite and smiling. Most will never know who those around them truly are, for we all present a false identity even to family and friends. It is one percent of a population who can be classified as a psychopath, yet there are many levels of this dangerous condition and it may be realistic to assume that up to twenty percent of us are, under certain circumstances, crazy. On these calculations, there could be up to seven hundred serial killers active in the UK at any given time. It seems that the ratio is much higher for the United States, but I think I have made my point.

Steven felt like an ordinary student in his third year studying biology at Jesus College, Oxford. He knew the ropes and had a comfortable apartment close to the city centre. He worked hard, combining his science studies with a passion for literature. The two subjects, rarely overlapping, made him feel like two people — one a rationalist and the other a lofty dreamer for whom all things could become reality. It was during his second year when Steven had nearly drowned in his studies, fighting for a first in his biology and rampaging through literature during his nights. He kept meticulous notes, which he filed in different coloured indexes on his computer. He was the biology student, and Charles was the name he chose for his alter ego that was in love with literature far more deeply than any man could love a woman. Through the intensity of his reading and studies, his health ran down. At first through laboured nights and then through an infection that retarded his efforts. Having mixed medication with alcohol, he studied on, yet was a hermit in the crowd. He kept interactions to a minimal. Shunning company and being a creature of habit, he walked the same route every day and lived to a repetitive order. Yet deep inside of him, he craved for something. That something grew like a need that would not cease. It was almost inevitable that his literature and science would merge, and the two entwined in his writing, driven by lust and a desire for company in a life devoid of human contact and love.

At first, he wrote brief lines of poetry that later spilt across his screen in imagined experiences, both painful and erotic. His self-restricted, shy personality became a demon of words that no other read. He had noticed a girl who was popular with her peers: a literature student who always carried books. She had opened a space in his mind that grew like nothing he had known before. The girl became an obsession so great he followed her in his dreams, sometimes waking near to her unable to distinguish reality from dreamt imaginings. He desired her but could not gain the courage to approach her. His thoughts tormented him beyond measure so much so that one evening he had followed her to a pub, frequented by students where she mingled with the crowd. At one point, he found himself standing next to her. He was paralysed by fear and shaking with nerves. Having reached out, he touched her arm and, as she turned looking up at him, she smiled and said, "I've seen you around. You're doing bio, aren't you?"

Steven answered with a, "Yes."

After some hesitation, Charles spoke. "I should have taken literature like you."

Charles was far more confident than Steven was and this made him jealous of the attention Carol was giving to his other self. Charles introduced himself, explaining his childhood fascination with the natural world and that later he had developed a love of literature. Their talk flowed, sharing thoughts about writers and what inspired their works, and the stories behind the words written. Steven, struggling, tried to butt in and bring his biology into the conversation, but there was no room in between Carol and Charles, who held an intense conversation. It was as if he wasn't there. Something had happened and Steven felt a jealous resentment of Charles who seemed oblivious as he grew in confidence to become the dominant personality. Charles and Carol met regularly, sitting at the same corner table in The Head of the River pub on cold wet winter's nights. They became close, enjoying the warm company of two people drinking glasses of heavy, warm ale. Theirs was a natural friendship coming from a shared love of a subject that had no limits. Somewhere out of sight, Steven's sense of inadequacy grew as did his frustrations. As Charles' confidence grew, too, Steven's shrank and he turned inwards upon himself asking how he could rid his mind of Charles. Unconsciously, he desired a death, that of Carol to punish Charles. It would be then that the demons could be exorcised from his mind. Carol's fate was sealed by the fact she was completely unaware of Steven, and Charles was almost ignorant of his other self. She was unable to distinguish between Steven and Charles, who had different motives.

One evening, Steven called at her hall of residence, and she welcomed him up to her room. It took one drink, laced with Rohypnol, to relax Carol who sat upon her bed, supported by her arms behind her back. Steven, sitting next to her, ventured a kiss on her full lips to which she responded warmly. He then raised his hands to her breasts and squeezed them rhythmically.

She gripped his hands tightly, sensing something was wrong and pushed him away. Feeling rejected where he supposed Charles had not been, anger rose and drove his inexperience and lust. A frantic struggle ensued as Steven unleashed his frustrations in one brief sexual act that climaxed with him juddering and jolting, and when he collapsed in relief, he released his hands from his victim's neck. This was his first sexual experience. Steven walked home almost oblivious to what he had done, yet feeling exhilaration that Charles' character had been reduced in his mind.

The shame followed days later as he read news reports of a promising young student having been murdered. He viewed the reports as if he did not know her, somehow being able to distance himself in denial. Something made him deeply uncomfortable and this feeling grew. Charles had all but disappeared until the day of Carol's funeral that he insisted upon attending. The police had interviewed Steven but were looking for a young literary student named Charles whom Carol had told her friends so much about. Steven, in a state-enraged confusion, set about removing his other self whom he blamed for Carol's death. It was then, for the first time, he considered suicide without knowing it.

From that moment on, Steven planned to hang himself to the point where Charles would die, for he could not in his own mind see Charles as an integral part of his own character. On a Friday evening after a few glasses of whisky, he set a noose lashed around the rafters in the loft above his room. Calmly, Steven approached the noose when Charles, realising what was happening, threw them both against a wooden roofing beam and pounded their heads against it.

Charles shouted at Steven, "I know your game. You can't live with yourself having murdered Carol. You are not going to kill me!"

These words hit Steven as for the first time he realised they were both the same person and he was fighting himself. Blood was flowing from his temple to gather in a pool upon the dark floorboards. Life was flooding into the dust and dirt before seeping away between the joints. His vision was fading and he knew he had achieved his aim: Charles was no more.

In the stilled, frozen silence of absolute terror, everything filters from a thought only to allow a focus of one thing through the slit of a mind's awareness. This is the fear when death is inevitable and desperation comes in an explosion of adrenaline. A moment that lasts forever — one that can never fade as time ceases and shock reverberates through the mind in an explosion that echoes its growing blast of energy, whilst blood pumps under great pressure, streaming urgency upon soft muscles that become as hard as granite rock. There is nothing that can prepare us for this moment that catches us all unaware. For some, they are dead before they have processed what is happening. Others, like Steven, lie exhaling their last breath as they process their terminal event. To contemplate suicide and set preparations in motion is one thing. To meet death by your own hands at the final point of life is something even more profound than anyone can imagine until they themselves have travelled beyond that point. It is then too late for a change of mind and none can ever explain or give an account. Even more shocking is to enact a suicide but be forestalled by another who kills before the victim can kill himself. To wish to die by one's own hand is, I suppose, the privilege of each individual. To be robbed of suicide by being murdered before the final act is a theft that has no measure or justice. Steven's life faded whilst clutching his head, and with his last breath, he proclaimed to an empty loft his innocence, for it is true that it was Steven who is a murderer, but he still blamed Charles who had died a few minutes earlier.

VOYAGE INTO THE VOID

The coal-black sea is calm, but the boat rocks steadily under the wash of the waves. It is a dark night and twelve people, who know each other well, sit in a circle talking, drinking and playing cards. They are part of a therapy group who have randomly been thrown together through a tragedy that has affected them all. Once every five years on the anniversary of a ferry disaster, they meet and take a boat journey to the scene at the time of the event.

The moon reflects its path, shimmering over the water, and all that can be heard is the slap of waves upon the prow and the low murmur of the friends' voices. Politics and love have been discussed as can happen in any gathering at a meal or in a bar anywhere in the world. There has been a slightly testy conversation between two women and a man. The women, each wrapped in a blanket, are of an age of active maturity. The man is older and more tired. He has been strongly challenged upon his assertion that social media relationships can be as influencing for some as are face-to-face communications. He has worked as a social worker for many years dealing with the tragic problems of others, often lonely and unsupported by the

221

system. By the time he retired, he had grown to feel isolated and undervalued by both those he sought to help and society as a whole. The younger women, who are avid users of screen communications, have protested that online comments have no effect upon them. Whilst talking, one keeps glancing at her screen, and fails to notice how the man winces at her rebuttal. George stands, braces his stance against the rocking of the boat and excuses himself to take relief at the stern behind the wheelhouse in private.

No one heard the gentle splash and his strokes as he swam away to meet his lost son who had been drawn into the deep twenty-three years earlier. Conversation and drinking continue in the prow as the group turn their attention to the event they are revisiting. They focus upon the cause of the sunken ferry. The question is asked what happened to the ship's engineer, a mild-mannered man who had fought valiantly to save many lives and survived the storm himself. The engineer had rescued thirty-six passengers, mostly children, and lost a hand freeing a woman who was trapped upon a collapsed iron stairwell. Despite his heroics and the court of inquiry praising his brave efforts, he had suffered years of abuse from the many bereaved families upon social media and through written letters. He was the only crew member to remain in the public eye and face the never-ending questions.

Maggie, a schoolteacher, shifts in her blanket and states she was friends with the engineer on Facebook. She looked for him, but he wasn't there. She then typed for an Internet search and found a local news report and obituary from exactly a year ago. He had drowned in the sea where they were now and had not been reported as missing for many weeks. The hate mail continued regardless. His suicide had clearly not satisfied anyone except himself. A silence falls amongst the eleven and each appears so focused upon their own state that they did not notice George's absence.

"Poor fellow," a second man says of the engineer. It could have been said of George.

A breeze rises from the east and the boat turns upon its axis rocking gently. This casts the moonlight upon the man who has just spoken and if anyone had looked closely, they would have seen tears in his eyes and upon his long, unshaven face. He was starting to notice the group was smaller. Having stood up, he walks to the back of the boat and realises George is missing. He takes his phone from his pocket and hits the speed dial for his now absent friend; no answer comes. When the call ends, he looks for his messages. It is then that he reads an aggressive response to a post he has shared highlighting how in modern times people had grown selfish. He throws the phone overboard, slips off his shoes and trousers, and then lowers himself into the comfortably warm water. *Why not?* he thinks. He wouldn't make the nine miles to the shore and no one would miss him. From his lips slips his long-lost wife's name and then the words, "It is time, Carol!"

A soft buzz breaks the silence that has settled upon the ten in the prow. It's the alarm that denoted the moment of tragedy so many years earlier. Each is so buried cold in their own thoughts that they haven't noticed the now absent friends.

Each in their own way have learnt to cope with the pain that had befallen them, yet never truly shared or reacted to the torment that still haunts them. In their own way, they had each individually compartmentalised the pain, suppressing it into a corner of their mind only to be reawakened once every five years. Over time, each would drown in their own private unshared isolation, unaware of how they were spilling pain into others by ignoring those around them.

There were no more memorial trips together after this one and within eight years, none of our passengers were still afloat in life. Out there, however, the ocean of pain continues to spill in the way we all ignore one another's needs. Each person is truly an island until recognised by another. Maybe it is love that gives us the will to live after all.

JIe

GIDEON

He said, "It's the same, nothing ever changes," as he swept his arms out over the gravestones indicating the dead land, then beyond past the small flint-built church into the land of the living. Pausing and looking down for a moment, he took a step back almost as if he needed more space between him and the church. Looking up and at me, rather through me as if there was something beyond who I am, he spoke again.

"They come here but don't know why, they just come. They bring the small ones and then the old ones who never leave, except for me that is."

The wind picked up and the rope whipped against its white flagpole in a thrashing motion as a stray piece of paper blew, scuttling past the head stones to plant itself upon my chest.

"Read it," he said almost in a wistful voice that I could barely hear.

Holding the page up, I struggled to read the small print. It was a page from the Bible, a very old page. After straining my eyes, I could make out that it was written in Hebrew and was probably from an early version known as Masoret.

Trying to not offend the stranger, I asked, "What does it mean and where did it come from?"

I had only been there some fifteen or twenty minutes, but the light had faded from evening into night and the air had grown noticeably cold and silent.

His answer came like a whisper on the wind. "Leviticus 11:31. These are unclean to you amongst all that creep: whoever touches them, when they are dead, shall be unclean until the evening."

I had looked back at the piece of paper that seemed to be a page from a Bible with a hint of gold leaf at its edge. Looking up, he had faded as if he was more distant, but he was as close to me as when I came across him. He was now backlit, for a faint moon had risen behind him, and as he was on the upside of the hill from me, he looked down on me.

I answered, "Yes, I helped with the burial of a boy this afternoon and had handled the body, but it is evening now, and so the ancient script must predict that I am no more unclean."

"You wanted to understand," came his answer. His hand then reached forwards and to my amazement, he took the hand of a boy of some ten or eleven years of age. The boy seemed to push close to the man as if seeking security.

I asked an obvious question.

"Why are you here?"

He had turned to walk away from me and the village but looking back over his shoulder, I heard him say, "I am here for my boy, Gideon. He is safe now having lived many times trying to find me."

With that, they withdrew as I stood shivering. I have revisited this memory many times and until today made little sense of it. Whilst out walking this afternoon, I passed the graveyard on my hike up Holders Hill to catch the sunset. On my return, I caught my foot on a stone and twisted it a little. Crouching down to massage my ankle, I noticed the stone, mostly covered in grass and moss, had a smooth surface. When I had ripped some of the grass and soil, the name "Gideon" was clearly legible and a few passages in Hebrew. I can only surmise that the man in my dream, if it was a dream, was his father. It is strange that I never feel alone when passing that churchyard regardless of the time of day.

THE BIG CONTEST

If I had known, things would have been different, but as it happened, I sat at that table innocently and it was only after my first drink that I realised it was the table next to the scary fairies. Well, they were dressed like fairies: frills and bows, wands and wings, but boy, were they big, real big and so loud! Loud and rude. I can swear but my, oh my, they were Olympians when it came to bad language. Then I noticed the boots: big, black boots, laced to the knees that held rippling, white flesh flowing out up into mighty thighs that any sumo wrestler would love. It was when the short one — with flowing, jet-black hair and a tattoo of a scorpion on her cheek — leapt in the air from a sitting position to kick the wine waiter in the balls. Spilling my beer as I slammed it down, I grabbed the poor man and pulled him away to safety. Then came my dilemma. Should I return for my chilled glass of beer by that overheated table of fat fairies? I did, sitting down whilst shooting a nervous smile at the table of dainty goblins.

"He bloody asked for it," said the black-haired one.

I couldn't help myself and my answer was out before I could restrain the words. "A bit of an extreme response, don't you think?"

With that, they all stood up as I shrank. Picking up their drinks, in the next moment they were all around me sat at my table, each looking directly at me.

"What's your name, sunshine?" asked a bleached blonde-haired woman with rivets in her nose, ears and hand.

"Colin," I answered.

The one with blue hair murmured, "That's nice."

"Colin," they all said in unison, "You're gonna order another round of cocktails, aren't you, dear?"

This posed the problem: to refuse and risk a kick in the balls or order drinks. As the waiter passed, I asked, "Five cocktails for the princesses and a pint of larger for me. Oh, and one ambulance please."

They freaked with laughter and drained the pink and green fluid from large glasses. Plucking up a little courage, I asked them their names. The answers came erratically from all directions at once.

"Annabel, Esther, Rachel and Fifi."

The titan of girth with black hair then spoke alone.

"My name is Burt."

With that, "it" cleared part of the wet table and challenged me to an arm wrestle. By then, we had an audience as the other tables in this busy open-air bar on the south side of the city's central square had turned their chairs to watch.

An elderly man called out, "Go on, my son!"

Now, I am a healthy chap who likes to keep fit, but the sheer laws of physics, power to mass ratios and maybe a stack of psychology made me shudder. After a long swig from my glass, I stood up and bowed to the audience, which now included the entire bar staff plus Mr Ball Ache. Next thing, my elbow was on the round, white, metal table and my sanitised hand in the grip of a black-clawed monster.

"Wow, you got some grip, girl!" said I.

She launched an attack and immediately my arm was over at forty-five degrees, knocking my beer that flew to shatter on the ground. The crowd booed. I mustered all I'd got, which wasn't much after four glasses at eight o'clock on a Saturday night. I pushed back and the large, white limb rose as the crowd cheered.

A barman shouted, "Twenty quid on the guy winning."

With that, money was changing hands and the crowd's blood was up. A smart, middle-aged man stood up and announced he was a bookmaker and was to take charge of the bets whilst clutching a large wad of growing money. Now the heat was on me and I was sweating. I stared into Burt's eyes and, unflinchingly, she stared back. Our hands had grown sweaty and the hairs on her upper lip were sticking out like broken glass on top of a security wall. I was holding my own as arms went one way and then the other. The table was shaking and the noise from at least a hundred people was deafening as passers-by stopped to join in. I even saw a vicar hand over fifteen pounds against me winning.

I held on and held on until Burt gave a little and said, "Quits?"

I shook my head as her mates were closing in on me, egging her on. Sweat broke out and ran black with makeup down over her cheeks to drip, staining the table.

Slowly through stamina, I got her arm over to sixty degrees and she was sweating and swearing like a drunken sailor. And then it happened. The crowd went silent, arms shaking, her arm gave out as I screwed my eyes shut and, by some miracle, I felt her let go and our arms slammed down onto the cold metal with my hand on top. The crowd went mad as a paper bag full of money was dumped in my bemused lap. Summoning the manager, I asked if I could buy everyone a drink. He smiled and nodded as the occupants cheered and queued to shake my hand. The bar staff leapt into action and drinks of many colours and volumes flew.

I now always sit in my chair at that bar whenever in the city. There is graffiti in the lady's toilets that reads: "Burt vs. Colin, the big contest 03/07/21."

JACK THE MARINER

All the way from St. Gilda's Church, the choir could be heard from the woods where wind danced; oak branches sending the odd leaf fluttering to the ground to join countless others from unfathomable generations of decay in a sea of leaf mould. The shrill hymnal voices of boys passed through the churchyard, rising to fade at a distance that no God would ever hear; the residents of graves also remained deaf. Inside the church, clutching the pew backs closest to the cold outside yard, the old and gnarled sang in gruff tones and prayed through selfish means. The collection would be light as it always was; the donations couldn't sink a boat made of matches. High above the ritual pantomime in the crumbling bell tower, jackdaws clucked and called in fun, looking for carrion to feed upon; the meat was always close in God's house of prestigious folly — a place where life often begins and mostly ends. A congregation of no more than twenty or so, which dwindled each year, gathered for some reason that most never considered, for it is a human thing to do as others do — we are all followers in faith. To be born, marry, produce

233

children and then die into a pit that was once where we played and ran over.

Jack had been a mariner, 1942, Arctic convoy duty, no more than a boy. He had worked for the Coastguard and later the Royal Naval Lifeboat charity. All he knew was the sea and he knew her well — every change in the water's colour, her meanness and softness, the cold and rippling sensual warmth. He could read the wind upon the sheeted surface and know the weather a day before it changed. It was the sea that had drowned his shipmates. PQ 17 was the code name for the allied Arctic convoys sailing from Hvalfjord in Iceland to Arkhangelsk in the Soviet Union. His ship, the Carlton, was bombed and went down; he was one of three survivors. The treacherous sea claimed his son when the trawler, the Rose of the Sea, was hit by a freak wave in a viscous storm in 1988. The loss had killed his wife whose soul now rested in the soil of sanctuary under a pink granite slab. For Jack, the church had lost all its meaning. He was there for one last time to bid his wife, Elizabeth Florence, farewell, for the sea was beckoning him to join his son and friends.

Time was slow and late life had dragged uncomfortably with the usual complaints of age. He still enjoyed a glass of whisky and the view over his erstwhile ocean friend that was ever-present from his cottage, perched high upon an eroding clay and chalk cliff. Each year, the sea carved a few feet closer to his old and only home where he had been born. Lighting his pipe, he added a few brushstrokes to his painting of the German Bismarck-class battleship, the Tirpitz. Only, in his painting, he had rearranged history for the Nazi behemoth, party to the death of his mates; it was sinking.

Summer passed and his garden bloomed. Many whisky bottles with messages in to lost fellows had been thrown in sacrifice into the summer, tender waters. Jack wrote one last note to take with him: "Oh hall of mariners' demise, it is my turn to return and leave the land behind. I know that you will come, for my life is done."

Weeks of waiting passed and autumn turned into late winter deep. On 23rd November 2017, a storm blew up through the English Channel, battering and flooding the coast. The cliff below Jack's cottage gave way, washing him out to sea. Whilst much debris washed to the beach over the following days, Jack's body was never reclaimed. However, a German captain's peaked cap was found in perfect condition, though sodden wet, washed up upon the sandy cove below where the lost house once stood.

TERMINAL WITHOUT REFERENCE

Along the run of corridors that dwindle to become passages, pipes, conduits, wires and optic cables, the wave-pulse radiation endlessly monitors all things required for me, the only organic intelligence, to survive and remain alive. Oxygen and water come first, then light and heat control, from shielding to generation. I am correlating this recording that will remain in the time-shield vault and be broadcast on the emergency eternity transmit. It is my last hope and effort that you hear or read my words. Clipboard in hand, daily I walk miles, checking structures and machines, the integrity of which are essential to the preservation of all human knowledge. I am the organic mind within the machine. The machine created us and now has the ability to preserve all that transpired — from a planet's creation to our destination, the long voyage that has distilled down to the last man on Earth. I hold my responsibility high, for it is possible to argue that, should I fail, all history will be wasted (and that is an infinite number of lives that were lived without purpose, lost into nothing).

There is no such thing as silence out here in the open space through which this ship sails. The vastness absorbs the journey into infinity in a way that any number of clicks or velocities of altered direction are lost because, regardless of where I am, everything remains the same. All things are relative. I now find sleep difficult. It is the whining of this planetary craft, built by nature and fashioned by skilled craftsmen who were directed by what might have been some of the greatest consciousness of all time, that keeps me awake. They knew the beginnings and, of course, the end. Yet, despite the futility, in the same way as our primate ancestors, they endeavoured like gods against all odds, battling, what may be, in vain.

As I sleep, I drift astronautical miles, serenaded by a myriad of minor earthquakes that cause the organic bone structures of my infinite cave to creak and groan as if I am an ancient mariner, held within the hold of some vast wooden sailing vessel. Sleep, oh sleep beckons me beyond all things, for it is here, travelling within a now cinder-bed planet, that I can move back into a time of life in escape of the burden that fate had gifted me. I am the last officer of the fleet. No others remain. I have the emblem of distance and balance woven into my tunic and programmed into my mind. I was not chosen in the same way; neither were you. You chose to listen to my words although the further I travel, the more I feel nothing is without purpose but, like the end of time, it cannot exist. I cannot meet the course of my journey without doubts that anything is of value anymore.

Unfortunately for you, by the act of knowing my story, the responsibility for a whole planet, the life that has been lived upon it and the billions of lives lived and lost, becomes your responsibility. Can you let that entire love and pain stop in the blink of an eye? Having fulfilled my task, most of the systems on this inner planet-craft will cease to function until you step on board and fly on to whatever awaits beyond the history of the planet that cradled a once human race. I wish you well and great luck. Godspeed to you, for time awaits. As for history, it is all yours now.

Undated message completed.

Signed: "Terminal without reference".

SUCCUBUS

*(In a letter from the first century AD, Pliny the Younger wrote to
Lucius Sura:*
*"... I am extremely desirous therefore to know whether you believe
in the existence of ghosts, and that they have a real form, and are
a sort of divinities, or only the visionary impressions of a terrified
imagination...")*

It was and it wasn't. She came to me in a dream from which
no man could awake. Yet, it hit me with pain and such
delight that I struggled to remain sane. I could never know
the time or how long she held me in that soul-ripping state
where I lost so much and made great gain. I slept deep, until
after a few hours she whispered my name so gently I flew to
her, aroused but not awake. She entered me through a portal
that I could not close. I felt her presence as I turned for her
embrace that opened me: the victim of her delicate grace. My
lips quivered against hers. It was hardly a kiss, but deep within
my heart, I could feel her hiss. Resist I could not, for the
nature of delight, within imagination's sight, is overpowering

as I sacrificed everything in fear that this enchanted pleasure would stall.

Calling out, I groaned within my restless slumbering night as she purred like a cat, me a mouse of her play. Brushing my chest, I felt the curve of her breast as her shawl fell while nakedly, we caressed. I wanted to escape, but I had travelled too far for any release. Held in her grip with one fingertip, I released my mind into a haunting time as she wiped perspiration from my brow and gave me a glimpse of an unearthly fight as I struggled in delight.

"Who are you?" I asked as waves of joy and fear travelled my static, writhing body.

Her silent spoken words made no sound, but I heard her loud and clear. "I am the spirit of your pleasure and fear. I will take you far or near. We were lovers once who could never make the sacrifice — that is, this love is not a vice, and in death we shall be free."

She had come to take me with her beautiful art, upon a dreaming lovers' flight into another life, where only one last breath can be drawn before the coming of another dawn. I was not aware of morning's bright, for I am no longer here. I fell victim of another's dream that passed beyond a sexual death within a sensual night of unfair play. I remember her dark eyes and raven hair that flew like wings upon her breath that so seamlessly ushered me to my death; her silken skin so pale in a shimmering moonlight that froze the chill of her breath from lungs so distant deep.

From the bed, holding my hand, we floated across a resting land as I at last came to know that Eros is her name, an ancient god sent for my heart to tame. I met her as I passed from a life insane beyond the restless human pain. She is my gain. Should you ever dare to dream, remember my endless night, for some spirit lover has you in her sight.

JOe

THE LAST CHANCE SALOON

Flickering light in dappled form falls through a tree canopy, casting light in between the bright and shade. Two men sit at a square wooden table that has a bottle and two glasses perched to one side. The bottle is nearly empty, and the glasses full of whisky that each man occasionally eyes with desire, fuelled by the spirit that they have already swallowed. There are cards being dealt into two piles, and the pack is split and placed face down in the middle of the table. One man is clothed in heavy, brown canvas overalls, which are the uniform of a farmer. The other wears tight cotton trousers and a white shirt, covered in a jacket in a style popular with businessmen and traders. Set to each side of this small table are two revolvers that rest, but are charged with energy waiting to be called upon.

The smarter man studies the farmer's every move with unflinching eyes that have the quality of evil. The farmer fidgets uncomfortably like an innocent man accused of a great crime he did not commit. A gentle wind passes, whipping dust from the dry dirt outside of this drinking establishment, and a few yellow leaves give way to float down past the table to dance along the street. From a short distance away, a dog barks and startles a tethered horse to bray impatiently for his gambling master. The smart man gestures with a cigarette in his hand for the other to take a card from the deck. He does so as beads of sweat break out upon his brow. He wipes his face with the cuff of his arm and nervously looks across the table. He then draws a card from his hand and places it upon the split deck. Each takes his turn at least another half dozen times until the farmer asks with a Spanish American accent, "Why my daughter as well as my home?"

The answer comes after a long silence.

"Is she not a fine young woman? And that farmhouse needs a woman."

Some people have now gathered to watch from what they think is a safe distance and out of sight, the town undertaker rubs his hands in anticipation of fresh business whilst he holds his horse in harness to his cart that contains a coffin. Above the door of the drinking establishment, written in block capitals, presented in a crescent like a lucky horseshoe, is its name "THE LAST CHANCE SALOON". A child runs from the clutches of a woman to stop behind the farmer and cries.

The smart man says, "Get the boy out of here!" After a pause, the well-dressed man says, "I call you."

The farmer looks at his cards that are now in a shaking hand, and then looks at his opponent and back again. He starts to turn over his cards: the first is an ace, the second and third are aces as well, and then he shows a king. It is then that the smart gambling man reaches for his gun but before he can clutch it, a shot rings out and he falls forward, knocking both the bottle and glasses to the ground.

From the far side of the street, a young woman drops a rifle and runs to her farmer father. She spits on the now dead man and says, "Pig!"

It is then that the undertaker's cart proceeds along the street to the table, and three men lift the corpse straight into the open coffin. Then the undertaker places the lid on it, mounts the cart and pulls away without a word. The farmer and daughter embrace as the boy gathers up the cards. They then walk to their cart upon which they ride out of town. In this small settlement, everyone knows the story. Yet it is never spoken of, for there is the law of the land, and then there is the justice that is witnessed by men.

DILLON

That's the day when I cut myself out of my life. It wasn't foreseen or planned, it simply happened. Early in the day, I was one thing, and then later, I was something else. What had happened and what I had become is open to interpretation. It had taken years to shed the shell of restriction that slowed me to tortoise levels of transit through life. I had learnt or been conditioned to consider others first, having held myself back time after time; humility became my trade.

I am a boot-polishing black man who is proud to work my pitch on Wall Street. I have polished many a celebrity and politicians' shoes, having regular customers such as Alan Greenspan of the Fed Reserve and Dick Fuld of Lehman Brothers. I have even spit and polished for George Bush Sr. and Jr. Once Monica and Bill lingered for a smoke and shine; the ash marked my jacket. Many have gained wealth and fame on this street, and more have lost everything.

I have been here sixty years, having followed my father into his pitch. Even the paving stones are stained from one hundred years of boot shine. My father had the moonshine under his stool. I have trained people in my simple craft, who then spread to polish at pavement level all over the world. The only thing I could never train into a person is a pride in humility. Days in the sun to days fighting with a parasol against cold rain. Eight hours a day, six days a week, and what do you know: at night, I study and write articles about people and then there is the poetry. The words fly out of me; they don't give me a break. Right now, I am writing to you about me and another me whom I should never have met.

One morning, I am polishing the hooves of some city type who can't even look down at me while throwing his few cents that roll out of reach. I refuse to collect them. I just watch the pig stroll away.

Next thing I know, a street kid picks up the coins and hands them to me saying, "Take care of yourself, special man."

I look at this vagabond of about eleven or twelve. He blinks and looks deep into me as if I just killed his mum or something.

"What's wrong?" I ask.

He steps a little closer and says, "Don't you recognise me?"

Of course, I don't and I say so.

"Take another look, Dillon!"

Yes, I've never seen this kid before and he knows my name. Right now, he's starting to rustle my patience. I then tell the little troublemaker that my name is my business and he's got no right to use it until he shares the drift of his game. Then I tell you that he says to me in a cool grown-up sort of way, which was kinda freaky, "I am you, aged eleven. You were me in '64."

Now, I can't process the meaning of his words, but then he shows me the treble scar on his inner left forearm that I got for trespassing in the local authority tip, scavenging for steel, aged nine years. I show him my treble scar from fifty-four years earlier. We look at each other and don't say a word for long seconds.

"Gee!" I say, pull out the flask full of whisky from my boot and take a long slug. I tell you, the kid then takes that flask from my hand and draws a gobful like an old lag as his eyes bulge like balloons. Then he staggers and coughs.

"Where's your mum?" I say, not believing the impossible is happening. His answer is cheeky but a good one.

"Why are you asking? You know what happened. Don't you remember?"

Then it hits me like a freight train at full locomotion, loaded with more shit than this city can pile in six months: the date is March 7 — the day my mother died on the Selma Bridge, following Martin Luther King Jr. in 1968. Sitting in my three-legged stall, my hands fall limp and tears well against my will to roll slowly over my cheeks and drip upon the pavement. All of the time, my younger self looks me in the eye unflinching. Unconsciously, I see myself and raise my arms as silently we embrace, while the world of people processes past us unknowing, unfeeling. My memory awakes, releasing long supressed feelings that have drowned in an ocean of sorrow to be lost behind the iron gridwork of pain buried deep. In my mind's eye, I know I have been here before. Is it a dream, or is it an awakened illusion? I still remain unclear as to what has happened. I ask my younger self where his father is — in part out of duty and mostly out of denial — for my father died six months before my eleventh birthday. The obvious question that most would ask is, "How did you get here?" I didn't ask because I sort of knew. I don't expect you to understand this, but I was him and he was me, we share time and memory. The strange thing about it is that he knows all about my seventy-six years, being eleven years old.

I ask my younger self where he's going and his answer is simply, "Dunno."

Well, I close my pitch and stack my kit into the barrow my father has bequeathed me, then hand in hand we bought shakes and drank sat upon the thick, granite kerb stones that wall the roadside of this treacherous street.

I enrolled young Dillon into school and we enjoyed the next nine years playing ball in Central Park and watching movies. We were inseparable, always knowing the other's wishes. We were rarely talking about our lives because we knew everything about the shared me. I became ill and could no longer work. Nobody missed me because Dillon was there just as my father was there before me. Oh, let me tell you about that day on 7th March, sixty-four years earlier when I was eleven and introduced myself to my older self. Well, I freaked.

EASING AND WHEEZING

Easing and wheezing, dark is this night's florid flight over primly proud chimneys that clatter, whistling silently while spluttering sooty breaths of smog from the ever-open round mouths that smoke and sigh thick, dark, cooling soot from an ancient burning fuel. The sinister dust greys the white fluttering feathers of old man owl as he glides from the ancient winter-stripped oak that rises above Farmer Gollup's ground, a meadow stream cut, water-levelled and icy-cold. With beatless open wings and one gliding swoop, three hundred yards are travelled before flaring upwards to land upon a telegraph pole beyond the callers whose ever-fading words race oblivious to their journey. It is a winter's deep muffling night, soft and dusty-black, wrapped in a scarfed silence, knitted and stitched between frosty air and moonlight that shyly peeps, glinting white between busy bundles of clouds that hurry in concern to chase time above a turning land that sleeps windless and stilled.

Hold still and listen to the silence now. You may hear the gentle quietness and wheezing sighs of death's dreaming souls as they snore ghostly breaths that settle in St. Mary's yard between the unkempt weeds and brittle green blades of grass that drink from beneath. Here, grey stones bear the faded chiselled names of now dusting bones. Those who are now shapeless and sleepless once drank and laughed in The Rose and Crown, dancing the jig on a late summer's harvest night when moths serenaded candles in sacrificial traditions amongst cigarette smoke and slopped beer. Lost are those revellers whose past breath is the air that creeps unseen between children's snuggling bedsheets with imaginings of who they will be before they, too, rest below white owls beside prickly lives that rummage amongst the earthen beds of this cold stone church. Sleeping and curled under the leaves, balled in dry, fluffy moss and missed by Verger Brian's rake, a first year hedgehog snorts his winter nights away as if he was never there. Into the silence, a creaking grows as the brittle bark of the church yew splits under the white, fluffy crystals of frosty fingers that claw at the surface of everything.

In defiance, Shopkeeper Bryman's boy slings a log upon the dying fire at the rear of the trader's home to send sparks rising like heralds that settle towards Granny Crowther's thatch, twinkling and hoping for fiery fun to purge a rat family whose home is above the warmth of a living room and below the chill of an open sky. A young rat squeaks and runs in fear. His family follow as the glowing stops and a small, burnt cinder joins many others in a fire waiting to happen.

Below and watching, Marmalade, a ginger cat of four and in his prime, bristles to lope away in search of mousey fun or scraps with other feline devils who relish the peace of night's mischief and freedom. Glistening-smooth and shadow-black upon the road, crisp footsteps come from North Street as Sydney, long in life and bottle to hand, wanders from kerb-to-kerb, footstep to unsure footstep, as he navigates to his humble cottage below the railway bridge. In passing Schoolteacher Halberd's cottage, he unzips and takes relief upon her beloved yellow rose bushes; he chuckles and is gone.

Flowing and flooding, white mist rolls over the stone walls that retain the proudly private land above Cross Road, north of the village. Bain's lower field is higher than the rest of the cottages' that lowly villagers occupy. The mist seeps snake-like under Joyce Langland's front door over the cold, grey Lias flagstones in her hall around Buster, her tearaway terrier, who sleeps with four paws stretched and touching at the tips, then to escape out through the cracks in the stonework in her home's rear wall. A white pool gathers on the river meadow to dance above the water in circles that fade to be replaced by more. Here, a vixen stalks Wise Rabbit, grey, lithe, sharp and fast. Wise is aware and nibbles grass whilst waiting and teasing to run at last with only the division of seconds between being a dinner and free.

Time pauses and all are asleep. Even the stones and the houses seem to ease with a gentle creaking resting, lullabied in the silent softness, watched by a lipid moon that hides its rimless smile from day. The rabbits snooze in their burrows, tightly curled with noses twitching, dreaming of spring lush grass, sunshine and baby bunnies. Mice, nimble and clustered, snooze grey and jigger against the cold under floorboards and in garden sheds, using stolen socks and old Syd's pants for a bed. High upon their twiggy rigs in the reaching branches of hornbeams under peeping stars, rooks hang like vertical bats with one eye open, waiting for dawn whilst smaller songbirds hide and quiver against dreams of hawks and a seedless bird table. Cuddling his teddy bear and sucking his thumb, baby Oliver dreams of his mother's warm milk, banging his spoon upon the family dog Charlie's head whilst hanging from his high chair before sharing his sloppy baby food that Charlie delights in withstanding blows.

The smell of burning wood shrouds this village as fires burn low and dawn sends a weak breeze that stirs the air to swirl the mist in warning of dawn's creeping light that grows in the colour of fire. Cocks crow and hens cluck as old Syd fills his kettle and soon the smell of buttered toast and coffee replaces the taint of night's lonely cold. A dog barks against dawn's creeping awakening as night slips tiptoeing into the horizon behind High Balcombe across the far level vale. In an instance, a robin shrill and plucky flits into song as another waking day turns her hand upon the tide of life in Bradford Adder. It is Sunday morning. The children are awake and mothers are stirring whilst husbands snore and elderly men lay smacking their teethless lips, craving the taste of the previous night's beer. Alone, the widowed old ladies pour boiling water into soon-to-be cosied teapots and cats creep home for another day of night's sleep in hidden corners.

THE WRITER OF SOULS IN A CITY OF WORDS

It is a bright morning. The sort of day when the dust rises from the ground, disturbed to float suspended in the air, illuminated by rays of sunlight. It is warm out there in the open on the street. Almost in silence, Hans Mecanter works away behind drawn curtains. Within his dark room, it is night, except for a few single rays of light that filter through those old, sad and dull, deep brown, hemp curtains. They hang still and heavy as is the atmosphere in his small and cluttered room. No one ever enters here and Hans only leaves the room once a week for essential visits. The room would have a musty, cloistered smell should anyone ever come in. Yet this room is a universe, populated with high living words that become people, who spill out through that ancient, wooden-framed window into the world beyond. The clock that stands upon a wooden fire surround has not been wound in nearly thirty years. Its silence is the stillness of frozen time unmarked. Within this room, the only change is the words — those that write characters into life. They start with a breath and then develop arms, legs and thought-filled heads that grow into actions.

Out in the city of Leipzig, the day is full of activity. Horse-drawn carts vie with incompetent motor vehicles as the dust rises to choke the air, lifted on aggressive thermals. Petrol exhaust blends with the smell of horse sweat and dung. All of the time, Hans' feathered quill is forever dipped into the magic of a crusty, enamelled inkwell that rests pensively, countersunk in an old wooden desk that was crafted in a village on the coast of the Milesian seaboard in ancient Greece. The inkwell has never been refilled like the words that come from it upon the broad ledger that Hans' hand writes. Both ink and words are without end. Pigeons fly in twos and threes to perch upon the apex roof of this compact ground level room. They coo and warble to one another, cosying up to the females in order to write more chicks of life. Hour after hour, worlds and populations would grow upon the blank sheets of stiff, white paper flowing from imagination. They would overflow to climb out of the room window and enter life.

Each person in this city of sun and dust had a writer. Without this, there would be not a soul to justify the buildings, shops and factories. All would have ceased to exist. Each feels that free will is theirs. Now through the window comes the voice of Frau Blamer. Flowery and high, she addresses a friend as to her errands of the day. She stands in Berliner Strasse. Perspiration is forming upon her well-formed upper lip and her dress is clinging to her over-bulging hips. She has to deliver a message to the mayor's office and then to collect milk without it curdling in the heat. Unbeknown, Hans writes her day along with so many others. From within a few rooms spread across this city, writers work. There are good writers and maligned writers. Good and bad vie to balance the people of all persuasions, shapes and sizes. This city breathes upon the unconscious will of secrets — those of written words and words that had meaning long before there were writers to transcribe them into the lives of the ones who would speak them. Dear reader, have you ever held a thought or even a conversation with your writer? Ah! That would be the conversation with your destiny, should you dare to challenge that, which remains unwritten. I had such a conversation once. I, too, travelled back into that inkwell of everything to be rewritten into a different time and place. I metamorphosed into the writer — perhaps the writer of your story. So please, when you pass me upon the street or sit next to me in a bar, maybe you should look deep into my eyes, for you will see who you are.

Leipzig burns and bustles so full of activity and life outside of this small room where I once sat. It is past midday now and the shop doors are closing for lunch. The draymen are leaning against time's wall to draw upon smoke, and the city's municipal workers sit upon park benches in Johanna Park to unwrap greaseproof paper revealing sandwiches of sustenance. Each written as it occurs to a writer of time's destiny. The coal carthorses drink from pails of cool water and bray to one another as the street sparrows steal seeds from their feedbags. Children play on during the school lunchbreak, heat and tiredness hasn't been written for them from the writer's pen yet. Shrieks of naughtiness disturb Hans' peace. As he writes, the school bell clatters its discordant blast and the children fall silent. From within Thomaskirche Lutheran church, prayers are being served to God as the bishop mumbles his daily routine. These words have no meaning, for they were never written and all who hear them remain unsure of meaning. The air is cool within this stone fortress of religion where writers never venture to interfere. People sit scattered amongst pews, lost to destiny, occupying a space static and excluded from reality. A place where the dead fear life.

Can you hear me, dear reader? Yes, this is me talking to you from the juncture between this moment and the next. Would you like to hold my pen and make it yours? To hold the quill that writes your destiny? Are you brave enough? This is a rare moment for us both, for should you take this quill, you will release me out into our city of words. I should be free to drink long cool draughts of Pilsner in the Emperor's Bar with other *Leute,* or cool in the church's sanctuary from the day's heat. I will be as you are now, unknown and unknowing. Here, reach to me and take this!

Evening closes upon the city. It is after eight and the louvered metal shutters can be heard slamming against the unchanging pavements. The sound of children playing with balls and the rolling clatter of cane hoops subside. The sun has now been written low and shadows stretch over the cobbled street into the park where tree shadows dance their branches in the cooling breeze that wafts the coming night's peace into us all. A stray dog sniffs the air knowing that Butcher Bremner will have closed his premises and is now cycling home. The sound of a bicycle bell tinkles from the distance as the rumbling of wheels passes away. The collie, cross black and white, heads with purpose to Bremner's bins. There will be only clean bones left in the morning. Each and every sound, every scent and molecule of air, every thought and every sneeze, all the love and life's confusion of streaming of hate, the sky and the seas, the children without care, the time and the space that is you — all is written by me, the writer of time's dream.

The city slows to a near silence, as night deepens. Yet, the tireless writer works on inexorably, for should he stop, all will cease. Perhaps, when deep in night's darkness, for a moment the flow of flowering future's words slows and for a fraction in time, it stops. You are asleep in the dreamtime of forever, suspended as only you can be, for in that splitting of a sleeping, slumbering second, just maybe you never existed.

Leipzig, 1920.

COMBUSTION IN AUSCHWITZ

(In memory of all the victims of the Holocaust. 25.01.2021)

The smell of burning gently permeated the air with that familiar warm, mellow scent which comes on a winter's night when frozen still air lays a sparkling cover of bristling frost that renders all stilled, brittle and icy cold. It is then that all things crave the comfort of deliberate controlled fire as memories of village life are drawn from where I grew up so many years ago. Along with that familiar aroma comes the thought of cooking that would have roasted meat in those open fire hearths. In that moment, I caught a hint of the sweet aroma of meat that only exudes when the outer layers of fat and flesh are crackling and charring black.

Our walk had been made easier by the ground-hardened frost as we tramped on through the forest. It had taken some hours after crossing the Sola River, beyond which we walked for several kilometres through cultivated farmland. It was then that hunger and tiredness set in and the first smell of death reached out to us, creeping around the old farmhouses and isolated dwellings that seemed like bastions of normality and comfort. It was only later that I discovered the source of the scent of burning.

I am Witold Pilecki, born on May 13, 1901 in Olonetsky Uyezd, Olonets, Karelia. I am a Polish cavalry officer and intelligence agent, a resistance leader. After the rapid defeat of the Polish army on November 9, 1939, I volunteered to enter Auschwitz concentration camp to understand the nature and purpose of the place. My report was smuggled out of the camp in 1942, covering details of gas chambers designed to kill seven thousand people a day, sterilisation experiments and untold horrors. My government exiled in London and the allied command found the information documented too horrible to believe and ruled that I had greatly exaggerated my findings. No action was taken. On April 27, 1943, I escaped from the camp but the resistance and allied forces again rejected any idea of helping those inside the camp.

January 27, 1945. The Auschwitz Nazi slave and extermination camp, where millions of people were murdered, was liberated by the Red Army during the Vistula-Oder offensive. The Russian troops were horrified at the hatred and evil the Nazis had shown to innocent people on a massive scale. Today, even on a still day, stood near to the crematorium chambers the smell of burning arises as the ash of millions of innocent, wasted lives is plucked by the breeze to blow the souls of those who were murdered across the pretty wildflower meadows in this unkempt place. All because society lost its way and good people were convinced it was good to do evil things.

GREENWICH FOOT TUNNEL

(01.01.1902)

As I slip upon those damp tiles, a clatter of echoes travels in the gloomy despair some three hundred metres through dark stagnant air. Alone and late, each night I travel in haste.

We met upon our passage. She came without a sound. Her dark laced shoes floating above the ground. Grey and black, eyes of the dead. She never bent her head, looking beyond me as I slowed in fear watching. She came in an instant. It ended the same. Shimmering so light. Hers was the moment. I had nothing to say. Within a vision that came not in a dream, was I conscious? Things were not as they had been. Where did she come from? Lips so pale. Hands white. Skin as cold as the brass plaque riveted to this soulless wall that tells of her plight.

Deep tunnel under water covered in dirt. I saw her go in a long, drifting skirt. Engraved forever. Through this tunnel of nightmares, she walks towards her last breath. Her destination has no name, for she enters each night to be murdered out of sight, never to leave upon the stairs. Yet somehow, she lives in my journey.

Ethel walks, for she has no grave. She is this time's tunnel slave. I felt her as she came each night just the same when I speak her name. She looks at me and is gone. I near the rising steps and the air changes as I tiptoe through a pool of blood. I never heard her scream.

LIPSTICK

Is she gonna stop? She's going too fast! The stupid bitch is now in a panic and her wheels are locking. Swerving up the grass verge, she goes. The radiator blows steam everywhere and a branch through the screen as the car rolls. Oh God, she's still coming at me sideways and I can't avoid her. I hit the brakes harder than ever. My coffee leaves its cupholder and launches against the windscreen in a moment of inertia as the belt yanks the breath out of me. I ram the stick into reverse gear, whilst still travelling forward, and there is an almighty sound of metal complaining about what I'm doing. Reverse engaged, foot to the floor, wheels spinning, and the smell of burning clutch and rubber asphyxiates me. I can't see out, for coffee's running down the inside of my windscreen, and I'm travelling in reverse at speed without looking in my mirror as a crazy, old bat in a Mercedes literally upends and rolls at high velocity after me. Coolly and most bizarrely, the thought that this is no way to travel crosses my mind. Then my old VW shudders and jolts as the tail crunches down upon my bonnet. Bollocks! I've only just washed the old banger and she was looking rather good.

The old bag's got to be dead! No! There, in front of my eyes from the rear window on the passenger's side of the upturned trashed car comes a head, and it's screaming and shouting. I get out of my wrecked pride and — somewhat in shock — approach the banshee, half-expecting to find a disembowelled corpse. But no, I find myself confronted by a smudged lipstick monster of a woman who, having failed in weaponising her car to kill me, is about to chew me up with the ugliest teeth and foulest mouth I have ever seen.

"Are you okay, lady?" I ask.

Her reply comes. "When I get this fucking door open, I'm gonna rip you apart."

I can tell she means it. She blacks out for a moment and as I open the door, she comes round and swings a fist at my head. This lady is whackadoodled out of her mind. I'm now retreating. She is staggering after me and I'm sweating and shouting.

"What the hell were you doing in the back seat?"

She screams, "Getting my lipstick! I've got an interview and I'm gonna miss it because you got in my bloody way."

It's then that she fainted.

*

"The next time I saw her is here, Your Worship. She is suing me for reckless driving, but it was her who tried to kill me, and that's after she had wrecked her car."

*

WELL OF SOULS

Something had gone wrong. Her mouth sank, emphasising the shape of the upper jaw, pulling thin pale skin over sallow cheeks so tight it gave the eyes an appearance of bulging decay with veins bursting red. In that moment, her facial features displayed those of a putrid skull. For a while, the true personality of this she-devil escaped and I knew what I was dealing with. Pleasant words met my ears yet this vision told of something sinister. The dull, oak-panelled room was oppressive absorbing light, and the raging fire overflowed heat into the stagnant air that held a musty smell of decay, that of the rats' nests I had cleared as a boy. She turned, reaching her hands out as if balancing precariously indicating instability. It was the hands of a corpse in decay with little flesh yet bony and pointing. Back turned, I could see her long, flowing, raven hair, that of a girl, falling from an age-haggard corpse. Such a contrast!

The journey to Mort Manor had been arduous over the fells from Appleby where the last train had arrived late afternoon. The carriage was rough, bumping and grinding along country tracks in the low light of late December. There was something of remorse in the cloaked, top-hatted driver who, when instructed upon the destination, seemed to shudder.

"None go to the

I asked, "Why is it called the silent house?"

"Well, sir, they do say that those who stay there, at least those who stay the night, return as mutes unable to tell of what they have experienced. But none, to my knowledge, have called upon the old witch of Mort Fell in many a year."

I asked another question, pushing for an explanation as to why the residence of an old dowager was named as a mortuary. The driver's answer should have made my attention peak, but I think I was tired from a day's travel up from London.

"That's where the plague victims were subsumed in a lime pit. On a hot summer's night, you can smell death from hundreds of lost souls."

I paused in thought and then asked, "Why there, so far away from the town?"

His answer was practical. He explained the old quarry carts would pass here and a disused slate open mine served as the burial pit that was covered with the waste slag. He went on to say the stench of over three hundred dead caused people to leave the town.

The rest of my journey was in silence with the exception of the rooks that flew in circling motions low over the broken, hedge-lined track. Approaching the building, the first thing I noticed was the broken stone cross that lilted high upon the apex of this stone monolith of a mansion against a dark, brooding sky dotted with black wings in flight. I paid the cab driver who turned and drove away at speed. No sooner had he travelled twenty or thirty yards from where I stood by my leather bag, he seemed to disappear without a sound. I walked over the gravel drive past a large, ornate fountain that had long since fallen into disrepair. It was clear it had not held water for a long time. At its base, where fish would have once swum, rested the bare bones of some poor animal that had died trapped within this carved-stone, circular prison.

I had written, enquiring about a distant relative who held the post of minister to the parish and resided at Mort House in the 1780s: Reverend Montague Morton who is recorded in the parish records as a firebrand preacher of sermons that lasted at times for over an hour. He was reputed to have lost his faith and declared God a fake from his pulpit before shooting himself at this old house.

Night fell quickly and the gas lamps were alight. I made myself comfortable and after a few hours reading by a large, open fire, I retreated to my room on the third floor. The wind was howling through the trees outside. Something had come loose and was tapping rhythmically upon the outside wall. Sleep came quickly and it was then that I slipped into a living dream. Was it a dream or did it happen?

At some point after midnight, I believe I awoke to a vile, pungent odour, the odour of rotting flesh. The rhythm of tapping had changed its tempo. I could hear the sound of railed carts trundling, accompanied by the clopping hooves of the beasts labouring the carts. There were muffled voices and when I peered through the warped glass window, I could see men with scarves over their mouths and nostrils, unloading bodies. I felt sure that one crawled from the cart at its own accord to collapse into a disgusting, gaping cavern in the ground. Below my bedroom window was a preacher, Bible in hand. I can only assume he was in charge of the macabre scene to offer comfort and the last rites to those not yet dead.

I must have frozen in shock at this vision, for the next thing I knew, it was dawn, and I found myself still standing at the window. There, below me, I could see the mud-spattered scars upon the lawn where the bodies had been dragged and an area of about eighty yards long and eighteen wide to the left of my view where a cut-off escarpment fell as if it had been recently infilled with some coarse slag and soil. Upon an old stone bench was a Bible sodden and open, the pages ripped and blowing against the boundary hedge. At this, I noticed movement. The thing moved like an animal, nervous and alert, yet stooping and faint. It was the dowager who gathered those blown pages and the Bible — printed words that had saved none. I believe she dropped them into a well that stood just in view at the opposite side of the house to the scarred pit. She looked up at me, lingering as if straining to see something. I waved, but my gesture went unacknowledged. This was a strange place indeed yet I felt no danger.

Having washed and dressed, I made my way to the house library that I had been introduced to the previous evening. This was the purpose of my visit, for many of the books had been the minister's. After some time of pulling heavy, leather-bound tomes and blowing dust from their tops, I discovered the diary of a butler who served here at the time of the plague. The script was handwritten and in a deep brown ink, not unlike the deep brown of dried blood. His words pertained to the despair and pain of the house grounds being used for mass burials. He described in his words: "a Hobb's cross that would never sit straight that had been carved from stone." I looked up the meaning of "Hobb" to find that it was old English for "Devil". I remembered the tilting stone cross upon the apex of the manor house. When I turned the last pages of the book, wafer-thin was a slither of slate cut into the shape of a cross that could have served as a knife with a blade long enough to pierce a heart. I left my reading and descended to the garden for a smoke and to rest my eyes.

Having wandered aimlessly around the immediate vicinity of the house, I found myself by the old well that was brick-built with an oak lid. The winding mechanism was in good order and the lid looked as if it had been lifted recently. I put out my cigarette and raised the well hatch — a square gate that gave access to the shaft. The stench from the night before and the sound of groaning immediately greeted me.

I called into the dark space, "Hello, is there someone there?"

A strong, silent draft rose, forcing me to step back. As it lifted into the air, forty or fifty crows made an awful noise before flying away. I was feeling most unsettled and forced the gate back, sealed the wellhead and returned to the library.

I walked along the rows of books until I felt compelled to pull a red, leather-bound book that, once removed, revealed what looked like a shrivelled crow's claw from behind it. I sat to read, refusing to touch the sinister, grasping object. The first words I read were as follows: "Only the dead can see the truth and it falls upon them as a duty to warn the living. Relative to relative, ancestor to the living and the living in return will join the dead."

As I read on, the scene from the previous night was revealed to me as if a prediction from many years past. I lost track of time in my reading, closing the book when my eyes hurt in the fading light. I hadn't planned on staying a second night but feeling exhausted, I decided to sleep in this odd hell for a second time. From my bed, I reflected upon the strange experiences of the previous night and day. There was no sense to be made of the tragedy and pain, which seemed to permeate the air I was breathing. Time here felt as if it had no order in the place where the past could become the present and wipe out tomorrow. Eventually, I must have fallen asleep to relive the previous night.

In my dreams, the minister came to me with a few words that I remember. "Stay away from the Diablo's Well, evil seeps from the deep."

I awoke long after dawn, tired as if I had laboured all night. I had decided to leave. I summoned the carriage, bid farewell to the dowager and walked the few hundred yards to the entrance gate. At the gate, I found myself unable to cross the boundary into the outer world. As I looked down, I noticed that instead of holding my bag, I held a black, heavy Bible. It was then I realised I appeared dressed as a minister. I awoke that night as

I have for every night in over four hundred years to administer the last rites to those plagued in limbo. I am the ghost of ghosts' deliverance in a place where time encircles like the dried souls of those who can never

WOLF TIME

(There are many pictures of wolves, but most are from captive creatures that look beyond the camera with longing, sullen eyes. Most shots in the wild are but second-rate glimpses of a king, for this beast cannot distinguish between camera and gun, hence the true king of the wild remains a mystery to all but a few.)

The sun slipped low-creeping shadow to soften the land as cooling ground made air sink, driving a wind that would blow night into this valley. The denser cold air conveyed the scent of a nocturnal predator, one who had just awoken, stretched blinking into the last light of a dying day. Lobo, a male wolf in his prime at four years of age, was awake to dominate his territory that stretched some four hundred miles across the Currumpaw, from Capulin Volcano to the turquoise Pacific Ocean. There is peace that washes across the land from this ocean, yet nature has a different intent from the name Ferdinand Magellan bestowed when he first navigated these waters in search of the Spice Islands. This vast expanse of water is the largest and most aggressive force on Earth, containing the energy of millions of years in fifty-nine million square miles of passive storming water that forms the largest ocean on Earth. With one leap of fluid movement, Lobo dropped six metres to the track that led from his den. He had no plan but to feed, for he needed the energy of life. He also knew he might not see his mountain cave for many months.

A wolf's mind comprehends what is in the moment and all that is in its past. When these come together, the scent of the future can be sensed. This is how Lobo chose his direction. West into the last light of day, this is the time of the hunter in nature's theatre of competition — this, after hundreds of thousands of man-free years. Man, the ultimate hunter who so often lacks the cunning intelligence of the wolf. Covering forty miles each day with great stamina, whilst conserving enough energy to expend upon great bursts of speed when hunting at dawn and dusk, Lobo, for reasons buried deep in his awareness, started the long trek that traverses the hills to the great plain. A route journeyed by only the most fearless of his ancestors that leads to the sea. He didn't travel in a straight line but zigzagged between springs and ponds for hydration, which he navigated through the extremes of his senses' abilities. There is a knowing in this creature, laid down from the old times, which has become embedded in a code, passed through each generation. This is the culture of wolves, the primal sense that enables generations long past to communicate survival: an awareness of water and where prey will hide. This way, jackrabbits have lived in the same warrens for as long as there have been wolves to prey upon them. Such is the law of life, a knowledge that cannot be taught.

On the seventh day, Lobo had crossed into the land of men, a place stolen from nature where fences formed unnatural divisions with creatures roaming in a pointless existence that appeared stupid to the wolf. He did not linger on such thoughts, for farmed chickens and young cattle were an easy source of energy. Lobo rested to allow the abrasion sores upon the pads of his paws to heal. Just one day of rest and gorging upon a calf returned him to his prime. Day and night had lost significance to this ranging creature. He slept when sleep was needed, resting up under the shade of a tree or in the undercut of a stream to travel on, loping with the ease of a land eagle in a gliding flight, alternating left and right limbs to take the driven force that gave motion. This way, limbs would gain partial rest minimising fatigue. Lobo had never confronted a man, having avoided the repellent, unnatural smell that conveyed their presence for miles. The scent of man was even more nauseating than the wolf's greatest natural foe — the mountain lion — that only a pack of his kind could defeat through the cunning of the intuitive cooperation that was the gift of his breed.

Joe, an outrider from the Hain's Ranch, was checking waterholes before cattle could be driven onto ungrazed, fresh pasture. The wind was against the man and away from Lobo, so sight was his first contact with a wolf of the human kind. It was hard for Lobo to respect such a hairless, soft-skinned creature that had fewer fangs than a domestic dog. But Lobo had never heard the ear-bursting detonation of a firearm and neither seen the instant delivery of death rendered without a fight. This is the most unnatural aspect of man. Joe, who was a good-natured forty-two-year-old, had never been a hothead and despite his awareness that the animal would be a threat, was reluctant to draw his gun. Lobo edged closer out of inquisitiveness and Joe lost his nerve, slowly pulling a revolver from its leather holster. Upon the sound of a clicking trigger, Lobo became rigid with alertness. Despite all the tales of men shooting wolves, Joe aimed to the left of this beautiful creature that filled him with both respect and admiration, tainted with a little fear. Pressure grew and the triggering point tripped the anvil that flew its energy against the rear of a cartridge as chordate unleashed enough power to kill, propelling a pointed lump of metal faster than thought. Having looked into the man's eyes to read his intent, Lobo was moving at the first break of sound, running to where the bullet ricocheted off a rock to impact upon the wolf's flanks, delivering sharp pain to leave an open wound that bled. He was gone, having learnt a lesson that he would later share with his young.

Joe wiped sweat from his face as his horse balked a little and said, "Sorry, fella."

Onwards the wolf loped in the full sun, only pausing once to lick the shallow wound that was now sealed with congealed blood. He was as resolute as a machine heading for the next waterhole some thirty miles away. There was an attraction drawing Lobo on, a deep need that pricked his canine consciousness, having left his family pack two years earlier whilst still a juvenile who was seen as a growing threat to the alpha male. Two years of lonely wandering but now ready to fulfil his destiny and start a new dynasty as nature demands. Something in the air was changing who he was and it fed a growing need that drove him to howl long and low at that eye so round and white in the clear night sky.

On the sixteenth night, as a full moon climbed to its zenith, Lobo threw his head back, releasing a long and low howl that had travelled to him from his mother, a large North American timber wolf, and his father, a slightly built creature who had developed a cunning intelligence to compensate for his lack of muscle. Lobo had wandered north from the Mexican border in search of a mate. When he ceased his howl into the wild for a long inhalation of breath, faintly from afar came an answering call that had travelled in a tradition down through generations into the now.

Lobo slept a restless sleep for six hours and then ran into an altered direction that took him south along the edge of the great ocean. His limbs moved with ease and his fur flowed as if each follicle had a life of its own. His nose, ever moist, pushed into the air, scenting for danger along with ears that folded three hundred and sixty degrees as if they were a ship's radar. The coastal forest was cooler than the more open hinterland and the soft, undulating hills consumed less energy than the rocky higher ground.

For six more nights under a waning moon, Lobo's nightly call was answered from over fifty miles south of him, inlands he and his family pack had never explored.

One afternoon, whilst crossing a highway, Lobo met his first truck. The road was deserted and the tarmac was cooking under the oppressive afternoon sun, setting a heat haze that played with light. Lobo paused and sat in the scrub that flanked the highway to study the phenomenon. Before any sound had met his ears, his eyes became aware of a distant monster moving in the contorted air. The sound of a Ford 1930 petrol internal combustion engine was rumbling along towards him. Cowering down and driven by inquisitiveness to stay and fear to run, his nerve held as he closed his eyes at the point of passing, anticipating some great calamity.

When he opened his eyes, he saw the rear of the flatbed truck was stacked with melons. As the truck caught a hole, a melon broke free to bounce on the road, rolling a few yards to stop in front of him. His nostrils became full of a sweet, intoxicating scent of a heaven he could never have imagined. In the heat, he cautiously pawed the fruit to see if it was alive; this released more of the delightful odour. He then took a bite, and as his teeth penetrated the thin, hard skin, they found the soft, sweet, internal flesh that exploded cool and fresh in his dehydrated mouth. Should a wolf ever smile, this wolf was grinning while lapping and sucking at this rich, lucky find.

For three days, there had been a faint, repetitive rumbling in the distance and a smell of space upon the air. Having climbed the flank of one of the higher hills to a bluff above the treeline, Lobo saw the ocean for the first time in his life. He was charged with challenge and headed along a cool river ravine, delighted in leaping through the shallow, cool water and occasionally swimming, submerged in the deeper outside of the bends where storms' torrents had gouged the golden gravel a few yards deep. He drank and played like a puppy under the shade of the sycamores that roofed the riverbed. Lobo travelled on so absorbed in the delight of being alive that time had no meaning as if fatigue could not catch him. He felt like the wind, no obstacle could touch him until after a few hours, the cool, golden gravel gave way to soft, yellow sand and the air grew saturated with the smell, salt and ozone. He burst upon the empty, southern Californian beach to run with his nose forwards and his tail as level as the pure sand along the waterfront, invigorated by the sparkling light and the power of the waves. Without any thought, he leapt into the ocean and swam as he had never swum before, matching the power his mother had bestowed upon him with the intelligence of his father's genes against the might of the Pacific Ocean. The delight of life filled every part of his being, for Lobo was now in his prime and he was close to fulfilling his purpose. Exhausted, he collapsed upon the sand just beyond the tide's reach, stretching his forepaws towards the water, casting his eye over the water's surface. Out of instinct rather than thought, he leapt forwards over and into the water, having seen a glint of silver amongst the waves. Upon returning to the land, he dropped a large fish some two feet long and proceeded to dine upon the energy-giving fruit of the Pacific.

Sleep now drowned his body, and he retreated to a small hollow in the soft, warm soil under a copse of trees adjoining the beach. Dreams raged through Lobo's wordless mind that recorded memories to speculate upon dangers in an ocean where wolves of the water in the form of sleek, great, circling, hunting, finned fish share the genesis of his ancestors. For the laws of life have always been and always will be such so long as there is a creature in need of energy. That night his howling had gone unanswered and this added a degree of anxiety that drove him forwards and brought him to the edge of a great human metropolis.

Lobo entered the city, navigating by the stars, for this place obliterated all other senses, being full of the stench of detritus and never-ending sounds. Artificial light tortured his eyes, and smaller family members of the truck ran fearless of his bristling snarls. One driven callously was steered at him to chase him thirty yards along a main street he was traversing until he turned and sank his fangs into one of the round legs as the beast hissed in pain, and a human voice could be heard cursing from within. He loped on past shops with their lights spilling yellow out into free spaces, skipping over a drunk sprawled upon the veranda of a now closed saloon. Here he prickled at the scent of whisky on the man's breath and found it so disgusting that he turned, biting the drunk's leg. He felt the deep, primal satisfaction when the enamel of his teeth clashed with the weakest constituency of bone. The man screamed, flailing at the wolf as the beast of nature glanced into the eyes of a failed species that had fallen far since the time of his heyday many centuries before. Disturbed sleepers arose, drawn to the drunk's yelps to see a one hundred and twenty-five pound wolf bounding along the sidewalk. The following day, the San Francisco Times headlines read: "Hungry Wolf Bites Drunk."

Having found a south-running railway track, Lobo made good time and by late dawn, the air once again smelt of dew-laden grass and pine trees. He was free of the human forest. The land rose as he travelled south and once above the treeline, great views yielded out across the ocean that appeared tranquil and passive from a distance. Lobo scented the air and shook his fleece to free dirt and to capture more air within his hollow, tine fur hairs for insulation. After resting for a while and watching the great, orange ball float down into the water's far edge until it had settled into its earth far away, he threw his head back in a motion as old as there have been wolves in the land. He howled long and low — a call that even in the still of darkness shimmered out of respect for some ancient deity who ordained that such a fearless wolf spirit should hunt the world. Instantly from the night, a long, haunting answer of a faintly higher pitch rose in a howl that he joined as two became one with the single-minded purpose of nature's demanded unity of creation.

Lobo rested for a few hours in the hollow of a fallen tree but awoke abruptly to a familiar scent he knew to avoid. The dank odour of a mountain lion filled the air. Some primal sense deep within his unconsciousness had triggered him to be alert, instantly rising in silence and ready to defend or run, backed up against a ridge of soil under which he had slept, formed by the ghost of a storm-battled, wrenched root of a fallen tree. His fur bristling, ears sharp as blades and fangs curled, every fibre and muscle of Lobo was tensed for the life-challenging combat that can only be enacted between two of nature's most skilled and desperate practitioners of life. The area in which this wolf was backed into formed a natural amphitheatre, enclosed on three sides by banks, covered in dense vegetation. On the open side lay the dull bones of a long dead wolf. Lobo had fallen into the trap of a great enemy of his kind. There was no route for escape in which through superior stamina, he could outrun the big cat just so long as he could avoid its greater surge of speed and power in the initial attack. First sight was the yellow glare of eyes, hanging about three feet above the ground, followed by a deep inhalation of breath that betrayed the wolf's whereabouts. Growling fiercely enough to cause the cat to hesitate, Lobo attacked, knowing his chance would only come once, launching in great cat-like leaps that confused his enemy, who expected a feebler creature trying to flee rather than being attacked itself. Lobo flew through the air, bounding upon the startled cougar's back to deliver a vicious bite, causing the cat to roll over in pain. He was now running with every pound per square inch of pressure against the forest floor he could muster, but the more powerful and much larger animal was catching up fast. Branches broke as the wolf crashed forward. Those branches shattered seconds later as the pursuer bludgeoned a larger space of travel. Through instinct, Lobo veered to his left, which opened the chance for the cougar to reduce his space of travel by cutting the distance between them. In a moment, Lobo felt the mighty claws lacerating his back, but the great beast had not yet got a deep enough anchorage to drag its prey down.

In pain and rage, Lobo turned to face his attacker and his almost certain death. The beast launched at the wolf, who leapt aside causing the cat to miss him, as Lobo braced again for another charge. When another of his breed appeared by his side, growling and spitting anger and vengeance, both ran at the cat's haunches, biting and twisting, causing great injuries as they acted as one. That made the cat flee bearing scars where no fur would grow and the cold air would forever bite as a reminder of the greatest wolf in the land.

Lobo had joined with his mate whom in his tongue he named Pacific, for he knew of the storms that both the ocean and she-wolf could rage in defence of a mate. The two wolves ran together, sharing a delight in companionship that grew into a single inseparable bond. The following spring, in the high hills that defend against Pacific storms, Lobo and Pacific raised six grey cubs.

Today, one hundred years on, on a night when the moon is brightest, an eerie calling can be heard that has travelled from a more innocent time into today. Life will never be passive as nature is of a temperamental character; however, those who have the spirit of nature within them will overcome, and survival will be theirs for many generations, for she loves her own. This is the love of life.

A SHARED PLACE, A DIFFERENT TIME

Leaning forwards from a straight-backed wooden chair made in a previous century, a man picks up a bottle that is two-thirds empty and pours a yellow spirit that flows over large ice cubes which will resist heat for long enough to take the sting out of the spirit and allow it to sting the man. A sparsely decorated square bar room whose main function is the consumption of drinks and little else with the exception of forgetting pain and the occasional fight. It is late outside, and the moon is casting shadows in short, sharp relief.

James drinks from his glass waiting for something that never comes and pours again as he has done for many years in the Old Relief Bar just after the edge of town. He is a regular here, but none know his name. He doesn't live in the town and if you can call it a life, he hasn't lived in any place around the town or at least stayed in one place for more than a month or two. James isn't a drifter either. He is one of the forgotten ones, who thought and fought often with himself until he was all beat up and out.

At one side of the room is the bar that runs a full fifteen metres, occupying the whole length as if one barman could serve a hundred thirsty throats. To the end furthest from the entrance is a plain wall with a hat and coat stand and a couple of posters upon the wall. One of the posters is an antique nailed up in 1870 with the caption in faded red and black of "Wells Fargo the Bank of Life". A blast of cold air pushes into the room as another man enters, leaving the door to swing open.

One of the few drinkers inside looks up and says, "Just 'cause you ain't got no feelin' in your bones, doesn't mean the rest of us gotta freeze."

The man hesitates out of pride, takes off his broad hat and closes the door. He turns to lean on the dull wooden bar as near to the door as can be. Nothing is said, but the pop of a cork can be heard along with a drink flowing into a glass. This place is a men's sanctuary where women rarely venture. The bar has been here for two hundred and thirty years to today. James is one of life's good guys who lost in love and refused to cheat in his work; others always used him. A man without a woman is a sad man indeed. Her nature can cut the sharp edges out of him and soften a snarling mind. The longer a man lives unloved, the more selfish and unlovable he will grow until he is a bitter old man.

We jump forwards from 1870 to 1999. The old lights are still casting an orange glow, but the bulbs are different; no one uses gas or candles today. The chairs might as well be the same. The poster is faded, framed and glazed and is accompanied by a picture of Bruce Springsteen holding a microphone. The bar has been made shorter to make room for a few more tables and there are a few people still out drinking on a cold winter's night. Even the moon casts the same light. Jon, a man of fifty-seven, reaches forwards and pours a bourbon over large cubes of ice, then sets the bottle that has a black label covering nearly all of one side of a square bottle with the letters JD upon it. The bottle mirrors the shape of the room and it settles, matching the line of the walls. Jon is down to his last forty-five dollars and wants to forget about the woman he loves but can't be with and the fact he lost his job yesterday. He drinks on as another enters the bar and doesn't close the door, letting cold air fill this space of alcohol and smoke. Jon stands, walks to the door and kicks it shut with a glass-shaking slam. He glares at the newcomer and sits to resume his drink.

I drank at the Old Relief Bar last year. Behind the bar is a list of customers stretching back over two centuries. James and Jon are there. They are also now up on what locals call Boot Hill below the church. James' grave cannot be deep because the soil is still piled high where he lies and has an old whisky bottle stoppered with a note in it implanted in the grassy soil. Jon, I am told, staggered out of the bar one cold night and fell asleep on the rail tracks. They gathered him together and buried him next to James. The only difference between the two graves is that Jon's grave has a whisky bottle implanted with a message in it, sealed with a screw on top. I moved on and found love, but when there, my glass was empty.

Jlu

TODAY IS THE DAY

R eality is on the move, and often we have no choice but to accept what is presented to us. Any day. A normal day. The sort of day when ordinary folks do ordinary things. But Jack wasn't ordinary and he certainly wasn't predictable.

The sun had risen at 6:22 a.m. as expected, and Mrs Goldberg had put her cat out at 6:30 a.m. as she did every morning. The early commuter train had rolled into town as it did every day of the week, and traffic had begun to roll along Main Street. Time did not matter. What mattered was that folks did as they do, and these are the things which form the routines that construct this human world. What mattered was to occur at 3:36 p.m., but we have six hours before the blast that changed everything.

Jack had laid in bed until ten and only then reluctantly got dressed, slipped out of his rented rooms and wandered unconsciously into Halley's Bar Diner where he'd eaten scrambled eggs on toast, washed down with a strong, black coffee. After a slow start, the town had come alive. Shops had piled goods in doorways to capture the attention of innocent passers-by. Market stalls had unfurled untold objects at the end of the street as people moved in all directions. When Jack left the diner, he screwed up his eyes against the bright light, slowly opening them to observe the absurd scene around him. All was so familiar, having been the same Wednesday morning for the last seventeen years. Jack was not a day older than when he had first arrived in the town of Stallworth. The people all walked as they always did, and the market stalls and shops sold the same artefacts. Nothing had changed and for some reason, Jack was aware of this but had never questioned it. He was quite simply stuck comfortably in a seven-day time loop. As he opened his eyes to the brighter-than-usual light, he felt different. Something had changed. His alertness jumped a gear when a large, brown labrador passed close to him. The dog paused, dropped something from its mouth and trotted on with purpose. This had never happened before and Jack shook as he stooped to pick up the roll of paper left by the dog. He opened it up to read the words: "Today is the day." Now Jack was scratching his head, because for years, each day had been the same.

Having been a first responder in New York, every ten minutes had been different — the scary, high-speed driving, the deaths and the messy emergency procedures. After ten years of trying to save so many lives, Jack had to save himself. He hit the road without notice and drifted into this time-forgotten, small town in the Midwest. It was that last emergency call that had pushed him over the edge — the heavy traffic and the mother's desperate pleading over the control radio link.

Upon arrival, he was confused to see familiar faces but was in his automatic professional mode. Having covered that gaping wound and injected adrenaline before fitting the oxygen mask, he had ignored his wife and the fact this was his seven-year-old daughter, Johanna. Once Johanna had been stretchered into the ambulance and the plasma bottle was doing its job, everything hit Jack, knocking the living daylights out of him. Time stopped. Johanna had died and seventeen years had passed. It was an ordinary Wednesday in hospital ward six as resident consultant Mr James walked through the ward in his immaculate, ironed, white coat. He paused at Jack's bed, glancing at the brown-backed, old-fashioned clipboard that hung at the foot of his bed.

"Ah, Jack, you have been more active of recent," he said as Jack stirred a little in his comatose state and settled back into his long, deep sleep. It is 3:34 p.m. and Jack opens his eyes to see beyond a dream for the first time in seventeen years.

At 3:36 p.m., his wife Lyn sits by his bed and reaches to hold his hand. She notices tears in his eyes and asks, "Jack, is it you?"

Turning slowly, he stutters and says her name, and then she hugs him as both shed bewildered tears. Seventeen years in an imaginary world into which Jack still, on occasions, wants to return to, if only to retrieve his clothes and wrist watch that will forever tick away upon some bedside table, which is as real as any artefact you or I use every day of our lives.

Ille

DARK NATURE, WHITE EVIL

From the front windows, the southern sun flowed in, striking the cream floor where the freshly mopped but age-cracked tiles glowed. Upon the ceiling, a bamboo fan turned steadily, mixing with each revolution the hot afternoon air with a steady but faint creaking sound. Kuno, not long a young man and still partly a boy, sat upon a high stool, contemplating the long, thin, heavy glass of cold milk that had just been placed in front of him. He had worked that day and the dust of the cotton fields was deeply engrained upon the skin of his toned, lithe arms. His hands were sore from cotton picking and a crust of blood had hardened on his left palm. The bar was empty except for this young man, who had eyes like a fresh-born calf, and the middle-aged bartender, who looked so thin he appeared half-starved.

A brown pickup truck abruptly pulled to a halt at the kerbside directly outside of the bar and three men stepped out. One man was in his late forties, clean-shaven, dressed in traditional lumberman's clothes. The other two smaller men followed him across the pavement and into the bar. Of the two shorter men, one had blonde, curly hair and a nervous disposition, his hands constantly fidgeting and fiddling with something; they found a loose thread upon his chequered shirt and started to play with it. Three beers were ordered and this was the only conversation until the lumberman spoke abruptly to the now tense barman.

"You ain't too particular about the sort of clientele you serve in here."

Kuno pushed the untouched glass away from him and said, "Save it!" to the skinny bartender. Pushing himself up on the bar, he made to leave. The fan stirred the air that had become tense in a now threatening atmosphere. Around and around it turned as the occasional fly landed upon its blades for a ride into nowhere.

The slight, blonde, nervous man stepped in Kuno's way, staring at him with his eyes bulging, and spoke. "You, boy! It's one of yours that walked with my sister. You're all the same, so you will do, there's gotta be payback."

Kuno felt the scars on his back prickle from where he had been whipped by a white farmer a few years before because he had got lost and trespassed inadvertently onto private land. He had sworn then that no man would ever whip or beat him again without suffering for it.

The big man said, "Let's have a little fun with this boy."

He stood and pushed Kuno against the bar — the thin bartender had disappeared. It was then that the nervous man punched Kuno in the stomach doubling him over. The third man had returned to the pickup and now re-entered the scene with a pick handle. He took a sharp swing with it at Kuno's head who ducked as the blow crashed into the bar, splintering the smooth, painted wood. Kuno leapt over the bar, took a beer bottle and threw it in the big man's face. Looking down, Kuno saw a handgun that he picked up enraged and shaking. Before he had thought, he had pulled the trigger. There was a loud crack of combustion and the nervous man fell staggering, clutching his face. The third man, who had not spoken a word, walked backwards towards the doorway with the still smoking gun following him. He tripped upon a table leg; there was a loud crack as his arm broke under the weight of falling awkwardly. With no witnesses (except for the bartender who was intimidated), Kuno had no one to defend him. He is now incarcerated in Unit 29, Mississippi State Penitentiary on death row.

A WALK INTO A DIFFERENT PLACE

Cold and amber, bubbling to a thin froth, condensation gathering to stream upon the outside of a glass. One stool. A man upon it with his elbows on a bar and his head bowed low. It is summer hot and outside is like a desert where not even the lizards will venture out into the cruel, parching radiation. Smoke rises in sporadic clouds as the man draws upon a slim cigar, holds his breath for a moment and then exhales slowly and deliberately. The air is full of nicotine as this man studies the glowing end of his cigar and focuses upon that small, red speck of fire. He is aware and appreciative of everything, even the bleached hairs on the sunburnt back of his forearm. He relaxes and in doing so, draws again and exhales after a moment of holding his smoke-filled breath. He puts the cigar down, freeing his shaking hand to lift that full glass to his lips. He hesitates, raises the glass level with his eyes and sees the world through the distortions of a beer; everything looks better than ever before. The cold glass stings his hand as he opens his mouth that kisses the lip of that glass, and he starts to drink. First, the cold freezes his tongue, as the gasses burst into bubbles, and he wants more. He gulps and gulps as if unable to get enough until the glass is empty.

Without a word, the bartender removes the glass, polishes another, fills it with beer and throws a cardboard mat upon the bar that has the words, "Cactus Bar, Mojave Desert" printed in sand yellow upon it. A second beer is placed upon the mat. It condensates, fizzes and froths, overflowing down the side of the glass to be absorbed into the sun-bleached wood of the bar top. Again, the man smokes and drinks, consuming six beers and three cigars in all. Below him, his dried and cracked pigskin leather boots rest his feet on a horizontal spar of the bar stool; his jeans are faded blue and sand dusty. He leans back stretching and looks to the door through which the burning, bright, cruel sun floods in as a reminder he had just walked forty-eight of the cruellest miles of his life, ending it at 3:22 p.m., having walked into and beyond the midday sun. Some fifty odd miles north of him is his truck that had broken its suspension in a rutted road. His mobile phone was out of range and the battery faded. He had drunk two litres of water in the first few miles of his trek, and it is only now that his body could afford to perspire again. His vital organs had been starting to show signs of stress and he had been delusional at times. It was only now the man realised the danger he had been in and how close he was to collapsing so near to this small outpost in the desert.

After draining the sixth beer, he rested flat on a long table and fell asleep. He didn't care for anything beyond the fact he was alive, and he knew he never wanted a walk like that ever again. He also knew a beer would never taste so fresh and beautiful again. But he did know he was going to enjoy the rest of his life and never waste a moment flirting with negativity or sadness. His walk was a walk from one state of mind into another. He had walked into and beyond death, and knew the value of his life. Now he was free to live as he had never lived before.

FLOWERS IN THE BLOOD

Absolute perfection, colour and symmetry formed in a season of growth yet destined to die. Beauty comes of creation, but beauty itself can be a killer. There are flowers that shine with colour, yet they can contain lethal poisons that are the harbinger of death. Passion, too, can kill.

The previous night's business had taken a toll on Federico's mind. It wasn't that he couldn't handle death. It was the way the butchery and barbarity required had lodged in his mind. He couldn't shake it and it was interfering with how he functioned. For some, death is a gift but never if it comes from the hand of a friend. Whom you trust in São Paulo beyond family was always a difficult choice for the dealers and shippers who supply the hard-core merchandise for thousands of addicts and demi-addicts in this Portuguese part of Brazil. Guns always made too much noise in the close-packed slums and favelas that climbed along the narrow, unlit streets of shanties and corrugated shacks. Knives and machetes were relatively silent and efficient at close quarters.

For a dealer to be an addict was always fatal, and Federico knew that by killing Joseph, he was only fulfilling the inevitable. This was business and he hadn't given a thought to the twenty years they shared growing up under the same roof. The harsh realities of life had to dictate a man's actions, and Joseph had already fallen victim to the white powder that had hijacked his pleasure and reward system, making him a liability.

Federico had held it together for some hours despite not getting any sleep, but when Joseph's partner, a slender, smooth-skinned beauty, had brought her child and asked where her husband was, he fell apart. Her eyes cut into him as deeply as his life had cut into the addict's throat. His last breath had gurgled through the gushing, crimson blood.

"I love you, Federico."

Somehow, the young woman had known what had happened. She knew her partner's addiction and covered for him on many occasions. The night before, she had begged him to leave the city and go to America with her and their son. There he could be treated to become clean, yet her reward was to be laughed at and beaten with a clenched fist. Love, even when subjected to long torments of pain, does sometimes endure, and the purity of Gabriela's heart had kept her love strong for a falling man.

It was only after he had withdrawn his knife that Federico realised he loved Joseph. It was then, as tears burnt his smooth cheeks, that he captured his mate as he fell and caressed him, and his eyes bulged in a vision that only the dead could see. In a city where a human life was as cheap as a labourer's weekly wage, the police didn't bother much with another dead addict. But Gabriela had made such a fuss that the investigating officer had told her that most deaths like this one were perpetrated by the dead man's accomplices.

Federico needed a drink, having wallowed through the day, feeling emotions that were driven by childhood memories. Sat at a small, open-air bar under a wooden frame draped in vines and bougainvillea, he was oblivious to the flowers and sweet scent around him. Gabriela paused as she approached and despite his mixed emotions, Federico's spirit lifted at the sight of her. He briefly stood and pushed a chair in invitation for her to sit. Gabriela pulled one of the perfect flowers to her nose and inhaled deeply, closing her eyes. She smiled as she opened them and with the feminine agility of a ballerina, her arm flew in a circumference of a hundred and eighty degrees. The knife in her hand slit Federico's throat in an instant. She dropped the knife as he looked at her and in his last breath before slumping forward, he said, "I loved him."

BANDULA

Silence falls like a soft, floating feather that drops wisp-like upon a seamless, placid pool of still water that absorbs all without reflection. There is no sound and there are no ripples to disturb this squared space. Only the unseen and unsettled turbulence of emotions fill this small, cluttered room of low light that dances through an opening cloud of cigar smoke. It is not the silence of peace but something that sinks far heavier, deeper and profounder.

In this cave of no more than sixteen feet square rests a large oak desk that dominates the entire space. It appears as if it predates the room. As such, it is far older as if the building had been built around it for its own sake. The desk stands upon four short, stubby legs that give way to two matching drawer units. Atop of this monument is a delicate, green leather surface that serves to absorb the pressure of a pen's nib as it is drawn over paper. In its soft, worn depths, the faded, fraying leather has absorbed written words of over a century of writing in impressions that remain elusive and secret for as long as the room may contain it. This desk, built by a master cabinetmaker, has an oriental feel although it is robust and practical in design. Upon the two outer legs are small Indian elephants and other hints of a further land. Should this desk be displayed in some well-lit showroom of an antique dealer, it would fetch a tidy sum of money.

There is a mystical sense that indicates a little magic in the way that, during the 1940s, the complete house which holds this small room was destroyed, but the desk suffered not a scratch, just a layer of dust and a few shards of glass. The later building was in fact built around it. It strikes me as unusual for an article of furniture to have a name; however, like all great characters, this one answers to the name of Bandula. We have been great friends for over thirty-five years now, and my palms have worn into the wooden surface's grain, blending with those who worked here before me along with the craftsman who put a little of his spirit into its form.

When working late, which is my usual practice, occasionally spilling red wine and ash as I write, I often talk aloud supposedly with myself and in the silence, I imagine an answer; I certainly get an idea that fits hand in glove into what I have been writing. My reporting and stories, all based upon truth, take me on long far travels, but I can never complete a work satisfactorily without Bandula. It is a strange truth that upon her comfortable inlaid leather my words come as if they are hers, fitting to settle like those silent feathers of an owl into what is needed. It is as if I am not the writer, but I am held in the same way that I hold my pen as the words come from another place. I often feel as if those articles and stories are not mine, and when I return to read them a day or two later, I do not recognise what I read.

I rarely open the set of four drawers, two on each side of the seating leg recess. They hold artefacts and objects long lost, forgotten and unused. One remains jammed and never opened by me. There is a long, shallow drawer as long as the desk is wide in which I keep pens, ink and cigars. I confess that there is an old revolver and a dozen brass bullets that were strangely there when I acquired Bandula who was here when I bought the house in late 1970.

I was able to learn a little about the desk many years ago when a housekeeper to a previous owner had informed me that in the years around 1800, a Burmese general had owned the property. His name was Maha Bandula. It was later when doing some basic repairs to one of the drawers that I found the name "Bandula" written upon a shipping note, stuck on the underside of the drawer. My relationship with Bandula has grown from fear to respect and now fondness. I have a suspicion that the desk may be indestructible and that some secret remains within that drawer which is jammed so tight. I wonder when it was last opened and what it conceals.

Of recent, my attention has been drawn to a nation, sandwiched between Bangladesh, India and China. Myanmar has experienced a turbulent past since British rule was withdrawn. Having been asked to write about the land once named Burma, I sat at Bandula to start my research. I worked late into the night, forming notes and starting my article that opens with the words:

"I sit here to write about a magical land that has mystified many an Englishman, once called Burma but now recognised as Myanmar. As I am composing my article, it strikes me as fitting that the desk I now write upon would have been made by a Burmese craftsman in the city of Rangoon two centuries ago. A renowned Burmese general who defeated the British Army owned this desk. General Maha Bandula was the commander-in-chief of the Royal Burmese armed forces in 1822 and served in the first Anglo-Burmese war. He fell in action and is regarded as a national spirit of the modern nation."

What happened next gives me a good reason to believe that that spirit is still a force to be reckoned with. After some time past 2:00 in the morning, absolute silence had fallen upon my modest office space. Having drunk a glass or two of Mouton Cadet Bordeaux, my head fell back and I must have slept for some hours. During my sleep, I dreamt of being a private in the British Army as a battle raged. Upon awakening, I found that jammed drawer had been drawn open and a small gun was upon the leather desk top. As I cleared my head filling it with wakefulness, I leant forwards to look into the open drawer that was hidden in darkness. At first, I thought I was looking at a smooth, rounded stone but rapidly recognised a skull. Having picked it up and placed it upon the desk top, I could see a hole in the right temple. At that moment, the gun fired and the desk appeared covered in blood and the skull was gone.

I never wrote again upon that desk. That vengeful bullet was mine. It is my skull, which I thought was the general's, that is now resting in a jammed drawer. Bandula is always waiting for another to write upon our leather-embossed coffin. There is a story engraved in the green leather that another will one day read and upon opening that drawer, maybe my written soul will be freed.

TOMBSTONE, ARIZONA, 1912

A nd then he stepped back one pace, momentarily held his face and drew in air deep through hollow cheeks as the pianist raised the piano lid and clear notes began to trickle in some order as if soft spring rain. The sound eased that of the previous minutes, and the combustion had faded, as the smell of chordate was slowly filling the still, static air. Removing a half-burnt cigarette from his pale, thin lips, his arm slowly fell to his side as fingers loosened limply, dropping the butt that left a trail of smoke which rose over his slowly fading form. It was then he realised his fate, yet felt no pain. A million beautiful things passed behind his eyes, most of which he could never have seen and now would be forever out of reach. Outside, a hot sun reached through trees into this small town square, scattering a leaf-filtered, dancing light that floated like free spirits between shadows and dirt-gathered time.

Hands now shaking and eyes misting, he started to crumble as his soul melted into the beyond-out-of-reach where he, too, would become dirt in the light. Few are here and none will speak of his passing. Silence is a convenience of death. His only memorial is this man's memory and a bullet hole that splintered a bar, having traversed through his life-giving heart. He never saw his killer who had been waiting fifty yards away, poised with a rifle trained out of a misguided vengeance. A single bullet had waited for the hammer blow of released detonation to travel in a fraction of time over a woodpile at the edge of a patch of weed and grass. It had then shattered a window before ending its journey on the other side of life. Falling slowly without knowing, he sprawled upon the wooden boards of the floor. Splintered and shattered, a bead of deep crimson life escaped to create a growing, irregular shape that overflowed into a narrow joint between those boards. I do not know what happened next, for I stooped clenching my revolver, stepping over an innocent man — a man who had minutes before asked if he could wear my star, the star of a US marshal. For that bullet was meant for me, and my would-be killer would never be taken into custody. He had forfeited that right. I am a killer of killers and my name is Wyatt. Now most know who I am and what I do.

(*Wyatt Earp (1848–1929) was a famous fearless American law enforcement officer who worked in many places in the American West, including Tombstone, Arizona Territory.*)

$\mathcal{Joe}$

TWENTY-TWO AND GONE

W as it a stylish death?" he asked, exhaling gentle cigarette smoke upon his last breath. "Hide the blood and let me clench my gun. Brush my hair and splay my legs, so that I look as if I died like a man."

I cushioned his head a little and buttoned up his shirt. Told him he was foolish, but many had done the same. His blue eyes glowed, reflecting the heavens beyond the sky.

I asked, "How old are you, son?" to which he told me he was twenty-two and then he was gone.

All that was left was the spirit on his breath and small tears in his eyes. We lifted him on a waggon and drew him along the path from which he had come.

His mother broke down, and his sister stood rigid and said he could join his father in a grave freshly dug in the ground. I saw the flowers upon the grave not thirty yards away. They made a wooden cross although he never set foot in any church. He did not have a coffin and no fancy words. His boots were polished and in his hand was a childhood toy. They slid him into the ground the way he had slid into this world.

I remember Geoff kindly, but he should have never had that last drink. I had come to fetch him at his mother's request; he did not want to leave. The barman had told him he would serve him no more. Having sworn at me, it was then he drew his gun. I got him in the heart and that was the end of his boyish, drunken fun. His family never blamed me. I do all I can to help. But boy, I hate myself. It was the bottle that made it him or me. I shot him fair, and I hope you don't judge me.

ALEKSEY

A leksey ran his life like an internal combustion engine. First, he used the energy of others to run down his obstacles and the vehicle of fear to carry his product into the minds of those whose dependency was their weakness. The weaker they grew, the more voracious they became, demanding more. It grew like a religious fever and even powerful people fell under his spell. As all engines, Aleksey's was destined to seize and it came to a juddering stop like a destination in time that served as a rock face for him to career into at maximum speed. He had become a victim of his own spell. The Dust, as it quickly became known on these winter streets of Moscow, seemed to fall like silent snow in the night upon the people who never awoke the next morning, having fallen under a sinister spell the previous evening. The city would never be the same again, having endured weeks of a particularly cold depression that had settled like a disease over its uniform suburbs. The minds of the people seemed to have frozen and even their hearts were demanding relief. It started (well, there was never a real start) not like a book or a race that begins and ends, for there can be no end to this and it was always destined to happen.

The drug exploded in the private apartments of a wealthy few to spread, detonating its consequences in the bars and nightclubs of the Tverskoy neighbourhood, overflowing into universities and schools. Finally, it permeated the factory floors and offices and no one was safe. The purest of white powder was synthesised from a genetically modified plant, *Eurotia ceratoides*, that naturally occurs only in a remote region of the Afghan Pamir. The original plant had travelled to Moscow with a returning soldier in the 1980s. When exposed to air, the volatile nature of this substance becomes airborne and inhaled involuntarily. Once affected, there is no cure for the craving need it generates in the pre-frontal cortex of the victim's mind. Productivity fell as workers lost motivation and many stopped working. Sales from shops fell and the economy was in free fall. Like the shockwave of an explosion, within a month, the addiction had spread to surrounding towns and settlements. Other cities were destined to fall; St. Petersburg came next. The only break that could slow the spread was the pace of the drug's manufacturing, which was produced and stockpiled by an industrial site in the Wuhan region of the Chinese People's Republic and smuggled to remote storage sites around Russian cities. There was enough of the stuff to kill a country of about one hundred and fifty million people who lived on the largest land mass of any country in the world.

Born of a Chinese mother and a Russian father, Aleksey grew up in the far east of the country in Khabarovsk. He had

320

studied politics in Beijing and law at the Lomonosov State University in Moscow. His loyalty to China was unquestionable, motivated by the realisation that all the productivity from eastern Russia was exploited and used by the Moscow political class. The Kremlin, thrashing about for answers, blamed it all on an American plot and promptly deployed its military on full alert. The Americans and democratic Europe responded, and a tense standoff grew, while the Chinese worked as mediators.

Having succumbed to the toxic dust, parts of the Russian military infrastructure rebelled next. Then the Chinese military entered Russia to stabilise an area that spread from the Ural Mountains to the Chinese border. From that point forward, Russia would never again threaten the world with its subversion and corruption. However, a greater threat had spread to the doorstep of Western Europe. As for Aleksey, his workers and warehouses were liquidated in a process of absolute denial, whilst in the United States, under several acres of glass, a specific Afghan plant was growing under the cover of a Chinese pharmaceutical research project.

PASSAGE

We passed upon the street late in partial darkness. High lamps, shedding orange, dull light, softened the harshness of the cold, wet, grey pavements and sharp-cut kerbstones. A cat peered, showing yellow eyes from a bin-top, while a rat rustled inside. Our footsteps echoed upon the flanking passage walls. Both paces shortened as we closed, each focused and tense with anticipation. I stepped down into the road to avoid a beat-up, old Ford, pavement-parked. He stopped, placing his hand inside his heavy greatcoat. My pulse grew faster as he tapped a cigarette upon its box; a lighter flame danced against his face. I saw a man of forty something, hat pulled low over his forehead. The wind blew specks of rain that misted the air. I coughed as we reached each other.

"Okay?" was all he said.

"Yep," was my reply.

His arm reached towards me and I took the package as our eyes met, not knowing, but understanding. At this moment, the alley felt like a deep, frozen lake where the rest of existence had ceased to have any relevance. I shook as we passed, quickening our steps, noticing something in the road ahead of me. It was trundling like a small truck, radiating dull, blue lights that scanned the ground in front of it. This was a mobile security unit that had obviously been detailed to intercept the handover, and I was now the carrier. I had no choice but to carry on, knowing there was no bluffing a machine. It was probably broadcasting live to the city control centre deep under Central Square, and more of its airborne brothers would be launching. In that moment, a laser flood-scanned me as an audio warning calmly instructed me to stand still. I could feel the tobacco package close to my chest.

"You are under arrest for infringement of the smoking laws. Please remain where you are."

For nine years now, smokers had been persecuted with the last members of an underground den having been ruthlessly tracked and killed only weeks ago. I am the last smoker in this fireless city in a time of machines. The cat lost its nerve and ran like a rocket past the droid distracting it. I ran at it, barging it over onto its side, as bullets glowed traces into the dark. I was away and running when a door opened in the darkness and I heard, "This way!" in low, desperate tones. I dived through the door that closed silently after me. In the candlelight, I saw the serious face of an old man, lined and frail.

"You got smokes?" he asked.

"Yeah," was my answer.

"Gee, they must be worth half the city."

It was true. People would kill for a cigarette. This was the case since United Tobacco had produced its Hallucino brand that could send any smoker on a hallucinogenic trip of fantasy and caused many to believe they could resist the regime. The system had shut down production, and for months, the citizens had been in rebellion, leading to the death of hundreds.

I am a smoker of resistance, Captain Robertson, No 288S, commander of S Division Central. The old man shook my hand and bid me luck as I exited the rear of his hovel home. Now I would be up against at least a dozen droids. I could hear the hum of the elevator closing. There was enough tobacco in this package to drive a revolution and the distribution network was ready to run. I was the last hope of thousands of smokers who were armed and ready. I ran zigzagging between walls and crouching beside cars as droids swept overhead.

Having lain low for an hour, I was able to get into an underpass and press the button on my distress beacon. Help would be on its way. Within minutes, I could hear the motorcycle engine of my pickup. It raced towards me as a droid entered the tunnel. Would I be the target or the rider? I held the package out as the rider snatched it and in the same moment, I fell. I never heard the motorcycle exit the underpass and never smoked again.

DIALOGUE WITH A STRANGER

The voice came to me in a muffled tone through the smoke and sound. Voices hummed in a background cacophony like an orchestra tuning up before a concert. Smoke blew from her mouth, hanging in a slow, diffusing cloud around her face. I could see contours of beauty but not who she was. This was the first bait and I took it. What lonely man drinking in the Parisian Latin quarter would turn away?

She spoke again through that shroud of smoke, lost in the babble and noise of so many. I thought I heard her, but it might have been my imagination. Pushing the second chair back from the table with my foot in a gesture for her to sit, she didn't. I took a sharp drink of the vodka that had been waiting in my glass for some time and looked at her again, this time paying attention. She was attractive. Her small nose and delicate eyes held me and I had to force myself to look away. She had a soft mouth that gave a fleetingly cruel smile. I shivered as I saw it, but cannot say why. It was after standing for a few minutes smoking that she sat without looking at me and lit another cigarette. Her coat was deep red and her hair dark. When I say dark, I mean more so than any black I had ever seen. I made a futile attempt to start a conversation by asking what she was drinking. She again sat for what felt like forever before answering in a low controlled monotone voice.

"Whatever you are drinking."

Returning from the bar, we remained silent until the waiter arrived with the two drinks. It was then she looked at me, speaking between sips and smoke.

"I've been here a long time."

This left me confused as it struck me as a rather odd statement that she left hanging. Considering what to say, I eventually found relevant words.

"What keeps you here?" I asked.

Leaning a little closer, which for some reason unnerved me, she answered, "My weakness of will and little resistance."

To which I asked again, "What undermines your will?"

Her answer came quickly as my question seemed to unnerve her too.

"Time. I do not exist beyond this bar."

With that, she announced she must leave, gave a fleeting smile, stood up and made her way through the crowd exiting onto the street. I had stood to watch this mysterious lady as she turned to wave, stepping back into the road. I grimaced, half closing my eyes, as a car (an old-fashioned type of car that would have been in use some thirty years before) hit her.

When I looked again, she and the car were gone as if nothing had happened. I ordered a double drink and sat for over an hour trying to understand what I had seen. It was then I noticed a small plaque upon the backrest of the chair she had sat in. It read: "Françoise, a lady who frequented this bar and wrote her novel, *Stuck in Time*, sat in this chair, 1924–1963." Upon the floor was a black glove with a silver F embroidered on it. I am now reading Françoise's story and will return some day in hope of catching a glimpse of her haunting beauty.

Jill

CHAIN REACTION

Days pass monotonously and seemingly full, yet with no specific event to generate a memory. Lives flow in this way through days that become years and eventually group together in decades. Yet all of the time, cause and effect roll on in chains in such a way that a simple action creates a flow that echoes indefinitely through generations. It is the hereditary consequence of what we do that can amplify into a sequence of occurrences, generating a wave of disturbance that may never have evolved should some minor event never have happened.

At ten minutes past eight in the morning, James stepped into his car, dropping his second cigarette of the day out of his Ford's partially open window. Turning left, he exited the car park that surrounded the 1970s bland concrete flats where he lived onto the highway that gave way to a country lane a couple of miles on. He was late and hadn't eaten breakfast. Having skipped his evening meal the previous night, he was hungry. Cruising at about forty miles an hour with one hand on the wheel, he ripped the lid off of his plastic lunchbox with the other hand and grabbed a ham sandwich. The car drifted across the lanes, but he soon drew it back and settled down to the heavy metal music that screamed from his phone into the car's music system. Having consumed his sandwich, he jettisoned four crusts out of the window, and they landed in the opposite lane.

Both hands upon the wheel and with the windows down, his foot drove hard on the accelerator as the car flew forward. He felt good with the sense of motion and the illusion of power that was driving him along whilst all of the time he screamed and sang to the music, "We're on the Road to Nowhere". The grass verges and hedges blurred as he whipped by. James hit the next bend hard with all four wheels squealing for grip. The centrifugal force willed the car over the central reservation while beads of sweat bubbles popped upon his forehead as a red Audi raced towards him. In a panicked reaction, he forced the steering wheel down to his left as the car juddered sideways and shot off the road, hitting a tree. James' head hung over the dashboard against a windscreen broken from the inside. The music carried on a loop and was still playing when an elderly man walking his dog bent down, looking in the car window while speaking into his phone.

"Ambulance please!"

The red Audi made it past James' Ford and accelerated on into an unforeseen revenge.

Jack had been out early, photographing deer from Lookout Hill. He had recently retired from thirty-eight years as a postmaster and was hell-bent on taking all the pictures he had missed in his life. Pottering along in his old but reliable Renault van, he rounded a bend to see a large, black crow was blocking his way. Jack didn't have to be anywhere and the beautiful, late spring morning had lulled him into a relaxed state of mind.

The crow looked Jack in the eye as it dropped a second crust of bread that it was picking up; one crust remained in its beak. Jack spoke to himself, but the clever crow heard him saying, "Go on, you cheeky bugger." The crow slowly and deliberately picked up the second crust and flew off low over Jack's van, letting out a call of thanks.

As the crow left the scene, Jack heard a brief squeal as if an animal was being slaughtered. It was a red Audi that slammed at speed into the back of his van. Jack had the shunt of his life that pushed him into traction in the local general hospital for three months. He forever more never stopped on a bend and spent more time looking in his rear-view mirror than he did through the windscreen of his new Volvo estate. The car salesman at Trusty Car Dealers had assured him it would survive a full-on barrage from a Royal Naval frigate at close quarters.

The ambulance on its way to James' Ford couldn't pass the crumpled Renault and the now conjoined red Audi.

Jacquelyn, bleach blonde and made up, was pleased with her early morning spray-on Bermuda tan that she had got out of bed early for. She had a job interview at 10 a.m. and was late, pushing her Audi hard to make time as she always did with her men until they took some other road.

The ambulance driver, a down-to-earth Yorkshireman who knew shit when he saw it after twenty-three years as a paramedic, radioed his control and explained the situation. James would have to wait for an ambulance to get to him from the opposite direction; besides, he had his music, but that was no defence against the cigarette that was smouldering its way through a litre plastic bottle of engine oil.

Adam, the paramedic, was not easily flustered. He saw Jack and spoke to him briefly in a Yorkshire accent.

"What made you stop here, you daft old bugger? Been photographing the crows?"

Having taken a pulse, he hurried but not too fast to the buckled Audi. Jacquelyn was a mess. First, Adam forced the driver's door open and fitted an oxygen mask. By now, his co-driver had followed him and they stretchered the brown and made-up mess to the theatre in the back of the Dorset Health Authority Ambulance. A drip was fitted in her arm. As a second response car arrived to help Jack, the ambulance was screaming away towards the local hospital with lights and siren at full welly. Jacquelyn was now delivering a very premature baby. Through the ambulance intercom it was announced to Adam, "We've got another passenger; she's just had a fucking baby."

Adam, a mountain of a man weighing sixteen stone and standing six three, swore and touched his lucky charm. The charm hung on a delicate steel cable around his neck. It was a link from the drive chain that he had removed from his Harley Davidson motorcycle after the chain had become slack. He called it his missing link in a chain reaction. Of course, there are no missing links, for chains are driven by a smooth or often not so smooth sequence of events. It is not for nothing that engineers call a "power chain" the process which delivers the drive to a machine from the power source to the wheels. Adam was fully aware of this after too many hours fixing his valuable vintage motorcycle.

Jacquelyn should have stayed in bed that morning because being late killed her (or was it going for a spray-on suntan that did?). Maybe it was because she drove too fast, or because Jack had stopped his old van for a crow. Or perhaps it was James' fault for throwing his stale sandwich crusts out of his car window on the bend of a chain reaction? He, by the way, was still sleeping whilst his radio serenaded him. Jacquelyn entered the hospital under a shroud and baby George entered screaming with indignation, having been jolted from careless comfort into a harsh world. Doctors checked him over, cleaned him up and gave him to Nurse Travis to cuddle before dumping him into a fish tank without water. George slept and God knows what dreams he had.

James jolted from unconsciousness to the heavy smell of oil burning. He couldn't see a thing, for the air was full of heavy, black fumes. He could hear the cattle that had come to inspect this most unusual intruder into their field. But seeing the fire, all twenty Daisys decided to gallop at full speed across the field to the safety of water that flowed obliviously along the river piddle at the furthest reach from the blue Ford Mondeo that appeared to have become intimately involved in a smoking hot relationship with a fence and a tree.

Adam, the paramedic, first spoke to him. "Well, you've had some fun this morning. Thanks for interrupting my bloody tea break. Don't fret now. I'm used to it, and I suppose someone's got to get you out of this field."

All of the time, Adam was working frantically to open the driver's door. He dragged James clear of the car as the upholstery flared up and the interior became full of dense smoke. James hurt. He could feel pain as he had never felt before. This would be a lesson he could never forget, and the permanent limp would forever earn him the nickname Loppy because of a lopsided walk.

THE DEATH OF TIME

In a bombed-out town at the end of a washed-out street, a time-spent man sits with a begging bowl at his feet. His company is a one-eyed dog that lies in the warm dust with his only eye upon the man. Both are as old as the hills that rise into the distance and each has lived by their wits and in fear from birth. They sit in the high street, which is empty, and the doors of the shops, lined as if soldiers stood to attention, remain closed. There is no life here beyond the man and his brown dog. There was a time when many would pass along this street and the shops would have been full of shoppers looking at items for sale. Cars would pass at intervals, dictated by the traffic lights that now hang rusting at the end of this street named Prosperity Boulevard. Begging in an empty street would seem like a futile proposition, which has been a symbol of life for so many poor people in the time before this. Our beggar, who knows himself as Ode and his companion that responds to the name Brown, are the last man and dog alive for hundreds of miles, and they appear to have no purpose for being here.

Sometimes we do things out of habit, and habit or routine certainly dictated Ode's actions, and his dog is a passenger upon his master's desires. To ask for something that cannot be given is on face value a stupid request; yet here they are begging without expectation. In fact, they both are hungry and defending against despair with an armoury of hope. Early spring sunlight strengthens as midday approaches and warmth pours into the man and dog, but the man does not remove the heavy, black coat that has faded to grey, displaying worn patches of weave and rips from where rats have chewed at the parts that are in contact with the ground. He doesn't feel the warmth or the cold of winter. The warm air lifts in a breeze that moves the man's hair so his eyes can be seen staring unhealthily towards the sun. Neither man nor dog have moved for some time, but, of course, there is no one to see if they did and perhaps no reason for them to move.

The begging bowl is made of stained silver, one taken from the church whose spire towers from a small green of grass from behind this street. In its day, that bowl has begged millions from needy parishioners for two hundred years or more. The bowl contains a hunk of bread that looks as if it is fresh and stands out pure white against the jaded silver of a once temporarily polished collection bowl. Written in a neat, engraved script upon the lip of the bowl are the biblical words, "The Lord Provideth". In some ironic way, for those who once had faith, the Lord, if you take the meaning of the word "lord" literally, did provide — the provision of pain and death on a wholesale mode of destruction. If there was ever a creator, it certainly excelled in creating pain in such ingenious ways of delivering it. Now there is only beauty in the natural decay that is the nature of all things, because there is no one left to feel the Lord's pain.

Both man and dog just sit there with no outward signs of being alive, but the bread has been removed from the bowl and the bowl is again dull and dirty. It is now afternoon and the shadows of clouds pass streaming over the decaying tarmac that is sporadically peppered with weeds and saplings, which force their way into life. As darkness falls, the man and dog are not there. Any observer, which of course there isn't, wouldn't have seen them leave because somehow, they are still there — not because they are invisible, but because they have chosen not to be seen. I can tell you this, because I know they are there and I have seen them many times, having lived at the northern end of Prosperity Boulevard. I would pass them on my daily walk to work serving coffee and snacks to commuters each morning from my coffee bar that had an open frontage and chairs on the pavement. I can see Ode and Brown, for only ghosts can see ghosts. Maybe it's a lingering figment of a memory in the three of us, who couldn't go somewhere else when the great ending fell upon so many lives. Ode and Brown will be sat there even after the buildings have turned to dust because the likes of them exist regardless of time. For them, time is a dead thing beyond which they live.

Ode

LUCK

A man's voice counting in a steady and deliberate way, "One, two, three." The explosion came in a deep thud. For a moment, the earth lifted, showering mud down upon the man who cowered under a corrugated sheet of steel, supported by a tree stump to one side and a rock pillar on the other.

Once the clatter of mud and rock ceased, coughing, he stepped out into the dusty air, drawing one hand over his eyes with the other waving to part air so he could inspect his work. As the bright sunlight returned, a three-yard crater could be seen. It had been blasted away from the bedrock that now stood out paler than the older, exposed face of the escarpment. This would be the moment of truth. Was there a vein of gold in those rocks, or was this going to be another day like so many before — another puny nugget, panned from a stream, a few fractions of an ounce, collected from the dirt after a storm?

Blinking dust from his eyes, the man studied the jagged rock face and there it was — a large, round nugget of yellow gold. It stuck out from the surrounding rock as he ran his fingers over its surface in disbelief. Glinting as if it had been polished, he chiselled away to free his reward. The nitroglycerine had cost him the last of his stash and after he had eaten his provisions, he would have been broke and hungry like so many others who came up to this wilderness, drawn by the false promise of easy wealth. Pick axing for two long days liberated enough gold for a man to live well for a lifetime. Having placed his booty in socks tied at the open end, he settled down for a night's sleep before travelling back into town where the dealers would weigh and inspect his gold before making an offer.

Night passed slowly with Jeff tossing and turning restlessly. Sleep came in brief bouts despite his deep tiredness. To one side of him was his gun and on the other was his gold. If he turned one way, he left his gold unobserved; to turn the other way left his gun out of reach. One dictated a need for the other, and the two seemed natural companions for a desperate man in a hard place. Tired and nervous, Jeff was up to meet the dawn, which crept like a native in silence along the valley. His mood was heavy, for he was a man who had nothing one day and wealth the next. His fear of losing his luck was growing. Having filled in the blast crater with mud and scree, he spread wet mud over the rock face to disguise his discovery. In town, he would stake a claim, but then everyone would know where he had struck lucky. He knew this would make life dangerous for him. Town would take a two-day ride arriving late after the dealers had closed for the night, so Jeff decided to spend a second night away to avoid getting his stash stolen.

He took a long look at the place that had rewarded him so well with what could so easily become a curse. He would not forget the triangular boulder that anchored two pine trees. The trail was a mixture of ancient native paths and animal tracks. Dust rose with each of his horse's steps and there were the first leaves of the autumn fall scattered under the horse's hooves. The horse could feel the extra weight of gold that rubbed her flanks making her sore, but, of course, she couldn't complain.

The first night's camp was well chosen in a small hollow under a bluff of rock, the fire being sheltered well and burnt steadily. Provisions were low, so a meal of rice and beans would have to suffice. Before sleep and alone with his thoughts, Jeff watched the small, red embers that lifted above the fire, rising to merge with the countless stars that filled the sky above him. He thought of the meal he would have in that posh hotel in the middle of town, then the hot bath and bed mattress that he would fall into, clean and full of food. Always in the back of his mind was the dread of losing his gold. He never let this thought far from his mind.

Jeff awoke late, but there was no need to rush. Then it occurred to his thinking once again that another might find the source of his luck and clean it out. A jealousy grew in his emotions that pricked at him in the way a man might feel about his woman in the company of better men. With this, he drove his poor, sore horse harder on towards town. As they drove on, the valley grew wider and more open as dense forest gave way to flowing pasture where a small river babbled and wound its way through. The land was fertile as if spreading itself out in the late summer's warmth in readiness for winter's sleep. The night before entering town, camp was set on the riverbank where Jeff could wash and his horse drink and graze on the fresh, lush meadow grass that would serve as a soft bed for him. A small fire was lit to not draw attention from any others passing through the valley. Jeff was conscious of his precious cargo and that the knowledge he had would certainly drive others to kill him if he shared it.

A town full of strangers who, for the most part, are down on their luck and all looking for a quick fix. Strangers are always wary of strangers, and this gave the town a tense atmosphere to the point of paranoia. The bars were always full and the main street hosted more brothels than bars. Jeff stabled his horse and, struggling to carry his gold without showing the burden, made his way to the Dancing Lady Hotel.

Entering the smoke-filled bar, he felt as if every eye in the place was on him. Having felt inconspicuous for a lifetime, he now felt as if he stood out like a sore thumb. He ordered a whisky that he slung back in one gulp and turned to see many men watching him. Having booked a room and a bath, he strode to the trade office to weigh in his gold. It was an ordinary-looking building with the exception of a man sat at the door with a rifle. Upon entering, Jeff was confronted with a bland counter that had a set of scales on it. Behind the counter was a short, portly man wearing wire-rimmed glasses with greased, black hair.

"Got a stash?" asked the man.

Jeff mumbled a little, wanting to play down what he had with him. "My partner has sent me in, looks like he's doing okay."

With that, Jeff unloaded his luck upon the counter, and the clerk lifted heavier scales from a shelf behind him.

"Well, I ain't seen lumps like them in here before. Where'd you get 'em?"

Jeff answered hesitantly. "It's my partner; I wasn't with him, only he knows where it's at."

The clerk cut into the gold with a knife, remarking that it was of good quality. Having weighed the stash, he disappeared through a doorway out back. Upon returning, he made an offer to Jeff of six hundred and fifteen dollars an ounce. Jeff screwed his face up and told the clerk he had to do better than that. After some haggling, they agreed to settle on seven hundred and ten dollars. Jeff walked out of the office with more money than he had had in his whole life.

Money is easier to carry than gold, but carrying so much money in a town full of poor folks made him feel uneasy, so he did what any ordinary wealthy gentleman would do and headed for the bank. As he entered the Wells Fargo bank, a man in a dark suit who blocked his way met him.

"What you doing here, prospector?"

Jeff, taken aback, having never been into a bank before, answered, "I wish to make a deposit."

With that, the man opened the door and told Jeff the bank didn't take deposits of dirt and dust and proceeded to show Jeff the way out back onto the street. It was then that anger rose in Jeff. He had been put down and kicked out many times before, but now he felt a great injustice because his newly found money was as good as any man's. For the first time in his life, he stood his ground calling to a man who stood watching from behind a counter that had bars separating customers from money.

"I have money and I need to deposit it safely. Do you want my money or not?"

The man behind the counter nodded and Jeff was let through. He made his deposit and had a bank bill to confirm it. Jeff carried that book close to his heart and his heart beat a little faster whenever his hand rose to feel it for reassurance.

The scalding water frothed with soap in the galvanised tub, filling the air with the scent of lavender. Jeff lay back, allowing the stinging heat to climb as he lowered himself in up to his neck. The shock of heat passed and he relaxed for the first time in days, washing and whistling with such a carefree manner that he could not remember having come over him before. The burden of poverty had fallen, but a new weight was growing upon his brow. The gold trader had spoken to the bank manager and they both marvelled at the quantity and quality of Jeff's stash. They sent the trader's guard to enquire at the stables where Jeff's horse rested, and later to the bar staff in order to learn where such fine gold came from.

Jeff slept long and deep with his bank bill under a pillow. In the meantime, rumours whispered through the brothels and bars of the town. A newcomer had hit an endless seam of gold, enough for everyone to be rich beyond their wildest dreams. Rising late and breakfasting for lunch, the bartender offered him a drink and asked where he found his gold. Again, Jeff told that it was his mate's and that he didn't know. An attractive young lady came to sit with Jeff, and he was flattered by her attention, but he had no intention of telling her where he had been. The town seemed to be closing in on Jeff. He grew claustrophobic, needing to get away from all of those questioning eyes. After three nights and three baths, he collected his horse, saddled up and rode out of town; bank bill secured close to his heart and a memory of where the means of wealth lay waiting hidden amongst dirt and rock.

Man and horse travelled on into isolation away from the greed and desperation of those who craved something they believed would make them happy, but only Jeff held the secret. Mindful of those who might follow him to discover the source of his luck, he travelled south away from his strike. On the second day, he swung west and after a few hours, he had rejoined the route he had travelled out on. Late in the second afternoon, he found the cold embers of a camp from the previous night. He was being followed.

Luck is a mysterious thing. It can shine its pleasure upon you, but it can also bring a darker colour, which dismantles that luck through the envy of others. Jeff had a growing awareness that his luck could fail as a silent battle grew somewhere in between his emotive desire for more gold and the natural caution of a man who has lived close to danger. Greed was growing in his heart, and fear hissed in his mind. He could not resist the ecstasy of gold and travelled to the place where the delight of wealth could meet the tempting danger of greed. On the third and fourth days, Jeff camped close to his gold. He kept his fire low, taking care not to send smoke with its giveaway plume into the air. All of the time, he thought of the gold but held off approaching it. He patrolled, looking to see if he had been followed, climbing high upon a bluff of rock that gave him a view back towards the town. All seemed quiet and empty.

On the sixth day, he rode in and pitched camp by the rock face that contained the luck of his curse. Excitement grew in him in anticipation of more gold. It was all he could think about like a fit of desire. Sat looking through the orange and golden flames of his fire, he scanned the low bluff of land that held his dreaming thoughts. He ran his eyes over every inch, looking for a sign that someone else had quarried there to steal his dreams. Despite having collected gold worth more than he had ever imagined he would have, he had a burning need for more. That need was a lust that sleeps in every man, the insatiable desire for wealth that once awoken can never be calmed. In his sleep, he ran his hands over that rock face caressing it like a lover, feeling every undulation and hard, jagged outlier. The eroticism of great wealth made him shiver in between dreams of jealous loss and the joy of what may be.

Morning broke with him in an agitated mood, and he arose alert as if threatened. He didn't notice the bright, yellow sun that warmed his face and he missed the beauty of the woodlands that stretched out below him. His only focus was a delirious fear that drove him to look for others who may have followed him — those who would remove him from this rich earth that was so barren for many. Jeff had always worked hard, and labouring for such rich pickings came easy. There was a great satisfaction in discovering each small lump of yellow metal. He had to be careful not to harvest more than he could carry; this was the balance of temptation and greed. Jeff had spent forty years drifting across the west, hiring himself out on cattle ranches, never making enough money to do anything beyond replacing clothes and feeding himself. Now at sixty-one, he had finally found his luck and he intended to live well.

Once he had deposited the cash from his second stash in the bank, he headed to his usual room in the Dancing Lady Hotel. Sleep refused to come as he lay restlessly in his bed, thinking about the place where gold awaited his hands to glint before his eyes. It had become a Mecca to him, the only place where he could find peace. Having finally drifted into a fitful sleep, something disturbed him as he blinked awake peering into the darkened room. The sound came again. There was someone in the room with him. Slowly, he reached for his gun, aiming it towards the source of sound and as he cocked the trigger, he spoke.

"Hold it right there."

An object crashed to the ground and a woman's voice, shrill with fear, spoke. "Don't shoot, mister. I don't mean any harm."

Jeff trained the gun against the voice and lit the oil burner that sat by his bed. A dull, orange, flickering light revealed a woman in her early thirties stood shaking against the hotel room door.

Jeff asked, "What do you want?"

Her answer came. "My name is Jessica. I have four children aged between three and eleven. We have no food, and my husband has been away for two years."

"So, you thought that you would steal my luck?" came Jeff's answer.

Since a woman thief had never confronted Jeff, and because she claimed to be motivated by her need to feed her children, he dithered and she left. As her footsteps could be heard hurrying away upon the wooden floor and down the stairs, he felt a shadow of compassion that pulled a pall of sadness over his mood. Again, he felt uncomfortable amongst the town's people and chose to leave. He stocked up on provisions and collected his horse in preparation for the ride to join his luck in an attempt to find peace.

As he headed towards the edge of town, he saw the face of the woman who had entered his room the previous night. She held a young child in her arms and looked away. Overcome with compassion, Jeff dismounted and asked her to show him where she lived. The small dwelling was little more than a shack with a circle of stones that served as a stove. There were bedrolls and a well-worn child's rag doll on the floor making a pitiful scene. The woman said little and Jeff was speechless. He reached into the bank bill that rested by his heart and fingered the dollar bills enclosed. There was nothing for it. Removing the money, he placed it on a broken-down bench that served as a table and left in silence.

It felt good to be back in the open with no faces pleading with him where the clear plain of the wide river valley smelt fresh and cool. There was purity here and the pleasure of being closer to his secret. Having set camp and being well-provisioned, he ate his fill and settled down for the night. It was then that the woman's eyes and the sounds of her hungry child returned to him, and he felt an anger he had never felt before. Why should he have to share his luck with others? He wasn't responsible for anyone but himself, and he had never asked anyone for anything but an honest day's work. The thought bounced around in his head like a bird caught in a cage. How could he reconcile his newfound wealth with the misfortune of so many others? He had never felt this way before, and he was confronted with questions he didn't want to answer.

Throwing caution to the wind, he travelled directly to his shrine of comfort on the second day. He felt more confident, having purchased a new rifle and enough ammunition to fight a war.

The owner of the gunsmith's had commented to his assistant, "That man looks worried. He's got something to defend and a secret to hide."

Again, Jeff inspected the rock escarpment in the way a banker would check the locks on his vault safe. All seemed to be undisturbed until he noticed scratch marks low down on the rock face. This made his blood race as panic rose in his mind. He climbed to the top of the escarpment with his rifle in a sweaty hand to survey the route back towards town. He was alone. It was only after twenty minutes that he realised how foolish he had been. The scratching was that of a wild animal, probably a mountain lion that had leapt at a buzzard.

Without purpose, he worked the seam for the following two days, retrieving twice the quantity of gold he had already banked. Whilst wanting more and more, there was nothing he could do with it. It was gold; simply gold that could no longer enhance his life, because he could already afford all he would ever need. At night, visions of great piles of gold came to him, intermingled with the woman's eyes. Only, in his dreams, the woman was eyeless and the child hung limp in her arms. He saw many faces looking at him and guilt planted its seed in his heart. A seed that was to wage war with his greed, the greed of a man who had never had to deal with such problems before. A man who for sixty years had owned nothing and owed nothing to his fellow men.

After two further days of work, pick axing and shovelling, Jeff was feeling his age. His enthusiasm for gold had pushed him to near exhaustion. He had worked relentlessly without thought, and it was tiredness that had overcome him and made him reflect upon his actions. There by his campfire, sat a dull pile that occasionally reflected a bright yellow in the fire light. In monetary terms, he had more wealth than any man could ever want or need. It was dawning upon him that he could not transport or bank all the gold he had mined, but this did not quench his lust for possession. Ever-present, the vision of the mother of four children hung close to his thoughts, eating its force into who he was becoming.

Not far from the escarpment of his luck, Jeff selected a place where the soil was soft, dark and deep between two towering pine trees. It was here he dug a grave for two-thirds of his gold, interring those yellow nuggets back into the ground from where they had come. The soft turf and soil lifted easily, forming a shaft some three feet deep in which he buried part of his soul. Somehow, something from his heart was left below that fertile soil, which would soon appear as if it had remained undisturbed for all time. Loading the remainder of his luck as he had done before, he set off for town.

The townsfolk had somehow anticipated the return of the quiet loner who appeared to have made his fortune somewhere out there in the wilds. Word had spread that he had helped the widow and her children, and that she had spent a sum of money in the grocery store, the dressmaker's and the hardware store. Jeff could not just be anybody anymore. He was to be looked up to, befriended and quizzed by all. His luck may rub off and become luck for others. Jeff followed his routine travelling from the dealer's to the bank and finally to his hotel room. Only this time small crowds gathered to watch him out of amazement and envy. Hidden in the crowd was the woman who had tried to steal from him, the lady he had helped with the money wrought from the earth that shed such hardships upon those who sought to rip her apart. All in search of her riches, for wealth was only of relevance to man and of no use to all else upon the planet.

No volume of gold can buy sleep and the loss of peace of mind comes cheap. Jeff could not sleep. He lay awake watching his hotel room door, fearing an intruder whilst regularly checking the blue bank bill under his pillow and the gun by his bed. The following morning, he left town, having left a false trail in the form of a map sketched upon a scrap of paper in his vacated room. It marked a place four days' ride south in the opposite direction from where he had buried his soul. He knew he would be followed. He had overlooked the anger that those who followed his map would feel after days travelling for nothing. They were as sore as if they had a hedgehog in their pants. No one followed Jeff but many followed his false map.

Slowly, the lust for gold left Jeff's mind like a virus leaves its victim weakened. It was not through self-evaluation or any thought processes that made him abandon his gold, which now lay hidden in rock and dirt. A fear had started to grow within him like an instinct that had been dormant awaiting the trigger to grow. He became afraid of what others may do to him because of what he knew and what he had. His gold had eaten into his brain and the damage was irreparable. Having worked so hard and fast for months, driving himself without any plan into exhaustion and having spotted other prospectors close by, Jeff buried his stash and rode without purpose far away from the place that had cursed him with great luck. Remaining within the back of his mind, he consoled himself with the thought that he would return. The gold would wait for him, but he overlooked the time he had to live with it. He simply drifted on.

Jeff moved south into Colorado over the high plains where once indigenous peoples wandered for thousands of years oblivious to the great value that others would later place upon a yellow metal. He settled into what he knew best, working on the ranches that were scattered in the wide, fertile valleys. He never drew from his bank bill, and late on in life he would look at a pencil-drawn map upon a ragged piece of paper to dream of where two pine trees stand aside of a rock bluff. It was there that his peace and turmoil settled to trouble his nights to the day he passed from this material world. His wealth remains his secret as does so much about this life that only reveals itself through experience.

Printed in Great Britain
by Amazon